SPARKS LIKE OURS

Reviewers Love Melissa Brayden

"Melissa Brayden has become one of the most popular novelists of the genre, writing hit after hit of funny, relatable, and very sexy stories for women who love women."—*Afterellen.com*

Eyes Like Those

"Brayden's writing is just getting better and better. The story is well done, full of well-honed wit and humour, and the characters are complex and interesting."—*Lesbian Reading Room*

"Melissa Brayden knocks it out of the park once again with this fantastic and beautifully written novel."—*Les Reveur*

"Pure Melissa Brayden at her best…Another great read that won't disappoint Brayden's fans. Can't wait for the rest of the series." —*Lez Review Books*

Strawberry Summer

"The characters were a joy to read and get to know. Maggie's family is loving, supportive, and charming. They're the family we all wish we had, through good times and bad."—*C-Spot Reviews*

"The tragedy is real, the angst well done without being over the top, and the character development palpable in both the main characters and their friends."—*Lesbian Reading Room*

"*Strawberry Summer* is a tribute to first love and soulmates and growing into the person you're meant to be. I feel like I say this each time I read a new Melissa Brayden offering, but I loved this book so much that I cannot wait to see what she delivers next."—*Smart Bitches, Trashy Books*

"*Strawberry Summer* will suck you in, rip out your heart, and put all the pieces back together by the end, maybe even a little better than they were before."—*The Lesbian Review*

First Position

"Brayden aptly develops the growing relationship between Ana and Natalie, making the emotional payoff that much sweeter. This ably plotted, moving offering will earn its place deep in readers' hearts."—*Publishers Weekly*

"*First Position* is romance at its finest with an opposites attract theme that kept me engaged the whole way through."—*The Lesbian Review*

"This book is thoughtful and compassionate, serious yet entertaining, and altogether extremely well done. It takes a lot to stand out, but this is definitely one of the best Traditional Romances of the year." —*Lesbian Reading Room*

"You go about your days reading books, thinking oh, yes this one is good, that one over there is so good, and then a Melissa Brayden comes along making everything else seem…well, just less than." —*The Romantic Reader*

How Sweet It Is

"'Sweet' is definitely the keyword for this well-written, character-driven lesbian romance novel. It is ultimately a love letter to small town America, and the lesson to remain open to whatever opportunities and happiness comes into your life."—Bob Lind, *Echo Magazine*

"Oh boy! The events were perfectly plausible, but the collection and the threading of all the stories, main and sub plots, were just fantastic. I completely and wholeheartedly recommend this book. So touching, so heartwarming and all-out beautiful." —*Rainbow Book Reviews*

Heart Block

"The story is enchanting with conflicts and issues to be overcome that will keep the reader turning the pages. The relationship between Sarah and Emory is achingly beautiful and skillfully portrayed. This second offering by Melissa Brayden is a perfect package of love—and life to be lived to the fullest. So grab a beverage and snuggle up with a comfy throw to read this classic story of overcoming obstacles and finding enduring love."—*Lambda Literary Review*

"Although this book doesn't beat you over the head with wit, the interactions are almost always humorous, making both characters really quite loveable. Overall a very enjoyable read." —*C-Spot Reviews*

Waiting in the Wings

"This was an engaging book with believable characters and story development. It's always a pleasure to read a book set in a world like theater/film that gets it right...a thoroughly enjoyable read." —*Lez Books*

"This is Brayden's first novel, but we wouldn't notice if she hadn't told us. The book is well put together and more complex than most authors' second or third books. The characters have chemistry; you want them to get together in the end. The book is light, frothy, and fun to read. And the sex is hot without being too explicit—not an easy trick to pull off."—*Liberty Press*

"Sexy, funny, and all-around enjoyable."—*Afterellen.com*

Praise for the Soho Loft Series

"The trilogy was enjoyable and definitely worth a read if you're looking for solid romance or interconnected stories about a group of friends."—*The Lesbrary*

Kiss the Girl

"There are romances and there are romances...Melissa Brayden can be relied on to write consistently very sweet, pure romances and delivers again with her newest book *Kiss the Girl*...There are scenes suffused with the sweetest love, some with great sadness or even anger—a whole gamut of emotions that take readers on a gentle roller coaster with a consistent upbeat tone. And at the heart of this book is a hymn to true friendship and human decency."
—*C-Spot Reviews*

"An adorable romance in which two flawed but well-written characters defy the odds and fall into the arms of the other."
—*She Read*

"Brayden does romance so very well. She provides us with engaging characters, a plausible setup with understandable and realistic conflict, and ridiculously fantastic dialogue."—*Frivolous Views*

Just Three Words

"I can sum up my reading experience with *Just Three Words* in exactly that: I. LOVED. IT."—*Bookaholics-Not-So-Anonymous*

"A beautiful and downright hilarious tale about two very relatable women looking for love."—*Sharing Is Caring Book Reviews*

Ready or Not

"The third book was the best of the series. Melissa Brayden has some work cut out for her when writing a book after this one."
—*Fantastic Book Reviews*

By the Author

Waiting in the Wings

Heart Block

How Sweet It Is

First Position

Strawberry Summer

Soho Loft Romances:

Kiss the Girl

Just Three Words

Ready or Not

Seven Shores Romances:

Eyes Like Those

Hearts Like Hers

Sparks Like Ours

Visit us at www.boldstrokesbooks.com

SPARKS LIKE OURS

by

Melissa Brayden

2018

SPARKS LIKE OURS
© 2018 By Melissa Brayden. All Rights Reserved.

ISBN 13: 978-1-63555-016-0

This Trade Paperback Original Is Published By
Bold Strokes Books, Inc.
P.O. Box 249
Valley Falls, NY 12185

First Edition: June 2018

Credits
Editor: Lynda Sandoval and Stacia Seaman
Production Design: Stacia Seaman
Cover Design by Jeanine Henning

Acknowledgments

Professional surfers in their skill, agility, timing, and athleticism have always amazed me, bringing me to these particular characters and their drive to be the best. But it's the love of the sport itself that keeps them coming back. In my opinion, there's a certain beauty to that, ranking right up there with the sun setting above the waterline, the tide ebbing and receding, and the mystery of the water itself. What a fun and intriguing backdrop it all was to write.

My editor and partner in crime on this series is Lynda Sandoval, who may know these characters even better than I do. I'm always grateful for her insight, humor, and guiding hand as we traverse the Venice landscape and cast of characters together. She gets me and she gets them.

Thank you to Bold Strokes Books for continuing to publish me, humor me, and support my creative zigzags along the way. I feel like I have a true family among you and am so thankful for the ongoing partnership.

My writing pals, friends, and family who support my work are what keep me going. They also provide donuts along the way. Bonus points forever.

To the loyal readers who have followed me to Broadway, strawberry farms, ad agencies, and beyond, I hope you'll stick around for what's next for Seven Shores and after. Hearing from you makes it all worthwhile.

For the Wave Chasers

CHAPTER ONE

Nothing kicked off Gia Malone's Monday more than charging waves the size of buildings. As she stood on the boat just off the tiny little island in the South Pacific, her heart pounded with the thrum, thrum, thrum of adrenaline-laced anticipation. Those were world-class waves out there and she had a major crush on them. She paused a moment to drink in the gorgeous view, fourteen footers at least, rising and breaking left like visual poetry.

This was why she loved to surf.

Even though she was ready to lose herself in those barrels, she made a point to slow down and keep her head calm. A decent breeze crept in and tossed her long, dark hair around, into her eyes and out again. Mostly, she surfed with her hair down. The feel of it whipping against her face and back was part of her process. Rituals were important to Gia. They kept her steady and alert in the face of pressure.

She'd arrived in Tavarua, the heart-shaped island resort in Fiji, two days before the Outerknown Fiji Women's Pro was set to begin. With the extra time, she'd been able to reacquaint herself with the conditions at Cloudbreak, one of the resort's seven surf breaks, and get her head in the game before the tournament. Jumping off a plane and onto a surfboard to compete at the world's highest level was a thing of the past. Rookie mistake. Arriving early before a competition was now another ritual.

She'd taken a few waves on the head during practice the day before, but overall, she was stoked with the conditions in Fiji. The colors were brilliant and the energy that came with this particular tournament was palpable. It was the fourth of a total of ten tournaments on the Women's Championship Tour, in which the top seventeen female surfers in the world battled it out throughout nine months of the year, jockeying for position, prize money, and more importantly, the claim that they were the top female surfer in the world. For Gia, that number one spot was everything, and she was so close.

No time for daydreaming.

She grabbed her board, hopped off the boat that had carried her to the surf break, and paddled out a distance to where she'd encounter the bigger waves. Next came the waiting, when that pent-up energy gathered like a tight little ball in her stomach. This was the calm before the euphoria. Nothing good ever happened in her comfort zone, which made high-level surfing the coolest drug she'd ever experienced. The seconds ticked by as she waited for her wave. Not that one. Nope, too squirrelly. Not that one either. It would fizzle early. Then she found some size heading her way. Okay, yeah. She felt good about this one, its speed, the way it moved. She and that wave were bonding. She zeroed in and made the call. This was it. Paddling for all she had in her, she set off, charging the wave, studying its swell, its breadth, the way it shifted. Once she'd found her position, she pushed herself up on the board to a standing position and started to glide, savoring the feeling of floating on air. Perfection. This was what it felt like to be on top of the world, and there was no greater joy. She took the briefest of moments to relish the power of the wave pushing through her board, propelling her onward. She checked her balance, crouched low, rode the turn. The breaking wave opened up, hollow and glorious, allowing entry to the barrel. While she'd love nothing more than to lose herself in the surreal experience, any loss of focus when the stakes were so high could result in her coming right off the board. A balancing act in more ways than one.

For Gia, this was a form of church. She honored the waves with the respect they deserved.

After a solid workout, she trudged to the shoreline from the boat, out of breath, muscles on fire, and on the kind of high she only encountered from waves in this part of the world. She spotted a couple of the tour's regular reporters watching her approach, most likely having assessed her session. The core grouping of press tended to be courteous enough when it came to practice time, giving her space, but now she'd be forced to walk past them on her way to change and shower at the resort. Part of the gig she hated most: trying to sound like a human in front of those guys. She didn't do the whole public speaking thing well. Sucked at it, actually. The few years since she'd been boosted from the

Qualifying Tour to the Championship Tour, she'd gotten a little better. But, God, not much.

"You ready for tomorrow, Gia?"

She pushed her hair out of her eyes and squinted at Shoshana, a staff writer from Surfline.com. Short in stature, spiky red hair, and tiny glasses she couldn't possibly see anything out of. They did look cool, though, which was probably the point. That was Shoshana. "Never felt better." She continued walking because she felt awkward and out of her element, but the comment didn't seem to be enough. Shoshana scurried after her, doing double-time due to their height difference. "You're looking a little cautious out there. More so than usual. Any particular reason?"

She forced a smile. "You gotta save something for the competition, right?"

The guy who'd been standing with Shoshana whose name Gia didn't know walked with them. "Gia. Charlie Kip from SurfTastic. Quick question for ya. You've had a great season so far, currently number three in the world. With number four Alia Foz injured, what do you think your chances are to take the whole thing this week?"

"It could happen."

"Do you think Elle Britton would agree with you?"

She suppressed an eye roll at the mention of the leaderboard's current number one. It was a provocative question, and she wasn't going to take the bait and speculate. "Hey, I just want to surf my best, you know? That's what I'm planning to do. The rest is out of my control." She knew it was the boring answer. Luckily, the reporters caught sight of Elle Britton and her signature blond ponytail through the glass in the lobby and raced her way like bees to their queen. Elle always gave them fantastic stuff, sparkling quotes laced with wit and charm and humor. She was born to play the part of media It girl. If Gia didn't loathe the woman so much, she might be impressed. As she entered the lobby of the resort herself, she watched as Elle burst into a smile and pulled Shoshana into a hug and squeal combo. A squeal? Really? And just look at her. She was pretty sure Elle had spent some time in the mirror, just to be ready for the attention she'd pull in the lobby. The peppy, fresh-faced look was why she landed gum commercials and late-night talk shows. Elle was not only the number one ranked female surfer in the world, she was the darling of the tour. Well, to everyone who didn't know any better. Underneath it all, Elle was plastic, opportunistic, and on her way to losing that ranking, if Gia had anything to say about it. Perky ponytail or not.

Elle caught her eye as she passed through the lobby. "Hey, Gia." She beamed. All part of the show Gia knew all too well.

"Elle," she said back evenly.

"Best of luck this week. You're gonna kill it, I know."

Shoshana and SurfTastic guy beamed at her. What a fantastic sport she was! What support she showed! Three cheers for the marvelous Elle Britton!

"I do, too," Gia said, and breezed by them with a nod. She closed her eyes briefly and glanced back to the surprised looks on the writers' faces. Not her best moment, but she couldn't resist. She didn't do fake. She wouldn't. And with Elle, that's all there was. Had the reporters not been there, she probably wouldn't have said a word to Gia. Maybe there would have been a smile, but it would have been just as plastic as she was.

Once Gia was safely on the elevator, she texted one of her best friends, Hadley, back in LA. *I was a cocky asshole to Elle Britton in front of reporters.*

Hadley, always Gia's number one supporter, was quick to type back. *Maybe they didn't notice?*

They did. I'm the resident bitch now.

Impossible. Come home soon, please. Autumn = pregnant and full of emotions and Isabel = workaholic, who is not paying enough attention to me.

Gia smiled at Hadley's description of their other two best friends. As pressure-filled as these tournaments were, she took comfort in the knowledge she had a soft place to fall when she returned home to Venice Beach in LA. Hadley and Isabel also lived at Seven Shores, the same apartment complex she did, and Autumn owned the badass adjacent coffee shop, the Cat's Pajamas. They were an unlikely foursome, given how different their personalities were, how widespread their occupations, but for whatever reason, they just clicked. She typed back her response. *Give me five days and I'm there.*

Don't kill E.B., Hadley wrote. *I'd miss you in jail.*

No promises.

She was kidding, of course. Kind of.

Over the next few days, she watched one competitor after another fall from the tournament, as the excitement about her chances grew. The further she went at Outerknown, the more points she'd be awarded toward her ranking. This was an important tournament to Gia, who didn't relax until she was the last one on her side of the board—right across from Elle Britton. Wouldn't you know it? While it would have been nice for Elle to go down early and not pull in the points, if Gia pulled out a tournament win, she would still take home more, moving her up a spot on the tour's leaderboard to number two. She closed her eyes and imagined how amazing that would feel. To win. She'd pulled in a handful of finals showings before, but it was the whole tournament she wanted.

Ousting every other competitor she'd come up against, and having the best year of her career, Gia still knew how hard it would be to take down Britton. The woman was a surf machine and had the kind of shred and tenacity that made legends. Even Gia couldn't deny her that, Barbie Doll smile or not.

The crowd was a vocal one that Saturday morning of the finals. The beach was packed and Gia could hear their cheers of support (mainly for Elle) all the way out in the water. She was the underdog in this matchup and everyone knew it. The waves weren't as generous as they'd been earlier in the week, so selection would be key. Elle had drawn first priority and would go first. She snagged a high arc and rode the front, carving into the pocket, taking it to the inside corner and ripping hard off the top for a fantastic first time out.

Shit.

That ride would pull in a big number from the panel of five judges who would score it on a scale of one through ten. Each competitor's top two waves from the heat would be added together to come up with their final score. Gia could take on as many waves as she could get in in the heat's allotted twenty-five minutes, but two of them better be awesome.

Gia's turn. She paddled forward. Her first wave fizzled early and would score low. Not something she could control, so she shrugged it off and wiped her eyes, clearing them of the salt bath they'd just received. But her second time out yielded quality. She set up a front side wrap in the pocket and came away feeling good, adrenaline surging. Her exit had been masterful. Yes! She'd just killed it on that one. Exactly what she'd needed. That would push her into the lead. She and Elle exchanged a nod across the water; that contact only made Gia want the win more. She cleared her head and prepped herself for the remaining minutes in the heat as the crowd screamed louder. Elle had ground to make up and struggled to find any real foothold on her next few attempts. On what would be one of the last waves in the heat, Elle didn't fully take advantage, playing it safe. Her timing was off. Gia couldn't take it anymore and followed Elle out to her wave, once she'd failed to capitalize. She stuck to the rules, however, and stayed out of Elle's way, honoring her priority. Gia made a meal out of the killer crest, shredding her way down with S turns to the bottom like a champ.

The heat concluded, and with a total score of sixteen to Elle's fourteen, Gia Malone took the whole damn thing. *Holy hell.*

The tournament win would contribute 10,000 points toward her ranking, moving her into the number two spot on the leaderboard. She cried out when the scores came down and smiled at the crowd screaming along with her. Elle, a few yards down the beach, nodded Gia's way and sent her a congratulatory smile. Love lost or not, Gia nodded back, because as a surfer, she had mad respect for Elle, and that's what today had been about, the work.

Now…it was time to celebrate.

Two days later, at exactly seven a.m., Gia's alarm went off. Well, her version of alarm, the morning surf report. Happy to be back in her own bed, she stretched and blinked against the hint of sunlight that slid in from the nearby window as she listened to Joker Johnny outline the conditions on the local beaches. God, it was good to be home.

"It's gonna be a gnarly one out there today, folks. Buckle up. Lots of morning sickness on the horizon."

"Perfect," she mumbled, and pushed herself out of bed.

"Check it, agros. You may be amped to hit the waves, but take it easy. Heavy winds and killer swells should dominate through the afternoon. Choppy stuff, so don't be a Barney. Stay safe, make good choices, and live to surf another rad day. Tide is peaking at a 5.29 feet at 6:30 a.m., then drops to a 2.03 feet at 12:38 p.m. If you're looking for clean waves, sit today out. Later this week has you covered. In the meantime, bumps ahead with thirteen- to fifteen-footers on tap."

"Well, that's what I'm here for," Gia said to herself in the mirror, with a smile. "Bring it, California. Game on."

Already dressed for the waves in trunks and her jersey, Gia pushed open the door to the Cat's Pajamas, the funky little coffee shop next door to the Seven Shores apartment complex. She lived on the second floor of the twelve-unit building and made daily trips to Pajamas for the best coffee in town. Hands down. The fact that her best friend owned the place, and her routine trips were just as social as they were functional, certainly didn't hurt.

"Wait," Isabel said, holding up a hand. "Is that number two in the surf world walking toward us?"

Hadley grabbed Isabel's wrist. "I think it is. She looks a lot like number three did, but somehow this woman comes with more championship swagger. I'm a little swoony to be in the presence of such a mega-athlete."

"All hail, number two!" Autumn called, and her friends broke into applause, followed by the morning patrons, most of whom were regulars.

"Knock it off," Gia said, though the attention gave her a boost, and the corners of her mouth tugged into a grin. She accepted the coffee from Autumn, cream no sugar, her usual order, and took a seat with her friends for Breakfast Club, their daily morning meet-up session. In just a short while, Isabel would head off to the television studio where she worked alongside her girlfriend, Taylor, writing one of the most kick-ass shows on television. Hadley would head to Rodeo Drive and open Silhouette, the posh boutique she assistant managed. Autumn would prepare her afternoon roast and dazzle customers with her warm and welcoming personality. And Gia would head to the beach. While Venice didn't yield the kind of waves Fiji did, practice was practice, and she was not about to let up when her momentum was so strong. But for now, and most every morning, the four of them started their days together chatting about anything under the sun before dashing off in different directions. She missed these mornings when she was on the road and had grown to savor them when she was on break from the tour.

"So, what did it feel like to go head-to-head with your archrival and win?" Autumn asked. "I mean, that had to be like a delicious cherry on the beach sundae."

Isabel frowned. "Now I'm picturing sand in a dish."

"Not as sweet as you probably think," Gia said. "It felt good, yeah, but it's almost like I can't revel for too long, as there's still so much work ahead." She pointed at Autumn. "What I'm more interested in is if they're kicking yet."

Autumn placed a hand over her swollen tummy and took a seat. She was four months along and already starting to show. "Flutters only at this point. Kate's obsessed, however. Stares at my stomach just waiting for that first little foot to give us a hello." Kate and Autumn had married less than a year ago and still existed in the happy honeymoon haven, grinning whenever they caught the other's eye. Gia was happy for them.

"I just need to know if these are little tiny boy babies or tiny girl babies or one of each," Hadley said with wide eyes and a sigh. "I mean, I can plan a variety of unisex outfits in the meantime, but the lack of direction is keeping me up at night. Do you think they like hats?" she asked Autumn. "Have they indicated at all?"

"Hard to say. But another week and you shall have your gender answer. In the meantime, I just pray these two don't turn me into the size of a Mack truck. At least not yet."

"You're gorgeous," Gia said. "I thought so as soon as I walked in."

Autumn offered a watery smile. "You're going to make me cry, Gia-pet. My hormones are on the attack and I have the weepies. No sincere compliments. None."

Hadley kissed Autumn's cheek with a smack and turned to Isabel. "Speaking of gorgeous people, Taylor isn't joining us today?"

"Nope. We spent the night apart because she has an early morning."

Hadley shook her head slowly. "You guys are the most pragmatic couple I've ever met."

Isabel's girlfriend was the well-known TV producer Taylor Andrews, who just so happened to think Isabel hung the moon. "Raisin has an appointment at the vet, so she has to do this whole pep talk thing with him. Who knew Dachshunds were so easily influenced? Not that it works for me," she said, and shrugged. "I can get him to chase a rubber pork chop, but she's able to change his whole life view in one chat. He's obsessed with her. I fault him not." Isabel turned to Gia. "Oh, and she watched your finals online from her office. Said to give you a hug just from her. We can get to that later."

Gia smiled. "Give her my love."

"Done."

Hadley, always one for following the surfing news, sat taller in her seat. "So, what do you think of the reports that you interfered on Elle Britton's final wave? Not at all true, by the way."

Gia sighed. She'd heard the speculation that she'd edged Elle out of her final opportunity to score by dropping in on her wave, but she hadn't broken any rules. That was just part of the sport. "Nothing I did stopped her from going for it. If I'd interfered, I would have been docked. I wasn't."

"Is that what she thinks, too?" Hadley asked, the always eager information-monger. "That you stole her wave?"

Gia passed her a look. "Are you worried about Elle Britton's feelings right now?"

"No way. I just don't like the idea of anyone being mad at you. It's not fair."

Gia softened. "In that case, hard to say. She sounded upbeat and perky at the presser after the heat. But then she always does, so..."

Isabel stared at Gia, tapping her chin. "She drives you crazy, doesn't she? I mean, I can just tell."

"She's my competition," Gia said plainly. "So yeah. Plus, her Miss Perfect persona is tired at this point."

Isabel looked deep in thought. "Right, but how does that make you feel? Physically, emotionally? How does the rivalry manifest itself?"

"Are you trying to put me in your TV show?" Gia asked, leaning forward. "You are, aren't you?" Isabel was constantly studying them for hooks, or story ideas, gestures, and reactions. The dangers of befriending a writer. In the year that they'd been friends, Gia had gotten better at catching her in the act.

Isabel sat back in her chair, shrugging in surrender. "It's possible we're working on a rivals-to-lovers storyline on *The Subdivision*. Just using your experience for the rivals portion I'm developing. I need sparks, you know?"

"Oh, sparks are good," Hadley said, resting her chin on her palm. "I love sparks. Write lots of those."

"No." Gia shook her head. "We don't have any sparks."

"Depends on the definition," Autumn said. "Sometimes you spot the sparks right away, like with me and Kate. Other times, they sneak up on you."

"Like with me and Taylor," Isabel said, with a smolder.

Gia shook her head. "By any definition, we don't have them. At all. None of those kinds."

Isabel studied her. "Does she hate you back?"

"Probably. I've never asked."

"Gotchaaaa." Isabel drew the word out, looking super thoughtful. "No sparks. But when you see her, how do you feel? Still applies."

That part was easy. "She makes my skin itch and my blood get hot and I just have this intense need to take her down."

"As in down to the floor?" Autumn asked, with a twinkle in her eye, as she swapped out the creamer.

"Maybe a bed?" Isabel joined in, with a sideways grin. She was messing with Gia. It's what she did to them all. The Isabel charm.

"Not even close," Gia answered dryly.

"You guys," Hadley said, waving them off. "It's not like that with them. They're like oil and water. Ursula and the Little Mermaid. Beauty and the Beast."

"Beauty and the Beast hooked up," Isabel said. "Big-time. Dancing furniture made it happen."

Hadley looked mystified. "Good point."

"Did you just call me a beast?" Gia asked.

Hadley shook her head apologetically. "I was on a cartoon kick and got carried away. Happens a lot."

"Mm-hmm." Gia downed the remainder of her coffee, grateful to have it back in her life even temporarily. Talking about Elle Britton just made her anxious to get to the beach and surf, remembering that every second of the season counted.

Isabel wasn't done and raised one finger, regarding the table. "Let's not forget the photo of Gia in which she appeared to be checking out Ms. Britton in a swimsuit." She turned her phone around to reveal the offending photo.

Gia closed her eyes. Not this again. A year and half prior, as Elle was speaking to the media, a photographer had captured a shot of Gia looking on. However, it appeared upon first glance that Gia was infatuated with more than just Elle's words to the press. The photograph had garnered a lot of attention and speculation. She loathed that photo to this day. "That photo can go to hell. We all know it's not what it looked like."

"Do we? And when do you see Ms. Britton again?" Isabel asked, sliding her phone into her bag.

Gia swore Isabel asked the question just to see how her features would react. "Well, nosy writer, probably not until next week. There's a Billabong party in Malibu I'll hit up."

"Who are they again?" Autumn squinted. "Pregnancy brain."

"Surf accessories," Hadley supplied. "Clothes, gear. They also sponsor tournaments and surfers." She turned to Gia. "Is this party beach attire?"

"Unfortunately, I think it's a little dressier than that." Gia glared at the thought. She hated wearing actual clothes.

"Perfect. When should we consult?" Hadley asked, always ready to put together the perfect outfit for her friends. Gia wasn't one to refuse that kind of professional help. "I'm thinking white. Your tan looks amazing in white, as does that dark hair."

"White it is," Gia said.

"I will put something together and we can play runway in a few days."

"It's fun when you get to play runway," Isabel said. "The time Hadley planned my look, I got lucky that night, and many nights after."

Hadley's eyes lit up. "That should go on my commercial! If I were ever to get a commercial."

"Well," Isabel said, with a saucy wink, "you'd have earned it." She stood. "I'm off to save Hollywood."

Hadley joined her. "Off to save Rodeo Drive."

"I'll stay here and save the good people of Pajamas," Autumn said from her chair. They all looked to Gia.

"Fine," she said, with a smothered smile. "I'm off to save…the ocean, I guess."

"Someone has to," Hadley said, beaming. "Go team!" The four of them headed off to their own separate corners of the world. Maybe they'd run into each other in the outdoor courtyard of Seven Shores later that day, or go for an impromptu dinner or a jaunt to the beach. If not, they'd see each other again at Pajamas the next morning.

Same bat time. Same bat place.

Gia smiled at that constant in her life. She didn't devalue it or toss it aside. Coming off the road like she just had made her understand more than ever how important good friends were. She'd slay dragons for Autumn, Hadley, or Isabel any day of the week. No one would have to ask her twice.

CHAPTER TWO

I think you should stop beating yourself up about it."

Elle pulled her hair from the ponytail holder and gave it a shake, noticing it was still partially wet from their earlier practice session. She turned to her best friend, Holly, who sat beside her on a chaise lounge, just yards from the ocean. "I've tried," Elle sighed. The depression over the whole thing was not letting up. "It's not working. I don't lose in final heats, Hol. I just don't. That's not the kind of competitor I want to be. So what the hell happened?"

"I think we know what happened. Someone dropped in on a wave that was supposed to be yours and wasn't penalized for interference."

"Not something I would have done, but it worked in her favor." She stared off in the distance, replaying that moment in her mind. She'd been about to attack the wave from the outside pocket when Gia Malone had shown up in her peripheral and knocked her out of concentration. Partially her own fault, but Gia had taken a pretty big liberty.

"Ballsy," Holly said. "You gotta give her credit. She was trying to apply pressure."

"Yeah, well, it worked." Elle shook her head. "Gia Malone. This tournament bumped her to number two. I'm so exhausted from it all that I can barely see straight, but now? There's no way I can lay up or take any kind of break. She's getting better, you know."

"I do."

"And I'm not."

Holly balked and tossed her bouncy dark hair that fell just shy of her chin. That bouncy hair was the most expressive hair Elle had ever seen. She envied Holly for it. "You're so hard on yourself that I don't know what to do with you. I want to smack you in your head over it.

Do you know how desperately I would kill someone to surf like you do, you little surfing prodigy?"

"Yes," Elle said glumly. "I should shut up, but I can't. I'm that competitive. My off switch is broken."

"No explanation needed. I've met you."

She and Holly had grown up together in San Diego, surfing every minute they had available to them before moving to LA just out of high school. Elle had always been the stronger surfer and had been good enough to pursue professional surfing at just sixteen. Holly had not. So while Elle hit up whatever tournaments her parents could scrape together the funds for, Holly had entered the world of finance, starting off as a teller at a bank and climbing the ranks to loan officer. Elle might possess the flashier lifestyle, but she admired Holly and the place she'd carved for herself in the world. Solid. Stable. Easy. Plus, she didn't have to travel the way Elle did.

"You're a wave weasel is what you are," Holly said, poking her in the ribs.

Elle grimaced at the childhood nickname Holly had assigned her and squirmed from her touch with a squeal. "I'm not a wave weasel. That's something you made up. I keep telling you."

"Don't argue. You're a wave weasel and always will be." Holly glanced at her watch. "Is it after four? It is. You know what that means? Rosé!"

"Four feels early when I'm in training."

"Well, that's dumb. It's not. I'll snag two glasses."

Elle shrugged. "You never listen to me. I'm the levelheaded one!"

"And I'm the fun one! So pipe down."

"Hey!" Elle called after her. "I'm fun. C'mon!"

"Once in a while. Not as often as you used to be."

Elle bristled at the probably accurate statement. Holly told it like it was. Yes, she'd been wildly focused on her career and the media responsibilities that came with it. Wasn't her fault the requests kept pouring in. She knew how to work the press, to smile in just the right way or toss her hair when she laughed. They were skills like any other that she'd developed over time, especially once she learned how valuable they could be. When Holly returned to Elle's deck with two glasses of rosé, Elle sent her a pout. "Am I really that bad? Please tell me I'm not. I don't want to become boring and set in my ways."

Holly stared at her. "You're an obsessed zombie hell-bent on world surf domination. You're admittedly exhausted from it all, but you won't give yourself a break. I, your much more carefree friend, miss the version of you that lived a little more. Allowed yourself a night out on the town."

"I go out on the town."

"You have a million dinners with acquaintances. It's what you do. Everyone knows your name, but how many people actually know you? Let me ask you this, when was the last time you went on a date?"

"I don't date," Elle said. "Look at my life. It never works. When would I date?"

"Therein lies the problem. You're turning into a spinster." She shuddered. "There are cobwebs on your lady parts. Allow me to remedy this awful trend and set you up with a buddy of Dash's from the bank. Finance guys are hot. We can double. Won't you allow me this pleasure?"

She didn't love the idea, but she fought the urge to decline. "What are Dash's friends like?"

"Probably a little like Dash, but he's a decent catch. You like Dash."

"Of course I like Dash," she said, already dreading the idea. Holly and Dash had dated casually for the last six months. The guy was good-natured enough, if a little boring for Elle's liking. Plus, the men Elle had dated in the past were often intimidated by her or interested only because she was well known. There didn't seem to be a lot of middle ground, which was why she'd shelved the process altogether. There were other things to focus on. More exciting things.

"You're never going to find the right one if you don't look for him."

"Fine. Set it up," Elle huffed. Though her expectations were dialed to low, at least no one could accuse her of not trying.

Holly took a moment. She turned her head and regarded Elle suspiciously out of the corner of her eye. "That was too easy. Is the other shoe about to drop?"

"I only have one proverbial shoe. You made a valid point, and guess what? I listen to you."

"And you won't cancel, even if *The Tonight Show* calls?"

This was hard. "I won't cancel."

"And when you marry this guy and have eighteen children you'll thank Aunt Holly and make everyone toast to her and her matchmaking ways."

Elle shook her head in wonder, not quite sure whether to thank Holly or slug her. "Sure. Whatever you say."

"That's what I'm talking about," Holly said, and clinked her glass to Elle's. "Two hot chicks like us, out on the town."

"I don't want to be called a hot chick."

"Yes, you do."

She grinned at her friend and took a sip of rosé. "Maybe a little."

Three days later and Elle had changed her outfit at least four different times. What was one supposed to wear on a date with a banker? Her dark pink flirty dress would make her look too frivolous, and her black pleated cocktail number seemed severe when she tried it on. Even her middle-of-the-road sundresses made Elle second-guess ever agreeing to this date in the first place. Indecision was so unlike her! In the end, she'd gone with her peach sleeveless dress with the thin beige belt. Simple meant classic, and that worked. If Christopher, or whatever his name was, hated it, well, that was on him. She sighed at herself in the mirror one last time.

When she arrived at Holly's house, a cute little one-story not far from Elle's place along Hermosa Beach, she didn't bother knocking. Their relationship was beyond knocks and doorbells. She found Holly standing behind her couch, remote control in hand and a giant version of Elle laughing on the television.

"Talk-show-you is so upbeat."

"Talk-show-me has to be."

Holly turned to her. "True. She's like regular-you turned up three notches. It works, though. I mean, look at your endorsement deals. You smile and show your abs and stuff sells. People like you."

"If it helps pay my tournament entry fees, I'm more than willing to add some pep to my step. I'm nervous." It all came out like one run-on sentence.

Holly took a moment to unravel the words. "You're nervous Christopher won't like you? That's insane. He's going to think you're as adorable and hot as the rest of the world does."

"No," Elle said simply. "I'm nervous we're not going to click, and you'll be disappointed in me, and think I didn't try and that I suck at dating, and I don't like to suck at anything. I'm type A. Get it now?"

Holly looked confused and continued to proverbially scratch her head as she rounded the couch to take a seat. "Humor me."

"Okay."

"Here's what I don't understand. Whenever there's any sort of event covered by the media, you have a guy on your arm, and you look like you're having the time of your life. But it never goes anywhere."

"Yeah, but those aren't *dates*. Those are friends or acquaintances who have agreed to go with me."

"You click with them?"

"I don't know if click is the word, but we have a great time. It's different. I don't know." She thought on it, looking for a way to better explain herself. "Those arrangements come with a much smaller commitment. One evening and some nice conversation versus working toward…more."

"And you don't have sex with any of them?"

Elle laughed. "Honestly, who has time for sex these days?"

"Riddle me this, Batman."

She was nervous about where this was going. "Okay."

"Do you want more? Level with me. If the answer is no, I'll stop trying to set you up."

"I do want more. Yeah." A pause. "I mean, probably." There was just never a person she'd wanted that "more" with. That was the core issue. Maybe not everyone was wired for an ongoing relationship, and while that made her sad on one hand, she also took pride in her self-awareness on the other. Maybe she was destined to focus on her career goals and leave the white picket fence and Facebook official relationship statuses to everyone else.

Maybe.

Or maybe she just hadn't met the *right* person yet. Maybe she would meet him tonight and put this whole issue to rest. That would be nice, right? To finally feel like a functioning person, like everyone else.

Twenty minutes later, she smiled into warm, dark eyes. The guy Holly had set her up with really was a looker. She had to give her credit. "Elle, meet Christopher VanCamp. He's a good friend of Dash's."

"Hi. Elle Britton," she said and extended her hand.

"Christopher. Nice to meet you."

She nodded and took in his perfectly tailored sport coat and color block tie. Not too flashy, but still fashion forward. "Likewise."

His hand was much larger as he closed it over hers. Firm, but not too firm on the shake. That was promising. Things were looking up.

"I've heard many great things about you," he said. "Dash and Holly are big fans of yours." He blushed, hearing how that sounded, and closed his eyes momentarily. "I am, too. Didn't mean to imply otherwise. I'm a fan of your *surfing*."

She nodded, letting him struggle. It was cute.

"I just meant that they spoke highly of you. As a person." He glanced from Holly to Dash and back to Elle again. "I'm a dolt, and hopefully, you can forgive the last thirty seconds."

"You're doing great," Holly said dryly, and then blossomed into a reassuring smile and shoulder bump. "Elle loves bumbling suitors. Tells me all the time."

Elle grinned. "I do."

Holly's humor worked and Christopher seemed to relax. "Then maybe tonight will be a good one for me." His eyes crinkled slightly and Elle decided she already liked him. He could be in a cologne ad. She passed Holly a secret look that said *well done*. Holly winked back.

Remembering her tricks of the trade, Elle made sure to light up as she turned to Dash, who she'd yet to greet. His sandy blond hair had less product than usual tonight and fell casually onto his forehead. She had no doubt that was Holly's doing. "Hi, Dash!" She pulled him into a warm embrace. "Are you caught up on *Game of Thrones* yet?" She kissed his cheek. "Say yes."

"Not yet. No spoilers."

"How are we ever going to bond over this show if you don't hurry up?" she teased. "You're turning into a TV slacker."

"I'm caught up," Christopher said.

"See?" Elle pointed at him. "The new guy is lapping you."

Dash turned to Chris and slapped him on the back. "Yeah, well, tell her what you do for a living, new guy."

"I manage funds, which means I can work from home."

"I work for the man," Dash said. "Chris's on his own schedule."

"How awesome," Elle said, looping her arm through his as they headed for the door. "Me, too!"

Elle had a fantastic time at dinner. While her heart longed for the fettuccini alfredo, her head made her order the salad with lots of extra chicken because victory didn't come to the weak. Luckily, the quality of the company made up for the loss. The four of them killed some wine and after-dinner drinks, and before she knew it, they'd been sitting around that table for more than two hours, shooting the breeze, laughing, as she got to know Christopher.

"You're really great, you know that?" Christopher said quietly in her ear as Holly and Dash argued about who had noticed who first at work. His breath tickled her ear and she resisted the urge to pull away a little bit. "I'm not just saying that. I was so nervous about tonight, but you really put me at ease."

It's what she did best. Elle had always been a people person and got along with most everyone. The fact that Christopher just happened to be an easy guy to talk to only helped the process. "I almost canceled," she told him and then pulled a face. A guilty one. "But I can safely say that I'm very happy I didn't."

The confession seemed to have inspired Christopher, and he glanced behind them. "This restaurant has a really cool garden out back, and a gazebo. Want to go check it out?"

She did.

He took her hand and they excused themselves to Holly and Dash, who grinned at them victoriously.

Once outside, they took a lap from the deck to the walkway, which was lined with tiny white lights. "I've always loved this restaurant," Elle told him. "But I've never been back here."

"So that means I've scored a point?"

She liked the way his eyes twinkled. Mysterious, yet proud. Elle smiled and squeezed his hand. "One point for you. Deal."

"Earlier tonight you talked about traveling for your job. Do you enjoy it?"

She considered the question. "Sometimes more than others. Seeing new places never gets old, but I miss the stability of home. Waking up in my own bed. I have a little house on the water not far from Holly's in Hermosa Beach."

"It's a great neighborhood. Maybe one day I'll see your place."

She slapped at his arm playfully. "Christopher, my word, you're forward."

He caught her lighthearted tone and laughed. "A guy's gotta try."

"Does a guy?" she asked. "Does he?" She was flirting. Even she could tell that much, and it was fun. *He* was. Their eyes locked, and it got very quiet. They could still hear the distant chatter and ambient music from inside the restaurant. He leaned in slowly, giving her enough time to say no if she didn't want him to kiss her. She appreciated that opt out, as a lot of guys didn't offer it. She stood her ground and met his lips when they hovered just shy of hers. The kiss was…fine. A little wet and soft. She wouldn't expound upon it later in a diary she didn't own. She wouldn't gush about it to Holly. Or relive it as she lay in bed that night. But *fine* was a big endorsement in Elle's book. She would chalk fine up to a win.

As he pulled his lips from hers, Chris met her gaze. "Can I see you again?"

She nodded. "I was hoping so."

The foursome laughed their way to Holly's place, where Elle bid them all good night. She needed to be up with the waves in the morning and had a whole workout planned beforehand. A run on the beach, weights, and her least favorite, abs. Christopher walked her to her car, and Dash followed Holly inside, no doubt for a little one-on-one time.

"Don't lose anybody's money this week," Elle said sweetly.

He covered his heart as if her words had pierced it like an arrow. "I will forgive you because you don't know how good I am at my job."

She leaned back against her white VW Beetle with a beige convertible top. She'd drop the top, she decided, once she got inside. The night was too perfect not to. "Thank you for dinner."

"I had a great time," Christopher said. "Even the part when you made fun of me for watching cartoons."

"Well, you are a grown man and should really look into that."

"Only because it was you who suggested it." His lips were on hers again. It was a good-night kiss and to be expected after the kind of date they'd just had. A simpler kiss this time. Less movement of his lips over hers and neither tongue made an appearance, though their lips were slightly parted. Was it odd that she spent the time analyzing the logistics of the kiss rather than focusing on the romance of it? Shouldn't she be lost in the heat? The exciting connection to another person she actually really liked? She wasn't, though.

Her end conclusion: the kiss was, again, *fine*.

She drove home, top down, with her spirits hovering slightly above status quo. Holly had done well this time, and she hoped to see Christopher again someday soon. In the meantime, she had two things to worry about. Three press appearances that week and massive amounts of training before the next stop on the tour.

Bring on the waves.

CHAPTER THREE

The Billabong party was packed, close to overflowing. The music pulsed and the drinks flowed freely as everyone who was anyone in the surf community mingled or danced or sucked up to the person they needed to suck up to most. All part of the game.

Gia knew there'd be a lot of industry folks in attendance, but the fact that she could barely walk three feet without bumping into someone who wanted to chat or take a photo with her had her worn down on smiles. She didn't mind the people themselves. They were great. But she had trouble staying "on" for an extended period of time. Regardless, she forced yet another smile as she and her agent of three years, Gwendolyn, made their way across the crowded warehouse of a restaurant, rented out entirely for the event.

Gwendolyn stayed very close to Gia's ear as they walked. She was like a hawk when it came to these events, looking to capitalize on any possible networking opportunity. While it was good for Gia's career in the long run, she'd much rather be surfing. "Don't be obvious," Gwendolyn said, "but over there is an up-and-coming tournament sponsor."

"Oh yeah?" Gia fist-bumped Lindy Ives, a fellow surfer, as they passed. She'd have to catch up with her later.

Gwendolyn wasn't done. "Some sort of new spicy corn chip company with tons of venture capital dollars to help put them on the map, and do you see that guy?" She pointed with her eyebrows, which was, c'mon, impressive. "That's Theo Trowebridge, their marketing guru. Make nice with him. He has money to spend."

"Got it." Gia nodded and sipped her sparkling water. No alcohol for her tonight. She'd noticed a dip in her timed sprints that she should remedy.

"You look stunning, by the way," Gwendolyn said. "Fantastic look."

Gia laughed. "Thank you, my friend helped dress me, but don't I pay you to say that?"

"Last I looked it wasn't in my job description, but it's true, sweetheart." Gwendolyn was a good fifteen years older than Gia and had taken on the maternal older sister role in her life.

"Well then, I will tell my personal stylist." In other words, she'd high-five Hadley, who had come through as always, putting together slim black pants with a flowing white top that showed off the physique she worked so hard on. She'd pulled her hair back and let it fall to her shoulders, which Hadley said was a softer look for her.

"Well, son of a bitch," Gwendolyn said in a huff.

Gia swiveled and followed her eye line to see Elle Britton chatting up the corn chip guy. She had to laugh. Of course Elle would already be in the know and two steps ahead of Gia, sparkling like the crown jewel. Gia watched as she laughed along with that Theo guy, touching his forearm briefly and nodding along with whatever he was saying. If there was a networking playbook, Elle had surely worn it out cover to cover, if she hadn't written the damned thing herself.

Gwendolyn gave her a shove. "We gotta get you over there."

Gia balked as they moved toward Elle and Theo. "Why?" she hissed.

"Because you never know when you're going to need additional sponsorship, and a juicy, plump endorsement deal wouldn't hurt your portfolio. You don't have enough of 'em. Now, get over there and play in the sandbox."

She hated the reality, but Gwendolyn had a point. Given her high ranking on the tour, she really should be pulling in more from external sources. She tended to shy away from those opportunities unless pushed. "All right. All right. I'll talk to him." She glanced back at Gwendolyn. "You're a bulldog."

Gwendolyn growled in response. It frightened her. She gave herself a quick shake and brightened into a smile.

"Well, if it isn't the rankings climber herself," Theo said as she approached them. He shook her hand heartily. "Gia Malone, your name's all over the place these days. Theo Trowebridge, marketing director for Trainers. Nice to meet you."

"Likewise. I'm a fan of your product." A stretch. Corn chips were corn chips. Apparently, Trainers were a healthy alternative to the stuff already on the market. That's about all she knew.

Elle grinned at Gia like they were best friends, but then she did that with everyone. "How are you tonight, Gia?"

"It's a good night. And you?"

"I'm having a fantastic time. Everyone looks great." Well, no one really came close to Elle. Her hair was down and a little wavy tonight in an understated, glamorous kind of way. She wore a patterned skirt and a sleeveless top that really brought out the blue of her eyes. Not that Gia had noticed. Though the men in the room sure seemed to, stealing not-so-discreet glances at Elle's legs as they passed. The world was a virtual meat market.

"Wait," Theo said, glancing between the two of them. "Have you two seen each other since Fiji and the big final?"

"Not since Fiji, no," Elle said sweetly.

His eyes widened. "So, this might be a little awkward. I read about the controversy." He made a face that said *yikes*.

Gia held her smile. Tried to. "I don't think there was anything too controversial about that final."

He seemed thoughtful. "Lot of folks thought there might be an interference call on that last wave of Elle's you dropped in on."

"I didn't drop in. I wasn't anywhere near Elle," Gia told him calmly. "I think she would agree that she had every opportunity to capitalize on that wave outside of any interference from me."

Elle held her thumb and forefinger close together. "You were a little close."

"That's not what you said at the press conference afterward." Gia felt her defenses flare, though she would hold that damn smile if it killed her.

"Well, that was neither the time or place. Did you take some liberty on that drop-in? Yes. But those press events should be more about the love of the sport." If there had been popcorn nearby, Theo would have grabbed a bowl as he listened in fascinated amusement. This was probably not what Gwendolyn had had in mind.

"I guess I try to be up front and honest with whoever I'm speaking with."

Elle's perfect smile faltered. "Why have you decided that I'm disingenuous?"

"You kind of just said so."

Theo's head swiveled to Elle for her response, and Gia inwardly cringed. She was behaving badly in front of a potential networking mark.

Elle scoffed uncharacteristically. It was nice to know she was capable. "You know what? Never mind."

Theo held up a hand. "I'm sensing some hostility."

"Not at all," Elle said, brightening, probably remembering where she was. "Just some post-tournament playback. Gia and I have always had a healthy, if not competition-laced, respect for each other. Right?"

Gia shrugged. "Sure." And then thought better and amended that. "Yes. We have."

"Just what I was hoping you'd say. I have a proposition for you both."

Gia and Elle exchanged an uneasy glance. For the *two* of them? "And what would that be?" Elle asked.

"A Trainers campaign featuring the two of you. Highlighting the rivalry in the water and out. You'd be joint spokespersons, and the stars of our campaign."

"There's no rivalry," Elle said, as if it were the easiest thing in the world.

Theo raised an eyebrow. "I beg to differ, and so do most surf fans. But even the people who have no clue who you are will love the spots we'll put together for you."

Gia was skeptical. "So, you're proposing an ad campaign based on—"

"The race for number one," Theo supplied. "Who's going to end up with the top ranking by the time this season closes out?"

Gia could tell from Elle's understated smirk that she didn't really think the ranking was up for grabs. Gia knew differently. If she could turn in just a handful of successful tournament showings and take Elle down another time or two, she'd have the points. It wouldn't be easy, but it wasn't outside the realm of possibility. She was currently two in the world. World champion was within her grasp, and she was making steady progress. Apparently, others had noticed.

Elle paused and adjusted a strand of hair off her cheek. "It's an intriguing proposition."

And would you look at that? Theo ran with the encouragement, looking like a dog with a giant, meat-filled bone. He stepped forward, energized. "I see commercials, magazine ads, billboards, all cleverly put together and all showcasing Trainers. Listen, the chips are about a healthier snack option, and what sport showcases athleticism and the human physique the way surfing does?"

Gwendolyn would kill her if she balked. "I guess I'm with Elle. Sounds cool, but maybe we can get a few more details to fully understand where you're headed?"

He nodded. "I'll draw up a formal proposal and send it over to your people." He pointed at each of them. "This could be a really fantastic partnership."

"I, for one, hope so," Elle said.

"Me, too," Gia lied.

"I'll leave you to your bickering, then," he said, eyes dancing, as if he'd just located his own personal pot of gold. "And please, whatever you do, keep it up."

Once they were alone, Elle turned to her. "If we do this, we have to pinkie promise each other that we'll keep it classy."

Gia turned her face and regarded Elle out of the side of her eye. "Did you just say the words *pinkie promise*?"

"Is that too pedestrian for you?"

"It's too sixth grade for me."

Elle sighed. "Fine. Blood oath at midnight it is. Whatever works for you. The point here is that this campaign could be a really good thing for both of us, if it's done right."

"Agreed. I want it to be just as tasteful as you do."

"As tasteful as you dropping in on that wave?"

Gia smiled. It was a good barb. Points for Elle. "Something like that."

Elle pushed a fist into Gia's shoulder as she walked away. "Train hard. Just know I'm training harder."

"Bet on it." Wait. That came out wrong. "Bet that you're *wrong!*" she called lamely to Elle's retreating form. Instead of turning back, she offered Gia a wave of her fingers over her shoulder. Damn that woman. How did she always seem to come away with the upper hand? Gia blinked after Elle and watched as a waiter did a double take as she passed, his eyes zeroing in on her ass, her long, tanned legs. Gia shook her head at him, not at all noticing them herself.

Deep breath.

Not at all.

Sometimes she really hated herself.

❖

Gia sat on a green cushioned couch in the outdoor seating area at Seven Shores while she looked over the Trainers paperwork Gwendolyn had sent over. It was late in the day, and the loss of the sun overhead left the air chilly. Gia didn't mind. For whatever reason, the window from late afternoon until dusk was Gia's favorite time of the day. It made her feel like something exciting lay in store as evening encroached.

The contract looked fine to her. In fact, it was a damn good offer, and with Gwendolyn's stamp of approval, and her attorney's, she was ready to sign. The i's had all been dotted and the t's had all been crossed. She tried not to think in depth about the fact that she would actually be working on this campaign with Elle. At least she would be paid a hell of a lot of money to do it.

"Oh! Is that the chip contract?" Autumn asked, joining her. She'd taken to working shorter days at Pajamas since the pregnancy and dropped her apron on the chair next to the one she'd plopped down in.

"Yeah, I guess we're a go."

"I have to buy them now."

"No, you don't."

"Do, too." Autumn ran her hand through her springy red curls as if to bring life back to them after a long day. "Understand something. If Gia Malone says I should eat these chips, I'm going to eat 'em."

Gia laughed. "I had no idea I had that kind of power. Gia Malone also thinks you should give her free coffee for the rest of time."

"Strangely, that one didn't work as well," Autumn said seriously, and then moved right along. "This means you and Elle, your number one rival, will grace the screen together."

Gia sighed. "Apparently."

Autumn raised an eyebrow. "Competition be damned. She's hot. You guys will look great together. That marketing guy is no idiot."

"She is not hot," Gia said, and felt the lie burn her tongue.

"Okay, if you say so. Except she is."

Gia let it go.

"So, when was the last time you got laid anyway?" Autumn asked.

Gia stared at her, water bottle stalled midway to her lips. "What kind of segue is that?"

"On reflection, it feels like an effective one," Autumn said. "We were talking about a hot girl and now we're talking about what one does with hot girls. So, dish. Laid. When? Go."

"I don't know." Gia shrugged. "There was a girl a few months back at a tournament in Hawaii. A local. Just a one-night thing."

"A groupie? You're doing it with groupies now? That's a thing?"

"No," Gia said, figuring out how to explain. "It's not a thing at all. It was a drunken, celebratory mistake after a big win, but you asked, and I don't lie."

Autumn grinned. "I got laid this morning."

Gia sat back against the couch with a laugh. "Aha. This was just a front for you to gloat. Isabel would call this sex-gloating."

"And sex-gloat I shall. It was glorious, G." Autumn's eyes lit up and she shook her head as if the mere mention transported her back in time. "There were stars and rainbows. Glitter fell from the heavens."

Gia shook her head in appreciation. "Maybe Kate deserves a medal for more than just firefighting."

"Good God, that woman does things to me. And with the pregnancy hormones hitting, let's just say it's happening a lot more often. Speaking of which, I'm feeling a little tired. Might head inside."

"I see straight through you, Carpenter."

Autumn grinned. "Yet I feel no shame."

Gia watched as her friend made the short trek to the apartment she shared with Kate on the bottom floor. The same apartment that had led to their meeting the year prior. There was a cosmic justice in that, Gia decided. It was also nice to have Autumn living so close by.

"Hey, is that the contract?"

Gia glanced at the gates to see Isabel enter the courtyard, hand in hand with Taylor.

"Yep, they want to get started right away."

"For the corn chips, right?" Taylor asked. "They're not bad. I gave them a try."

"I'll take not bad. What are you two up to?"

"Just here to grab some clothes. I'll be at Taylor's for the next few days, since it's closer to work and we'll be pulling some long hours. Fat Tony is coming, too."

"Cool." Isabel's cat, Fat Tony, had slowly become the hateful little mascot of Seven Shores. They took turns feeding and tending to him on weekends when Isabel spent her days and nights at Taylor's. When it was Gia's turn, she'd stay an hour or two and play hide-and-seek with the moody cat, allowing him to leap out from under the couch and attack her feet. She feigned surprise for his benefit, but let's be honest, he was fooling no one. As far as Isabel and Taylor went, Gia wondered why the two of them didn't just bite the bullet and move in together already. They seemed adamant about not rushing but were so insanely in love, she didn't really get the point. To each their own, her mom always said.

"Do you know she has her own calendar?" Taylor asked. "The other surfer, Elle Britton."

Gia nodded. "I've heard that somewhere." She'd heard it everywhere. They sold that calendar at vendor stands at the tournaments. Those things flew off the shelves and people lined up in droves for Elle to sign them. Some of the photos had her in action, shredding like she was born to do it. Other months were a little more…sexy in nature. Elle in a swimsuit, simply holding her board. She'd thumbed through it once or twice, purely out of curiosity.

"How did you come across an Elle Britton calendar?" Isabel asked, scratching her head.

Taylor scoffed. "One of my writers used to have it pinned to their cubicle at work."

Isabel turned to her, amusement plastered all over her face. "And you just happened to notice one day as you breezed through? 'Oh, would you look at that! A hot girl in a bathing suit!'"

"Not hot," Gia supplied.

They ignored her.

Taylor held up both hands. "I will completely admit to finding those shots…motivating."

Isabel laughed. "That motivation is causing you to blush. Oh! And it's spreading. This could get embarrassing. Look out, everyone."

"You're awful," Taylor said, now the impressive shade of a tomato.

"Of course I am. I don't have my own calendar or anything. Not even a desk version."

"There's always Christmas," Taylor said innocently. "I'll need something under the tree. I don't think you even need the swimsuit."

Isabel's mouth fell open. "And now *I'm* blushing. Perfect." She shook her head. "I think posing naked might be a little beyond me."

Taylor smiled. "Not if memory serves."

Gia held up a hand. "You guys get that I'm sitting here, right?"

Isabel laughed. "My fault. C'mon, let's get my stuff," she said to Taylor. "G, you're in charge of the complex until I get back. No loud parties, understand? Larry Herman rule."

"On it."

Gia rolled her shoulders, wondering what was in the air that had her friends all sexed up. If there was time to be jealous, or the smallest burst of energy available, she would have been.

"Oh, wow! Is that it? Is that *the* contract?"

Gia stared hard at Hadley as she approached, keys jangling from her hand. Her hair was swept up in that posh way she did it for work in some sort of blond twist. Her designer clothes only confirmed where she'd been. "You guys planned this? Isabel put you up to this, didn't she?"

"Planned what?" Hadley asked.

"To all open with the exact same sentence? It's like Groundhog Day."

Hadley shrugged, dismissing it. "It's cuz we all live together. Mind meld. It's real. Now, is that the contract we've been waiting on?"

"It's the contract."

Hadley stared in awe. "Can I hold it?" she whispered.

Gia passed the stack of papers her way. "You're so weird."

"I'm *reverent*." Hadley held the contract to her chest as if to soak it in, swaying slightly as if backed by a choir. "There's a difference, and this contract is huge for you, which makes me extra happy. Next level stuff, Gia. I'm proud of you. You should be proud of you, too."

Hearing Hadley gush made it hard to hide her own smile, because Had was right. This was the kind of exposure she'd been looking for, and with exposure came opportunity, and those were the kinds of things that kept a career afloat and tournament fees covered into the future. Leave it to Hadley to remind her of life's little business truths. "Yeah, well, sometimes I get caught up and forget to celebrate the small victories."

"Not small. Huge. This is a huge victory."

Gia swallowed the urge to downplay and nodded instead. "Huge."

"And in preparation for this campaign, have you figured out your Elle strategy? You probably want to if you'll be working together a lot. I can't even imagine how that's going to play out. You two working side by side."

Another valid point. "I was planning to just be professional and not let her get to me. Probably not the best plan, though, because she always seems to."

"We could do better. Maybe we need a poster board." Hadley

looked skyward. "Not to get off topic, but it's intriguing what Iz said a couple weeks back, isn't it?"

"That Ms. Pac-Man should be allowed to have boobs? The only problem with that is where would they go?"

Hadley held her eyes closed for several seconds. "No. Gia. Strangely, not that."

"Give me a hint."

"I meant the part where she said you and Elle had *sparks*. Apparently, this corn chip executive thought so, too. Interesting series of events is all."

Gia felt her defenses engage. "Please tell me you're not going there. Not everything is hearts and butterflies, Had, just because you want it to be."

"First of all, ouch. And second of all, I'm not going there," Hadley said quickly. "I know you hate Elle and how always put together she is. But maybe that's part of it. That tension."

"I see through her. That's all. I'm not her number one fan. That part is true, but it certainly doesn't mean we have sparks. The whole idea is stupid. Isabel's just projecting her glamorous, fictional world onto my life, and the fit's not there. It's lame."

"Understood," Hadley said, with an affirmative nod. "Won't mention the sparks again. Will mention nachos, though." Her eyes took on longing. "Let's get some on the boardwalk. Please, with sour cream on top? My day smacked me on the back of the head rudely. Cheese will help me love everyone again."

Now, nachos on Venice Beach was an offer Gia couldn't pass up, so she softened, letting go of the bristles from the conversation with a sigh. "You just said the magic words."

Hadley broke into a grin. "This way, superstar. It's time to celebrate your chip deal in style."

Gia nodded. "With more chips."

"Duh."

CHAPTER FOUR

Elle tunneled a hand through her untamed hair as she studied the nondescript building through the windshield of her car. Her call time for the photo shoot was not for another ten minutes, but she was stringent about leaving a cushion in case traffic was unruly. It hadn't been, and as was often the case, she arrived at her destination early. She rolled the window down on her Beetle and let the afternoon breeze drift through the car.

She had a third date with Christopher scheduled for that night. The shoot for Trainers would likely go through the afternoon, leaving her a small window to get home and changed before he'd pick her up. She'd need to do a few stretches first, as her morning workout left her muscles beaten and sore. She grinned, loving it when her muscles pulled. A sign of her hard work.

Things with Christopher had remained pleasant enough. He was witty, and kind, and knew how to dress himself, which was sheer bonus. They'd taken to texting in between dates, and he was a solid conversationalist. So why wasn't she more excited about tonight? She was seriously starting to wonder about herself and her ability to stay interested in a guy for long.

After checking the clock, she headed inside and found hair and makeup ready to doll her to pieces for the shoot. She took a seat in the folding chair as they went to work. Loud rock music blared from nearby and her gaze settled on Gia, who stood in front of a green screen several yards away, posing for the photographer in a black and blue two-piece that made her look badass and feminine at the same time. She wasn't sure who had chosen the suit, but it was a good call. Elle had almost missed the bag of chips in her hand as she stared at the tangle of dark hair pooling at her shoulders—that was how great she looked. Lights and reflectors framed the space around Gia, and a myriad of assistants dashed here and there adjusting props, lighting, and Gia's hair. As her hair was styled, Elle strained to hear the conversation above the volume of the music.

"Hit me with a competitive gaze," the photographer called to Gia, who adjusted her grin into a hint of a glare. It wasn't close to the look she got on her face in the heat of real competition. The one that said she'd come to win. Elle knew that look all too well. Thinking about it now, visualizing it, got her worked up, and remembering the finals loss in her not-so-distant past only bolstered the effect. Nope. She wasn't a fan of that competitive gaze at all, and rolled her shoulders to rid herself of the strong physical reaction.

Half an hour later, with her hair shiny and her makeup in place, she joined Gia under the lights. They would do several different looks together before Gia would head out and Elle would shoot her solo shots. The schedule was designed to make maximum use of their time, which she appreciated. She also knew that she had more experience at this kind of thing than Gia did and would likely finish her part of the session faster.

"Looks like you're having fun over here," Elle said, standing off to the side of the shoot.

"Oh, I don't know about fun," Gia said, passing her the briefest of smiles between shots. That smile was probably forced, she decided, even though it didn't seem so. Would Gia afford her a real smile?

She and Gia Malone had never had the best relationship, and for whatever reason that went beyond their competition in the water. Elle had gone out of her way to be nice to Gia on more occasions than she could count, only to have that friendship branch stepped on, snapped in half, and handed back to her in pieces. Gia didn't like Elle, and after all was said and done, she wasn't especially fond of Gia either. She found her hyperfocused and closed off for the most part, though she did seem to have lots of friends on the tour. Didn't mean they couldn't have a cordial working relationship. Elle planned to make sure that happened.

"Oh, come on. It's not so bad."

"For you, maybe," Gia said. "Mugging isn't my thing. I just look like an asshole."

"Then don't think of it that way."

While she could see that Gia was nervous and outside of her comfort zone, she hid it well. Plus, her looks would be killer in print. She had these large brown eyes that just didn't quit, thick dark hair, and a sculpted body people killed for, that *Elle* would kill for. The camera was going to love her, which was great news for the success of the campaign.

"So, what's your suggestions?" Gia asked.

The photographer stepped away from his camera. "That's good, Gia. Let's take five and then we can do the two-shot with Elle."

"Cool. Thanks, Jake."

"Elle, good to see you," he said, dashing over and kissing her cheek.

She beamed. "Always a good day when I get to work with you, Jake." They'd done a handful of shoots together in the past, and he was easily one of her favorite LA photographers.

Elle walked all the way onto set, now that it wasn't in use, refocusing on her conversation with Gia. It wasn't like she had much else to do. "It's all in how you approach the day."

Gia eyed her skeptically but seemed intrigued, as if she could use a lifeline, even if it did come from Elle. "What does that mean?"

"You just tell yourself that you own the room."

She laughed. "Yeah, but I don't."

"No one does. But that projected confidence helps you get through it."

"That's what you do?"

"Always."

Gia smiled and glanced away. "Well, that explains a lot."

Elle laughed, and accepted the barb. "There's nothing wrong with playing to the crowd. I'm not sure why you look down on it."

Gia took only a moment to answer. She smelled like fresh cotton. "I would just rather focus on the surfing."

"Yet here you stand."

Gia offered a nod in surrender. Elle had her there and knew it. "Are we gonna get through this together?" Gia asked, her guard coming down. Thank God for that, because going toe-to-toe every time they worked together was going to get old. She hated conflict and would go out of her way to avoid it.

"I think we'll be fine."

"Good," Gia said. "Me, too."

Jake clapped behind them and joined them on set. "Okay, we need some rivalry shots for the chip folks to choose from. The slogan for phase one of the campaign is apparently 'There's only room for one at the top.' I don't know if you've met the ad exec on the project, but—"

"Mallory Spencer," a striking brunette said, joining the conversation. She wore a tailored business suit, and came with a kind smile. "Pleasure to meet you both. I'm an admirer of your work." They said their hellos and Mallory detailed the goals for the campaign. "So essentially, phase one is all about the competition, the rivalry between the two of you. Hard-core, intense, the battle for the number one spot. Theo's got it all worked out. We're simply implementing his vision."

Elle chuckled quietly, but Gia caught it and raised a questioning eyebrow.

"What?" Elle said in response. "I just don't really feel the title's up for grabs."

Gia held her gaze. "You won't. Until the moment I take it from you."

The banter was lighthearted but laced with an undercurrent of truth that Mallory clearly picked up on. She pointed at them. "Use that in that shoot. It's golden."

"Shouldn't be hard," Elle said with a grin.

"Let's do it, Britton."

She was surprised Gia didn't shoulder check her as they turned to position themselves on set according to Jake's instructions. For the first round of shots, they faced each other as if advertising a Saturday night fight. What that meant was that they were forced to stand face-to-face in challenge. She attempted the glare Mallory had asked for, but it was hard to sustain and she felt the edges of her mouth turn up. "I'm sorry," she called out and readjusted, giving her arms a shake. "You're a badass," she told herself out loud. "Look at what a badass you are."

Gia laughed. "How am I supposed to keep a straight face with you saying stuff like that?"

Elle looked at her innocently. "That part's on you."

"Are you serious right now?"

"As a badass."

Gia shook her head, they readjusted and went at it again. Hardcore stares. Serious attitude. It worked for a few clicks, until Elle dissolved into giggles. Embarrassed, and unable to stop, she held up a hand. "My fault entirely. This is just not me. I'm usually…happy. It just comes more naturally."

"Not today you're not," Mallory said. "Because this woman is about to take what's yours. Got it? Rip it the hell away from you."

Gia raised another eyebrow in appreciation.

What was with all the eyebrow raising and how was she doing it so effectively? Elle harnessed the outrage, planted her feet, and faced Gia, competitive stare firmly in place. The camera clicked, clicked, clicked as Jake moved around them, offering encouragement. He was talking, but she wasn't really listening. Her focus was on Gia, because when told to stare at another person for an extended amount of time, you start to notice things about them. First of all, Gia's skin was flawless and soft-looking. It almost made Elle want to reach out and touch her cheek briefly just to find out how soft. Because of their proximity, she could feel the heat coming from Gia's body. She took a breath. And then there were her lips—

"Wow. Perfect. Let's adjust for look two," Mallory said, shattering Elle's concentration and pulling her back into the here and now. She blinked hard and forced herself to focus on Mallory. This woman seemed to know exactly what she wanted and had a warm, yet knowledgeable, way of expressing herself. Elle appreciated her moving them along. After all, she had a date to get to. "Let me just adjust this one strand of hair," Mallory said to Elle, moving the strand off her forehead. "And we're a go. Gorgeous."

The rest of the shoot went surprisingly well. Gia found her stride, and Elle's individual shoot was a piece of cake. She thanked the hair and makeup staff, Jake, and of course Mallory, who would apparently help oversee the campaign from New York as they moved forward. Feeling accomplished, if not a little tired, she headed to the parking lot where the sun was setting and the temperatures dropping. She expected to hop in her car, put the top down, and jam out to some tunes. What she didn't expect was to find Gia sitting on the curb. Elle passed her a questioning glance.

"Won't start," Gia said blandly, and gestured to her black Jeep Wrangler. Her shoulders drooped and her eyebrows were drawn.

"Do you want me to take a look?" Elle asked, approaching. She was quick when it came to troubleshooting cars, something her father had made sure she and her two brothers were adept at.

"You know about cars?" Gia asked. She stood and pushed her hands into the back pockets of her cutoff shorts.

"Not everything. But enough to help diagnose."

Gia hesitated, and Elle was confident it was hard for her to ask for help.

"Do you mind?"

"No. That would be…great. Thanks."

It took her only a few moments to ascertain that the engine on the Jeep would crank but not start, narrowing down the problem. "When was the last time you had your battery replaced?"

"Maybe three months ago?"

"Then I'm going to guess this is an ignition issue. Unless, of course, you're out of gas."

Gia balked. "I'm not out of gas. I'm not a total dumbass."

Elle placed her hands on her hips. "No, not totally."

The shot pulled a grin from Gia, who had an amazing smile. A shame she didn't employ it more frequently.

"Unfortunately, you're probably going to have to have it towed to the shop."

Gia tucked a strand of hair behind her ear as Elle exited the driver's side of the Jeep. "I was afraid of that. Thanks for the diagnosis. I'll call it in and see if I can get a friend to pick me up."

"Cool. Yeah, okay." Elle wasn't sure what to do in this moment. Should she just walk away and leave Gia there on the curb, knowing a friend would come along eventually? Nope. Not her style. Even where Gia was concerned. "I can drop you."

"I live in Venice."

Right. There was that little haul to consider. "It's cool. I honestly don't mind."

"Are you sure? I mean, I'd appreciate it."

"Hop in, Malone. I hope you like Bieber."

Gia paused. "That's a joke, right?"

Elle stared at her. "I realize you think I'm a vapid Barbie Doll, but give me *some* credit."

"No, not *totally* vapid."

Elle laughed. "I see what you did there. Maybe there's hope for you after all."

"Oh, well, if Elle Britton thinks so, then I'm golden."

"Shut up and get in the car."

They drove in silence for a while, listening to the classic rock station. Gia stared out the window. Elle focused on the road. They'd never really been left together for too long on their own. Now what? Elle wasn't the type to sit in silence for extended periods, especially when it felt awkward. In fact, she couldn't stand it. Her social compass was screaming at her. Minutes passed. Still no one said anything. She felt like she might explode, and then did.

"I have a date tonight."

Gia turned to her. "Oh yeah?"

"I don't know why I'm telling you this. You hate me," Elle said, shaking her head at the personal direction of her comment. Why couldn't she have said something about surfing or groceries or the weather, for God's sake? Her mouth had a mind of its own.

"I don't hate you."

"You do, too. In fact, you've gone well out of your way for years now to be sure I know it." She cringed again. Why was she making their car ride a therapy session? She had excellent people skills. Why were they failing her where Gia was concerned?

Gia seemed to soften. "For the record, we're just different people. You're perky and peppy and love the media. I just want to surf and leave it at that."

"So you're saying we don't speak the same language?"

Gia shrugged. "I guess that's probably a big part of it."

A long silence. "It's not a crime to be upbeat."

"I guess not." Gia seemed to consider the comment further. "But you can't tell me you're feeling 'on' all the time. Some of that is manufactured, right? It has to be. The smiles, the toss of your hair, the endless hugs to everyone you see."

"Okay," Elle said, nodding. "So now we're getting somewhere. You think I'm fake."

"I didn't use that word."

"But you wanted to."

"Maybe a little."

"Well, don't hold back." They were really going at each other now, and it felt quite satisfying.

Gia sighed, decelerating their exchange. "Look, it's likely we're going to be tossed together a lot because of this campaign, so maybe we should find a way to—"

"Get along."

"Not kill each other," Gia said simultaneously.

They smiled at their different approaches, a common ground moment.

"Deal," Elle said finally.

Gia nodded. Another silent stretch hit. In a plot twist she was not expecting, Gia saved them this time. "Who's the guy?"

Elle passed her a glance as she exited for Venice. "What guy?"

"Your date. You mentioned having one tonight."

"Oh, right!" Elle smiled. "His name is Christopher. We've gone out twice before. I like him. I think."

"Does he surf?"

"He does not. He's in finance." Out of the corner of her eye, she saw Gia wince. "But not boring finance. Exciting stuff. He's smart."

"And hot?"

"He's good looking, yes."

"The full package, then." Gia pointed. "I'm up here on the right."

Elle followed Gia's directions until they pulled up to what she could only describe as a boutique apartment complex. A post stood in front with a cute hanging sign that said Seven Shores, which made sense as that seemed to be the address, 7 Shores Drive.

Elle nodded, studying the building. "This is where Gia Malone lives."

Gia glanced up at her place. "It's not fancy, but it's blocks from the beach, which as you know, is important."

"I'm guessing you're training for Swatch Pro." It was the next tournament on the Championship Tour. This time they'd stay stateside in San Clemente, California.

"Only day and night."

Elle nodded. "Me, too. It's like I never sleep."

"Bring it, Britton. I'm ready for you." Gia raised her eyebrows in a challenge that was only half in jest. Elle shifted, knowing that as much as she scoffed at Gia's recent rankings climb, it did increase the pressure. She pushed that much harder during her workouts knowing that Gia was only a handful of points away from taking her title as they neared the end of the tour. While motivating, it also left Elle nervous and a little off-kilter, which wasn't her favorite place to be.

Gia tapped the top of the Beetle once. "Hey, thanks for the lift. I appreciate it. You didn't have to come all the way out here. Very cool of you."

"Anytime," Elle said, brightening to her typical smile. "It also gives me a chance to scope out your practice beach."

"Totally my territory. Don't get any ideas." The comment was playful and a good note to end on.

"Be good," Elle said, and pulled away from the curb, realizing that that whole thing could have gone a lot worse. Maybe they'd made a little progress today. At least, she hoped so. But it was time to push Gia Malone from her brain altogether. She had a date to get to and an outfit to settle on. She cranked the music and drove toward the setting sun, wondering just what delicious possibilities the night had in store for her.

❖

"Freeze. Don't move a muscle."

Gia glanced up to see Autumn standing in the entryway to the courtyard. "Why am I freezing exactly?"

"Oh, don't play innocent with me. We saw you get out of Elle Britton's car. What gives?"

Gia glanced around. "First of all, who's we?"

"The three of us," Autumn said, gesturing to her stomach. "As in, me and the twins."

"I didn't realize they kept tabs on me the way their nosy mother does."

"Well, they do. They're advanced for their age. Now spill."

Gia walked on, passing Autumn, who turned and followed her, hot on her heels. "There's nothing to tell. Jeep's getting towed, which sucks."

"Did she do something to the Jeep?"

"No."

"Did you guys do something *in* the Jeep? Together, perhaps?"

Gia whirled on her. "You need to stop hanging out with Isabel. She's a bad influence on all three of you." She made a circular gesture in the direction of Autumn's stomach.

"And why is that?"

Gia turned at the sound of Isabel's voice and found her lounging on one of the courtyard couches, probably trying to steal some sun for that pale skin of hers, a common and genuinely futile occurrence.

"What did I do now?"

Gia marched over to her. "You're the one getting both Hadley and Autumn going about Elle Britton and sparks and conflict."

"Saucy conflict," Isabel amended, matter-of-factly. "You guys have the recipe. You're the ones with the rivalry. I just pointed it out. I can't help it if the romantic and the busybody have both run with it." She shrugged. "Not on me."

"Totally on you."

Autumn raised her hand. "Which one am I?"

"The busybody," Isabel and Gia said in unison.

She nodded. "I own that. The busybody would formally like to point out that this one just got out of Elle's white convertible Beetle. Saw it with my own busybody eyes."

"Get out of town," Isabel said, intrigued now. "The story heats up." She squinted at Autumn. "What else did you see? Report."

"Nothing," Gia told them. "Because there was nothing to see. Stop being dumb."

"I saw them laughing," Autumn said. "Most definitely. And smiling. Gia touched the car fondly like this." Autumn imitated the tapping of the hood, but drew it out in exaggerated fashion.

Gia rolled her eyes.

"Wow," Isabel said nodding, as if taking it all in. "That's progression from wanting to kill each other. Right on schedule, too. I couldn't write this any better."

"I hate you both," Gia said calmly, and headed to the outdoor staircase that would lead to her second-floor apartment. Let them speculate all they wanted. In fact, let them drown in curiosity. But then…she couldn't hate them for long. In fact, it lasted about ninety seconds. Her ability to hold a long-term grudge against her friends was embarrassingly lame. "*Ms. Pac-Man* in twenty?" she called down to Isabel, who glanced up. They'd bonded hard over their love for retro video games and never looked back. Isabel was not only competitive, she understood the treasure that was *Ms. Pac-Man*. A rare find.

"Done. My place. I'll tell Kate."

Barney, the beach bum who lived next door to Isabel, strutted from his apartment and looked up at her. "Surf chick?"

"What's up, Barney?" Gia called down.

"Can you introduce me to your surf friend in the car?"

She stared at him. "No."

"She's the girl of my dreams," he said happily, and ran his hand through his shaggy blond hair. "Got her calendar on my fridge. She's in a swimsuit."

Isabel and Autumn exchanged a grin and a fist bump on the couches. Their muscle-bound neighbor was generally a happy-go-lucky individual, if a little random. You could always count on Barney to lend a hand when you needed one, making this the first time that Gia wanted to murder him. She took a moment to gather enough energy to not do just that.

"She has a date tonight, with a guy named Christopher, so I'm thinking she's not in the cards for you, Barn."

"Boo, Christopher," Autumn said.

Isabel nodded. "We hate him."

"Who is this dude? I'll take him down," Barney asked, flexing. Seriously? Did the guy ever wear a shirt?

Gia lifted a shoulder. "Got me. I just report the weather." She pointed at Isabel. "Pac-Man with a bow in twenty."

"Eighteen now."

"Do you at least have her digits?" Barney called.

Gia chose to ignore him. She let herself into her apartment and crashed temporarily on her couch. With thirteen minutes to veg, and five to make sure her car was brought to the shop, she used the time to relax and unpack her psyche from such a weird and unexpected day. The shoot hadn't been nearly as awful as she'd expected. She and Elle had sparred a tad, but nothing overt. The one detail she couldn't shake, however, was Elle's assertion that Gia had gone out of her way to be unfriendly. While true to a certain extent, hearing it played back was like a punch in the gut. She wasn't raised to be a mean-spirited person. She didn't want to be. In fact, she'd always tried to be kind. Yet she'd let her sense of competition override those instincts when it came to Elle and her bubbly shtick. Yes, Elle and her perfection annoyed her no end, but she didn't deserve poor treatment.

Gia sat up and ran a hand through her hair as self-recrimination swept in. She'd have to find a way to change her behavior where Elle was concerned. And you know what? Maybe Elle wasn't as bad as Gia had built her up to be. Today they'd actually had fun together on the ride home. She seemed…genuine during their conversation.

Gia would focus on the good. She could do that. She lay back down and gave it a shot.

Okay. Elle could be warm on occasion, like today when she'd gone out of her way to help Gia out. She was a killer surfer, with the kind of shred and precision Gia worked long hours to emulate. She was definitely pretty, and when she stood near Gia in a swimsuit, like today at the shoot, it was hard to remember the annoying stuff. She visualized that moment now, taking note of her own very acute reaction. Gia covered her eyes and shook her head. What a complicated scenario she had herself in. She gave her face a scrub to wash away the image of sparkling blue eyes and the swell of cleavage, and reached blindly for her phone.

Time to rescue her car and forget about the rest.

As if that were an option.

CHAPTER FIVE

He had constantly moving hands. Like rovers. All over the place." Elle sipped her Sauvignon Blanc, appreciating the crisp reveal of flavors. "A lot of touching going on."

"Thank God. I hate it when a guy just grabs hold and goes for it." Holly grinned, enjoying the details from Elle's date with Christopher two nights earlier.

If only Elle could enjoy them as much. She'd hadn't thought much about the night since, which told her it hadn't made much of an impact.

"What else?" Holly asked. Her hair bounced as she readjusted to sit cross-legged on her brown leather couch.

Elle noted distantly that Holly's house always smelled of cinnamon and apples. Homey, like her. She sighed from her spot on the floor and searched for more details that she hadn't filed away, realizing she was failing at girl talk yet again. "That's not enough?"

"Not nearly. I'll help. So, his hands are on the move, what then? Spare no detail. This has been a long time coming. When was the last time you got laid?"

Elle thought on it. "A year ago. The guy with the beard, remember? It's when we learned I hate beards. They're so awful, Hol."

"Right. Don't remind me about your facial hair issues. Back to Chris's hands."

"Well, he has big hands and they're clumsy."

"I love big hands." Holly closed her eyes as if whisked away to a magical sex island. "They give me thoughts."

"He tried to unbutton my shirt, but he couldn't quite kiss and do that at the same time. Tons of fumbling, which is not his fault. Don't get me wrong, but again, big hands. It kind of ruined the mood."

Holly went still. "What do you mean ruined the mood?"

Elle stood and walked to Holly's kitchen, where she dumped the rest of her wine and filled her glass with water. Her early morning workout would thank her. "We just talked after that. He's an awesome conversationalist, really. Did you know he studied abroad in Rome when he was twenty? He can still speak Italian and apparently makes a mean veggie lasagna. He's going to make me dinner one night soon."

Holly looked like she'd just announced *Game of Thrones* was moving to the Hallmark Channel. "Hold everything. You're saying you didn't have sex? This story doesn't end in sex?"

"It doesn't," Elle said. "But I still had a great time. We really click."

"I thought this was gonna be a sex story. This was hugely misleading."

Elle inclined her head from side to side. "It's kind of sexy, though, right? Making out, a little bit of groping, hands on the move. No?"

"Yeah, until you stopped them." Holly paused. "Have you ever considered that you're just not that into him?"

Elle had considered it. In fact, she still considered it, because if she were into him she wouldn't have been balancing her checkbook while he attempted to get her naked. There was a disconnect, but then that wasn't exactly new. Sex just wasn't as important to her as it was to other people. The other stuff mattered more. Not a big deal. Some people also liked broccoli, while others were less enthused. It's what made people different from one another. "Sex isn't everything, Hol. Besides, and hear me out, *maybe* I just need to take some time for me and focus on surfing. The season is right at its midpoint, and this is probably not the best time to get caught up in anything overly romantic anyway. Christopher and I can keep it light."

"And compare lasagna recipes." Holly pouted, which she did exceptionally well. "Whatever you say. Allow me to hang up my matchmaking cape."

"You don't have a cape."

"Maybe that was part of the problem. What do I know about matchmaking anyway? I was totally improvising. Oh!" A lightbulb seemed to propel Holly into action. She grabbed her laptop. "I almost forgot. Did you see yourself on SurfNuggets?"

She hadn't. In fact, she avoided SurfNuggets as much as possible. That website reported mainly gossip from the surf world, and usually got it wrong. The last story she'd seen about herself said she'd gained twelve pounds and was leaving the tour for a health camp. Total lies. She loved media attention, just not that kind.

Holly whirled the laptop around to face Elle. She stared down at the headline. "Declaration of War." The article went on to detail a tumultuous relationship between Elle and the number two ranked Gia Malone. It described an all-out feud in which they fought for the Trainers endorsement deal. The short paragraph ended with the line "The claws are out and boy do they sting."

She pointed at the screen, laughing it off. "Ridiculous."

"Well, only a little," Holly said, studying the screen. "They got most of it right. You guys do have a rivalry going and Trainers is a legitimate endorsement deal. You just happen to be sharing it."

Elle rejected the notion. "No way. There's no backbiting, no underhanded tactics."

"Yet," Holly said, with a grin.

"That story is an inflated tabloid piece. Plus, Gia's actually not so bad, it turns out. I mean, she's not great, don't get me wrong, but we had a chance to talk at the shoot." She thought back to their conversation in the car.

Holly looked surprised. "Oh, yeah?"

"I think we came to an informal understanding. We're different people, and that's not going to change. There will be no kumbaya session, but the campaign should be fine. We'll be able to work together easily enough, but there's no way she's coming close to taking my ranking. By the end of the season, I will be this year's world champion. SurfNuggets should put that in their pipe and smoke it."

"I'm glad to hear you still have that fire, Wave Weasel. Keep it. Did you shame her for that late drop-in on your wave in the final?"

Elle grinned, remembering the party and their exchange. "In my own way. She knows how I feel on the subject."

"Well, prepare yourself for the world to start asking questions about your hatred for one another. I have a feeling the gossip is only going to get bigger after this write-up."

Elle shook her head. "It's all so stupid."

"It is." Holly nodded. "But I'll need you to leave now."

"What?" Elle froze the application of her lip gloss, mid-gloss. "You're kicking me out?"

Holly ushered Elle to the door. "All that big hands talk got me going, and Dash is on his way over."

"You were secretly texting him while we talked? You were

summoning your booty call and planning my departure in tandem? What kind of person does that?"

"Me. It's a skill I'm quite proud of."

"You're going to hell."

"Tonight, I'm hoping for heaven. Now leave, so I can change into my sexiest underwear and get some much-needed action. Something you should put on your to-do list at some point."

"Meh. I'm good."

"Honestly, Elle, if you got laid once in a great while, I think you'd be much happier."

Elle scoffed. "I don't know what you're talking about. I am happy. I'm at the peak of my career and enjoy what I do. Take in the noticeable smile on my face. My life is good."

"Please. You're status-quo happy. I'm talking off-the-charts happy."

Elle grumbled as she hit the sidewalk. "Yeah, well, I don't have your sex drive, okay? Not sure what I can do about that. Just a part of life."

"Maybe you just haven't awakened it yet. Stirred that inner, naughty yearning. Food for thought. Now scram. I got yearnings of my own happening."

Elle smiled at her friend and headed down the walk. She'd not brought her car, since she and Holly lived close enough to walk easily to each other's homes, by design. It also allowed them quick access to the beach for impromptu surf sessions. Surfing with her best friend reminded Elle how much she loved the sport. When it was just her and Holly out for a fun Saturday, catching waves, she lost herself in the day, in the sun, the recreational side of an activity she'd forced firmly into the job category years ago. They needed to make a date to do just that soon. Elle needed it.

She checked her phone as she walked, daylight all but extinguished, finding an email from her manager, Kip. *Did you see the latest on you and Malone?*

Elle laughed because she had seen the latest, and Kip was overreacting. There was nothing to talk about. The feud article would be fodder for about ten minutes. Then the world would move on to the next new rumor. She clicked the link just because Kip had included it, and paused right there on the curb.

This wasn't the same story from SurfNuggets.

This was a piece from *Surf Magazine*'s online arm, which came with much more clout. Way more people would stumble across this article. She scanned the words in front of her, not quite believing what she was seeing. At the top of the page was a shot of her and Gia in Elle's car, pulling out of the studio's parking lot. There were a few more shots of them smiling, one of her looking rather adoringly at Gia. How in the world had they managed these shots? She'd seen no one with a camera. The headline read "Canoodling Much?" and was followed by a short paragraph under the photos. Elle read on, flabbergasted.

Spotted together in West Hollywood, Elle Britton and Gia Malone shed their tour rivalry for a flirtatious afternoon of fun. Sources close to the women say they've discovered a new appreciation for each other and are getting in lots of one-on-one time. Are we witnessing a burgeoning romance? How will this new pairing affect the race for the number one?

Beneath the article was that old photo of Gia watching Elle talk to reporters, the one that had received all the attention for Gia's gaze, which had been totally misconstrued.

A romance? She scoffed, then scoffed again to be sure the universe had noticed her scoff. How ridiculous. If anything, they'd done their best to achieve civility. Elle had to laugh. How in the world had two opposing articles hit the internet on the exact same afternoon, both making claims about her relationship with Gia Malone, of all people?

She called Kip, if for no other reason than to figure out an approach to handle the attention that at this point could continue to grow, given the one-two punch.

"Thought I'd be hearing from you," he said, upon answering. They'd worked together for years and could skip the polite greetings.

"So, what's our plan?" Elle asked. "I gave her a ride home when her car wouldn't start. Something with the ignition. That was it."

"I figured. Any clue who these sources are that put you together in a romantic sense?"

"No idea. It's crazy."

"It's not *that* crazy. She's gay, even if you're not. You've not been linked to anyone romantically for more than one outing. They're making a leap and hoping to hit pay dirt."

"Well, they haven't. Trust me on that. Did you see SurfNuggets? They're claiming the exact opposite. What is it they say? Any publicity is good publicity."

He paused. "That part is true. I think we don't comment on the rumors. Any of them. At least for a little while. Let the world wonder and clock the attention."

She laughed. "Interesting angle. All right. We'll try it your way. Gay is trendy, I guess."

He laughed because he was. "Don't ever forget it."

"How's Peter?"

"Handsome and waiting for me to get off the phone."

She laughed. "Don't let me keep you."

❖

A shiver shot through Elle as she ran a hand across the most magnificent naked body she'd ever seen. She relished the feel of heated skin beneath her fingertips. The curves that were on display to her. As their bodies came together, she began to move her hips. Oh, yes. This was good. Slowly at first and then with more purpose, doing everything in her power to draw out the pleasure she sought and losing the battle. She couldn't help it. She rolled her hips faster now, furiously. She wanted it *now*, needed to be touched, to be filled, more than she'd ever needed anything. The delicious ache was all consuming. She bit her bottom lip and slipped her hands between their bodies, cupping two perfect breasts. She held on to them tightly as she was at long last filled, taken, owned. The orgasm ripped through her in an intense rush, leaving her limbless, breathless, and reveling in ecstasy. She reached for Gia, wanting to touch her one more time, needing to…but she was gone.

A distant beeping infiltrated her thoughts. It grew louder with each passing second. She resisted, loving this wonderful place she'd found herself in but losing that battle. Elle blinked several times and stared at the ceiling, attempting to right herself. A dream. She understood that she'd been in the midst of a sexual and incredibly realistic dream. Her heart still hammered away as she glanced at her surroundings, anything to anchor herself in the present. Hyperaware of her body, her accelerated breathing, and the fact that she'd just come in her sleep, something she generally couldn't even do during sex, Elle took a moment to savor the aftershocks that still took their turns with her. This had never happened to her before. Nothing even close to this. The details of the dream floated back to her, and it was then she understood exactly who she'd been dreaming about.

No way.

She'd just had a sex dream about a girl. A woman. Gia. And it had been *good*. They'd been in some sort of press conference, as usual, then a locker room, and somehow ended up in a hotel room together. Gia had kissed her in the hotel room, and she'd given back just as good, thrusting her tongue into Gia's mouth. They'd touched each other until there were no clothes, or thoughts, or cares other than following their own desire and where it led them. It had led them to some pretty decadent places. Elle threw an arm over her head and marveled.

Well, this was certainly an interesting twist.

It was likely that the article from the night before had inspired the dream and all its salacious detail. That's what happens when your mind runs away with itself. You get crazy dreams. She pushed her sated and boneless body out of bed, needing to shake herself awake and back into the here and now.

Fifteen minutes later, after a quick protein shake, she was on the beach and on her way to five hundred sit-ups and a five-mile run with ankle weights. As she ran, her muscles screamed and her brain flashed on the details of that scandalous dream, examining them, curious as to why they'd had such a potent effect on her unconscious body. Why they still did.

The waves jostled her free of further reflection, and she lost herself in the sun and ocean spray. Surfing always helped center her. In the shower, just before lunch, she ran the soap across her heated skin. This time, the touches came with new meaning, and she remembered the sensations of someone else's hands on her body. Her stomach dipped, and she placed a hand on the shower wall for support. What in the world was all this about? It was just a damn dream. It had nothing to do with reality.

An hour later, phone pressed to her ear with one shoulder as she assembled a turkey sandwich with tomato, she decided to bounce the whole thing off Holly. "Have you ever had a dream about a girl?" She popped a sliver of tomato into her mouth. The tomato was key. Without it, why even have a sandwich?

"Um…all the time. The other night, you and I held up a mall dressed as Mr. and Mrs. Panda. It was epic."

"I'm not talking robberies. Or shopping excursions gone wrong. Or drinks with your girlfriends, who are friends."

"That's a confusing sentence."

"What I'm asking," Elle said, changing the phone to her left shoulder so she could slice her sandwich, "if you've ever had a *dream* dream, if you follow."

"Listen, I have about eight minutes left on my lunch hour and three tiny bites of chicken salad before Stan-the-teller comes to lean against my door and ask what time I get off and what perfume I'm wearing, so you're going to have to be more specific, and fast."

Fine. She'd just put it out there. Say it really quick, like ripping off a Band-Aid. "Have you ever had a sex dream about a girl?"

"Definitely." A long pause. "Are you saying that happened to you?"

So she wasn't alone. These things happened. "Yes. I've just never had one of those before. No big deal." Well, not anymore it wasn't, now that she knew everyone had them.

"Well, they are a big deal if they're good. Was yours good?"

Elle felt the blush that no one was around to see. She flipped around and faced her refrigerator for no real reason and then flipped back. "It wasn't *not* good."

"Hey, I'll take that. Not-bad sex dreams count." Holly's energy dropped noticeably. "Oh, hey, Stan."

Elle suppressed a smile. "Stan-the-Man is right on time. I'll let you get back to work. Thanks for the help."

"I didn't do anything."

"You were my sounding board."

"Then I'm brilliant."

Elle laughed. "Sure. We'll go with brilliant. Bye to Stan."

"Don't encourage him. Can we do a surf date this weekend?"

Elle mentally scanned her calendar. "I'd love to. Let's book it."

"Done. Hey, wait. Who was in the sex dream? You didn't say. Was it me? It was, wasn't it? You've always loved my hair."

"Sorry, Hol. Definitely wasn't you. Bye." She clicked off the call before she was pressed further. She preferred to keep the identity of her dream companion in the vault. She didn't know why, but it mattered.

Speaking of, she had an hour to be on her way to the Trainers shoot, this time for a short commercial spot that would air in a handful of markets in the coming weeks. She scanned the short script on her phone as she ate, realizing distantly that seeing Gia might feel… weird, given the past twenty-four hours. She shook her shoulders as a pleasurable chill moved through her. She needed a plan. Walking in blind was a bad idea. Okay, she should certainly reference the news articles, at the very least in jest, just to get it out there. Keep it from being weird. And she should smile a lot. Be a laid-back, breezy person just enjoying an afternoon commercial shoot. The more personal details of her night, she'd keep to herself. She'd focus on the work and her job, and wait for time to wash away the memories of last night. Maybe after the shoot, she'd call Christopher and see if he was free for dinner.

Status quo was firmly in place. Nothing to see here. Her plan was perfect. Airtight.

What could possibly go wrong?

❖

Gia sat in her small dressing room, waiting until they needed her on set and clutching the script Trainers had provided. She'd practiced her lines with Hadley at least a hundred times in preparation for the shooting of this commercial spot, knowing full well that Elle would walk in and nail it. She was not about to draw attention to herself as the surfer who could only surf. If she prepared enough, and she *had*, she'd get through the afternoon looking every bit the champ Elle was.

"These photos of you and Elle are amazing," Hadley had said the day before.

They'd been rehearsing at Gia's kitchen table when Hadley spotted the proofs from the recent photo shoot on the counter. When Gia had first scrolled through the ad agency's favorite shots, she'd had the same reaction. They'd truly made the two of them look fantastic. Elle was obviously made for the camera, but the photographer had made Gia look great, too. Seeing the close-to-final results of the shoot had her feeling more confident in her role in this campaign, like maybe she'd emerge from this thing without looking like a fool, and wouldn't that be a relief?

"Yeah, they came out all right," she said to Had. "I'm relieved."

"All right? No. Not all right. These are smokin' hot." She flashed one of the prints at Gia. "Look at the challenging smolder you guys have going on. The menacing grin, the slightly raised eyebrow you sport. They are going to sell so many chips off this thing. There will be a chip shortage. You think this country needs more jobs? Nope. Not after this ad. Everyone will be hired to make more chips. Speaking of," she glanced around sadly, "I'm hungry."

Gia smiled and grabbed one of the fifteen bags of Trainers the company had had delivered to her. "Knock yourself out."

"Can't. That photo already did the job." Hadley fanned herself and fell back into her chair.

A production assistant pulled Gia from the memory. "Ms. Malone, we're ready for you on set."

She smiled and gave the college-age girl a nod. How official did that sound? On set. She followed the assistant to the small soundstage, where she found Elle smiling and laughing with Colleen, the director Gia had met earlier.

"Is Timothy five now? He must be, what, in kindergarten?" Elle asked. Apparently, these two had worked together before.

Colleen beamed. "You have a good memory."

"Like I could forget that adorable nugget."

"Hey," Gia said, as she arrived next to Elle.

"Hi, Gia." Elle offered her a smile, but it was brief and didn't come with the normal Elle Britton wattage. Odd. The production assistant handed Gia a bottle of water. She stole glances at Elle, who continued to chat with Colleen, as she drank it. The wardrobe department had them dressed in athletic wear for the commercial. Gia in running shorts and a hoodie, zipped halfway. Elle in running capris and a sleeveless spandex top that showed off her shoulders, which were…nice. A small number of freckles were visible beneath the tan. She didn't have any on her face, just those shoulders, which piqued Gia's interest. Why only there? The hair and makeup team had pulled Gia's hair back into a ponytail. Most likely for contrast, they'd left Elle's down and given it a soft curl that fell past her shoulders.

"And what about you?" Colleen asked Gia, smiling.

Oh, she hadn't been listening. She'd been… "I'm sorry?"

Colleen laughed. Loud, too. She had a great energy and seemed more than approachable. "Asking if you're ready for a quick rehearsal before we start shooting. It should give you a chance to walk the space and learn your marks." She pointed at the floor, where small pieces of colored tape had been applied. "You have three."

Ah, yes. She'd been told in an email from Mallory, the ad exec, that there would be marks and had mentally prepared herself to screw that the hell up. She and Elle exchanged the briefest of smiles. Things just felt back to weird between them. She shrugged it off and focused on Colleen. "A rehearsal would be great."

The walk-through was easy enough. The premise of the spot had Gia busting in on Elle watching footage of herself in competition, all the while eating Trainers from a bowl. Gia joins her on the couch, they engage in smack talk, and Gia eventually steals the chip bowl for herself. It was short, snappy, and mildly amusing depending on your standards. Apparently, the witty dialogue had been written by one of Mallory's agency partners. It had a good rhythm.

When the director called action, Gia was ready. The preparation with Hadley had truly helped, and she allowed herself to have fun with the lines, with her "character." On the flip side, Elle seemed to struggle through the rehearsal, looking pensive and serious. Not at all her typical bubbly, vivacious self.

After four failed takes, they went again. Gia entered the apartment, hit her mark, said her line, took her spot on the couch as she had been directed, and waited for Elle to nail her with the zinger from the script. But as their eyes locked, Elle faltered, attempted to play it off, and faltered again. She pulled her gaze from Gia's and looked to Colleen for a lifeline.

"I'm sorry," she said, defeated. She ran a hand through her hair and let it cascade back onto her shoulder. "I don't know why I'm off today, but it's embarrassing."

Colleen waved her hand. "You're doing great. Don't give it another thought. Want to take a break or go again?"

"Again."

Gia nodded and reset herself. They got a little further this time, but again, right in the middle of the shot, Elle shook her head and stopped them short.

Was it wrong to relish the fact that she wasn't the problem, because she fully expected to be? She couldn't wait to tell Autumn, who was always fun to gloat with. But looking at Elle, her eyebrows drawn and the edges of her mouth downturned, she felt a slash of guilt for that kind of thinking. Clearly, the shoot was getting to Elle, and somehow, that was getting to Gia.

"Maybe that break after all?" she asked Colleen weakly, ten minutes later when they'd yet to make much progress.

"Of course. Let's take fifteen, everyone," Colleen called.

Once the set cleared, with production folks scurrying off in a million different directions, Elle's demeanor seemed to slip even further. Her guard was down and she looked...vulnerable, and lost. She didn't move from the couch on set but remained very quiet, pulled into herself, staring hard at the ground. Gia decided to give her some space and walked a small distance away to the craft services table.

Silence. The kind that didn't feel good.

"I don't know if you've tried the hummus, but it's killer," Gia said, with way more enthusiasm than she felt. Elle didn't answer. "As killer as hummus can be. Never really considered hummus to be the star of many meals. Or snacks. But this particular hummus takes the cake. Or carrot, as the case is." Why was she attempting small talk with Elle? Not only that, but stupid small talk. Totally not necessary. Except that Gia felt this pull to get Elle through this, make her feel better. In a sense, they were partners on this whole campaign, and the teammate in her stepped forward. Plus, she'd always been a softie underneath all the competitive bravado, just not necessarily where Elle was concerned. Apparently, things were shifting as her heart now tugged. "Yep. A hummus for the ages."

She tossed a glance behind her to Elle, who attempted a nod and smile at her ridiculous hummus analysis, but it wasn't at all convincing. Gia dropped the carrot in the trash and headed back to the couch. She met Elle's gaze and those luminous blue eyes. "Do you know what I do to get through this stuff? Not that I can believe that I'm offering you advice. This is more your area than mine any day of the week."

"Not my area today, apparently." Elle looked back at her. "What do you do?"

"I think about Ms. Pac-Man."

Elle scrunched her face up in confusion. Gia had to admit it was endearing. Cute, even, if it had been anyone else. "Not sure I'm following."

She laughed, playing it back in her head. "No, and why would you? Sorry. I happen to be a fan of the game and believe there's more than one life lesson there."

Elle met her gaze. "Who knew Ms. Pac-Man was so wise?"

"Very few people. Trust me. But she's helped me."

Amusement rang apparent in Elle's eyes. "Okay, tell me more."

"She has a lot going on, right? Pellets to eat, lives to store up and protect, ghosts to avoid or take down given the moment. But she can't stop to think too much about it or she loses it all. She's this bodiless creature with a hair bow, already at a disadvantage, just trying to make it in the world."

Elle nodded, as if trying to take apart what it was Gia was driving at. "So, you're saying…"

"Just eat pellets and avoid ghosts." She nodded to affirm her words, because it really was that simple. "Don't think about it."

Elle laughed. "Right. Got it. I think." She shrugged and took a fortifying breath. "Not sure what's going on with me. But I'll try and stay out of my own head about it."

Gia pointed at her. "That's probably the better way to put it."

"To each her own." Their eyes held, and the sincerity that passed between them was not lost on Gia. She nodded and returned to the craft services table with an uptick in energy at their forward progress. "Hummus?"

Elle threw up her hands in mock exasperation. "Well, if you keep peddling the damn hummus so hard. Sure. Let's have hummus."

Gia wasn't sure if breaking bread and dining on hummus were synonymous, but once everyone returned to set and they picked up the shoot, Elle seemed lighter. Fun, even, so maybe her efforts had been worthwhile.

"Oh, I think you just smashed into a ghost," she said quietly, when Gia had trouble with the prop door a few takes in. "Wanna try that again?"

"This damn door shall not defeat me," Gia said, with a raised eyebrow, and stepped backward through it as if on rewind.

"See? Now that was way more impressive," Elle called. "Colleen, maybe Gia could do her part in reverse?"

"I think we'll stick to the script," Colleen said, with a wink.

"Hey, Gia," Elle called through the door. "If you put that same kind of finesse into your surfing, you could really make something of yourself."

Gia stepped back through the door, her mouth agape. "You won't be laughing when you're number two in the rankings."

"No, I definitely won't," Elle said serenely, "because that will never happen."

"Did you work out today?" Gia asked, recalling her own four-hour intensive session at the gym.

"I work out every day," Elle said simply. "That's not even a question. I'm like Ms. Pac-Man on Red Bull."

Gia laughed. "Okay, but not even close." She shook her head and reset herself for the shot. The competitive banter was light and surprisingly fun. Not only that, but it seemed to liven them up. Take after take, their comedic timing and give-and-take came together all the more.

"Am I wrong or do we have another one of these next week?" Elle asked, as they walked together down the hallway to their respective dressing rooms.

"You're not wrong. We're back on Thursday for the second commercial."

Elle paused in front of the door that was hers, her facial expression sincere. "Thanks for bailing me out earlier."

"I didn't do much."

"You did, and we both know it." She sighed and ran a hand through her hair, pushing it off her forehead.

Gia was learning she did this a lot. Hair moves.

"Just a weird day."

She wanted to ask why, to find out what had Elle on her heels in a manner Gia had never once witnessed in the past, even in the midst of the most intense pressure imaginable. She didn't, however. That information didn't seem to be hers to ask for. "Well, you rebounded nicely."

"Thanks. I guess I'll see you Thursday?"

"I'll be here."

Two down and only a handful more to go. As Gia made her way to her own dressing room, she took note of the smile on her face. Somewhere along the way, she'd started to enjoy these little promotional shoots.

How had that happened?

She glanced behind her at the closed door to Elle's dressing room, shook her head, and went inside her own. The olive branch was nice, but this didn't mean she wasn't still going to take Elle down at the next tournament stop. Nope. That part was still on. Hummus or no hummus.

CHAPTER SIX

W e need our own bar," Autumn mused, glancing around the décor of Dive while sipping her virgin daiquiri. "This one's fine, but it's not ours, you know?"

"I like it," Gia said. It had been her turn to pick the locale for their night out, so of course, she'd chosen Dive, the little spot off the water that catered to locals. Okay, mainly the surf crowd, but she knew her friends would assimilate well enough.

"What do you mean, our own bar?" Isabel asked Autumn.

"Somewhere that just says us, you know?"

Gia scoffed. "So, no surfboards lining the walls, then?"

Autumn squinted. "The surfboards are a nice touch. Very Venice."

Isabel nodded. "Very you. Just not *us*. Speaking of, aren't those friends of yours?" Isabel inclined her head to the table across the way made up of some surfers Gia hung with on Venice Beach.

"Yep. That's Ozzie, and Ricky, and Marilyn D," she told them.

"What's the D stand for?" Hadley asked.

Gia shook her head. "No one knows."

"Mysterious. I think at some point tonight, we'll need to find out," Autumn said. "Speaking of our neighbors, I wasn't going to mention this, because sometimes you get a little bent out of shape, but Elle Britton walked in about five minutes ago and is sitting two tables behind you."

Isabel's eyes lit up. "Fuck, yeah. The plot thickens at Dive." She sat back in her chair with satisfaction as if ready to take it all in.

Gia stole a quick glance behind her, and Autumn hadn't been messing around. Elle, wearing dark jeans and a black camisole, sat at a small table with two men and a woman. One of them was probably that guy from the date she'd had the week prior. Patrick, Jason, Trevor. Something bland enough for Gia to forget. Aha, yes, that must be him, the one with his hand on her forearm. They were drinking from carved-out pineapples generally reserved for tourist types and laughing at something. They were actually laughing *a lot*. She was hardly the cool police, and tried not to be judgmental about the pineapples. She lost the battle.

"Guess you're not the only surfer who knows about this place," Hadley said, with an interested grin. "You going to go over there and say hello soon?"

"What? No," Gia said adamantly, and shook her head. Then she thought on it. Maybe it would be rude not to, now that they kind of worked together. Elle seemed the type to be cognizant of etiquette. Was there protocol for public sightings of your work friend? She'd never had the kind of traditional job that required that skillset. "Should I?"

"Your call," Isabel said. "Might be weird later if you don't. Aren't you two trying to get past the hateful toe-to-toe grudge match of old?"

"Yeah," she said, reluctantly. Isabel had a point. She glanced over and caught sight of Elle walking to the bar with the slightest sway of her hips. She had her customary smile in play and stopped to chat with a table of in-awe college kids who had flagged her down for an autograph. "Be right back."

As Elle leaned across the bar to catch the bartender's eye, Gia took the spot at the rail next to her. "Of all the surf bars in all of Venice, you had to walk into mine."

"Oh my God," Elle said, brightening and looking around. "You came out of nowhere." A pause, followed by a growing smile. "Hey."

"Hey." Gia smiled back. "Just stalking my competitors in my downtime and surprising them when they least expect it." She needed stronger social skills. She'd pay for them if she had to.

Elle turned, leaned back against the bar, and dropped her tone to sincerity. "Sorry for crashing your turf. I wanted to show Christopher a little bit of my world. My people."

Ah, yes. Christopher. That was his name. She committed it to memory for stupid reasons not worthy of reflection. "What's the verdict?"

Elle glanced back at him, her brow furrowed. "He's still taking it all in, I think. He's a little more buttoned up. You know the type."

"Nope. But I've seen them around." Gia tapped the bar. "I won't keep you. Wanted to say hi and all. Have fun tonight."

Elle nodded as the bartender approached. "Thanks. You, too."

The night played on, and more and more people jammed the small space. They'd taken one of the walls down, which allowed a nice breeze off the water to keep everyone cool and comfortable. As Isabel expounded loudly about Taylor's uncanny ability to know when she was craving Chinese food, Gia politely excused herself to the restroom, which was not as awful as she was imagining it might be.

Her second surprise came when she emerged from the stall and ran into Elle, who stood at one of the sinks...not looking too great.

"Too many hollowed-out pineapples?" she asked, washing her hands at the sink next to Elle's.

"How did you know?" a bleary-eyed Elle asked.

"Just a hunch. You okay?"

"Nope. I've had too many, I'm afraid. I don't normally do this when I'm training. Drink more than one or two. Today was weird, though." She held on to the countertop for balance.

"You mean the shoot today?" Gia turned off the faucet and reached for a paper towel.

Elle nodded about eight times. "It was awful. I was ready to see you, and then I did, and it was...whoa, and then so hard to act normal, you know?"

She wasn't making sense. "Not sure I do."

Elle covered her face the way girls did when they were making a decision that embarrassed them. "Okay, why not just say it, right?" She laughed. Her cheeks were pink, and it was spreading into an impressive blush.

"Right," Gia said, still not following.

"So, I had a dream. A crazy one."

"Gotcha." She waited. Nothing. "Was I in this dream, or...?"

"Oh, yeah. You were definitely involved."

"Ah. Well, I hope I didn't do anything too crazy or mean." She nodded and turned to go.

"It was one of *those* dreams," Elle said. "God, I can't believe I'm telling it all right now." She seemed to refocus as Gia turned back and met her gaze. "And then seeing you on set was so...odd. After we'd... you know."

Wait. Gia stopped and played the whole thing back. She took a step toward Elle, and even though they were alone in the restroom, she made sure the coast was clear and dropped her tone. "Are you saying you had a *sex* dream about me?"

Elle pointed at her, seemingly more confident and exceptionally drunk. "Bingo."

"Oh." And then, "Wow."

"I know," Drunk Elle said. "No idea why. Well, it might have been that online article that we were dating."

"The internet prompted this?"

"That's what I said. Like, more than three times to myself. Because we're not. Dating."

"Didn't see that particular article." But then Gia didn't really pay attention to what was said in the press. "Let me get this straight. You're saying that there was an article about you and me that inspired a dream in which we were—"

"Naked, and kissing, and it was really good." Elle gave her head a shake, as if the details were all consuming. "Sooo good." She then glanced around, realizing her hands were still damp from the faucet. "Are there paper towels in here anywhere?"

Gia retrieved one for her, trying to figure out how to play this cool and keep everything status quo with her thoughts moving a mile a minute. She decided it was best to just check in on Elle's state of mind. "Are you okay with everything? Just a dream, right? Nothing more."

Elle put her hand on her heart as if relieved. "Right? A silly dream that messed with me temporarily. Feeling so much better now if only the floor would stop doing that. Maybe I need another drink."

"Maybe not, though. I'm feeling like that would be a bad idea."

Elle nodded vaguely and pointed at Gia. "You're very wise. I never knew how wise you were until now and the Ms. Pac-Man advice. And you're much nicer than I ever thought, too." She downgraded to a whisper. "And very pretty. Like…don't get me started."

"Thanks." Gia shifted uneasily. "I should get back to my friends now. You going to be okay?"

"Yeah. Sticking with water, I think, so I don't make any other embarrassing confessions."

"I think you're in the clear." A pause as they stared at each other. "Take care, Elle."

"You, too. See ya out there."

Gia, wanting to make sure Elle made it back to her friends safely, took a spot at the bar where she could observe the restroom door. It was only a moment or two before Elle emerged and joined her friends. Just as promised, she latched onto a giant glass of ice water. Knowing that all was well, Gia headed back to her own table, where she found her friends musing about Autumn's future menu prospects.

"I'm just wondering if you decided to offer a few actual entrees, like French toast in the mornings, if you would make a killing," Isabel said casually.

Autumn held up a finger. "Except I would never do that, because Pajamas is about the coffee. The coffee is the star. Nothing can overshadow it. You just want convenient French toast."

"Is that a crime?"

"You guys," Gia said, in a bit of a fog.

"I get Autumn's point, though." Hadley chimed in. "It's a branding issue. She can't confuse the message just so your life is more convenient. Though I do love French toast. Hey, Gia's back!"

"Depperschmidtson!" Isabel yelled and pointed.

Gia stared at her, lost.

"Marilyn D's name. We gave Hadley five dollars to go and ask."

"I get why she just goes with D," Autumn said, sadly.

Isabel winced. "Wouldn't you? Think about it. Hi, I'm Marilyn Depper—"

"I think I just discovered why Elle was so out of it at the commercial shoot today."

"And why is that?" Isabel asked, still clearly in the land of Depperschmidtson.

"She apparently had a sex dream about me."

Three faces froze.

"More," Hadley said, with the come-here gesture. "We're going to need so much more."

Autumn nodded, setting down her virgin daiquiri. "A bomb has been dropped."

"Can I just say that I've been waiting patiently for such a bomb?" Isabel said with a know-it-all grin.

"No, not like that. This is a *straight girl* bomb," Gia said, still trying to laugh off what she'd just learned and wrap her mind around it at the same time. "And no, you can't say that," she told Isabel. "You have to stop with the harassment."

"I'd like to know how I'm harassing you so I can be more effective at it."

"Well, to start with, you're constantly insinuating with the—I don't even know. With the sparks talk and the whatever, the *tension*—"

"Do we know that she's straight?" Hadley said quietly, attempting to regroup the conversation. "Do we know for sure?"

Isabel shrugged. "We were all straight once. Just saying. Don't get me started on Cindy Mackleroy tossing her hair in the seventh grade. She changed my entire life for the better. I should send her a gift basket, now that I'm thinking about it."

"Not me," Autumn said. "Not even for a swift second. Women from day one."

"Prophetic," Isabel said, and fist-bumped Autumn. "Doesn't surprise me. You've always been ahead of your time."

Autumn grinned. "Right? I knew hot chicks were destined to be my calling, and in the end, I nabbed the hottest one and now we're happily knocked up." A second fist bump, this time from Hadley. Gia struggled to follow the thread of the conversation, as her mind was on the events of the last fifteen minutes.

"While Kate is extra yummy," Hadley said, gesturing to Gia to take the floor, "I think we need to hear more about this dream. The details need coloring in."

"Oh," Gia said. She paused as her three friends stared at her expectantly while she tried to figure out how to articulate the random, drunkenly dropped details. "She didn't give me much. Just that there was kissing and we were apparently naked and that it was good. Wait. I think she said sooo good." The *sooo* stuck out in Gia's mind. For some reason, it mattered.

"Doesn't look like she was the only one who was surprised."

"I'm not surprised." Damn. She couldn't sell that. "Okay, maybe a little. The thing is, I've never imagined myself naked with Elle Britton, and now I am. So, yeah, I'm figuring it out." Even hearing those vague descriptions played back had Gia...affected and dealing with the creative images they inspired. Her face felt hot. She sipped her apple whiskey, hoping it somehow contained the antidote to right her shell-shocked ship, because things were extra upside down.

Elle Britton had a sex dream about her? Really? That was reality?

Regardless, the knowledge should have rolled right off her back. Instead she was imagining herself *on it* beneath Elle's touch. This wasn't good and so shallow. She felt dizzy from the aggressively battling emotions.

Meanwhile, her friends continued to patter back and forth about the dream and what it meant. Luckily, they kept their voices quiet enough that nearby tables wouldn't pick up on the direction of the conversation, which was rare for them. All the while, Gia tried her best not to look over at Elle. But that was hard because she really did radiate tonight, all loosened up and less "on" than Gia had ever seen her. She was just…a person. Apparently, the after-hours suited her. And it wasn't like Gia was lusting after Elle, either. It so wasn't. She was merely intrigued by the week's series of events. Hostility, friendship, support, and now…this. Gia thought back to a phrase her mother used often when she was a kid. Will wonders never cease? Yeah, that one. And would they? Fucking wonders.

❖

Why was there a drumbeat inside her head? Elle opened her eyes. Oh no, that felt awful. Opening her eyes had been a bad idea, and who was doing the drumming? And why wouldn't they stop? The searing pain when she tried to sit up was enough to keep her lying down for the foreseeable future, which was unfortunate because she really needed to train. She looked around and attempted to get her bearings. She was on the couch, apparently. How had she ended up on her couch? She didn't remember that part.

There was a glass of water and two Advil on the coffee table across from her with a note that read *Take me, please.* Aha, Holly's handwriting. She smiled, as much as one could when their face was about to fall off. She'd left the exact same note for Holly last year when she'd gotten blitzed on New Year's Eve. So, that was it. She'd had way too much to drink last night and Holly and Christopher had made sure she was home safe and sound. There had been pineapple margaritas, chips and queso, the memory of which turned her stomach, and some sort of running joke about her loosening up and how nice it was. And oh, she had, too. That was the problem, and she was paying for it dearly. She wouldn't drink a margarita for the rest of her life. She promised the heavens, offered them this sacrifice, if they would just take away the awful.

With determination, she sat up…slowly, drank the water, and took the Advil. More details from the night floated back to her. Gia had been there and they'd chatted at the bar. It had been nice. She pushed herself up and headed to her bedroom to see about a shower. But there'd been more with Gia, she reminded herself as she stepped under the hot stream of water. As the heat caressed her skin, waking her up more fully, she froze. No, no, no. The bathroom. The confession. The horror!

Naked, and kissing, and it was really good.

Surely she hadn't actually said those mortifying words to Gia in real life. This was just something she imagined, or dreamt, not *experienced.* Except she had experienced it! She placed both hands on the wall of the shower to steady herself as panic and dread threatened to drown her right in her spot.

"Mayday," she said, as soon as Holly answered.

"Well, look who's alive!" Holly said gleefully into the phone. "Was just about to call you. Wanna go to breakfast? Pancakes, butter, bacon."

Elle swallowed the nausea. "You're a cruel woman."

"Among other things. But as your bestie, it's my job in life to make fun of you, and that opportunity comes about so rarely. Let me have this."

"This might be your lucky day, because I did something really stupid last night."

"Oh, you did a lot of really stupid things last night. You're going to have to be more specific." She could hear the smile coming through the phone. It wasn't helping.

"I told Gia Malone I had a sex dream about her. I used the word *naked* and told her it was really good."

A pause. "I am so goddamn impressed with you right now."

"Really? Because I want to hurl myself against the rocks in the ocean. I'm mortified."

"Why? She's probably flattered. I would be."

"We didn't get along a couple weeks ago and now I'm announcing I'm dreaming of her naked?"

"Tell me you really used the word *naked.*"

"I did!" Elle yelled as she walked circles around her living room, wincing against the throbbing headache. "And honestly, who knows what else I may have said? I should just never leave my house again at this point. I can't be trusted."

"Or maybe just fewer margaritas."

"Yes. Yes! I blame them, and whoever invented them."

"That seems a little extreme. They were just trying to give the world the gift of tequila in a sugary glass." Elle could hear Holly shut off the music that played quietly in the background, which meant she was ready for the day and leaving her bedroom. "Want me to come over?"

"No," Elle said, softening. It was nice to know that she would, though, that she could always count on Holly when things were tough.

"Gonna rest, try not to think about what I've done, and salvage what's left of the day. Maybe I can get it together enough to train this afternoon, at least."

"See?" Holly said. "All is not lost."

"Not so sure about that."

Elle played it low key the rest of the morning, poring over the internet to read about the various bloggers' speculation about the next tournament on the tour, Swatch Pro at Trestles, which was just a few weeks out at this point. Luckily, she wouldn't have to travel any farther than San Clemente, which took some of the headache out of the whole thing. While she loved seeing new places, time on the road wasn't as much fun as it once was. Maybe she was just getting old.

Because she couldn't seem to stop herself, and she was honestly curious, she clicked through to the gossip section and checked out the stories from the week prior, the ones about her and Gia. The write-up about their rivalry had scored quite a few views, but that paled in comparison to the one about "their flirtatious day out." While it went against everything she believed in, Elle broke her own rule and scrolled to the bottom of the article for the comments, blinking in surprise at what she saw.

Please tell me this is true—SurfJunkie89

Hottest. Hookup. Ever.—BobbiBoBobbi

Okay, my head just exploded. Can someone confirm this?—WavesToBurn6

It just got wayyyyyy too sexy in here. Can I watch?—YoMammasShred

Wow. People were latching onto their fictitious coupling, which was insane. But apparently, Elle hadn't been the only one to have a strong reaction to the article. Hers had just been a little less deliberate. Still, reading those comments back now had her stomach tightening in an uncomfortable (okay, but not entirely) sort of way. Her cheeks flashed hot and a commanding shiver moved through her as she remembered, for the briefest of moments, the details of her dream. Slamming her laptop closed and moving away from it with purpose, Elle had yet another reason to never read the comments section again.

Christopher checked in on her that afternoon, and they made plans for dinner later that week. She managed to recover enough to spend ninety minutes on the beach with her coach and trainer, Bruce, who was not thrilled about their canceled morning session. All the while, she remembered Gia at the bar that night. Flashed on it every few minutes or so. She'd seemed carefree and…happy. Elle had stolen glimpses here and there, merely out of curiosity about a girl who'd mystified her (and continued to do so).

"You gonna stand there with your hands on your hips and a faraway look in your eye or are you gonna drop and give me a hundred pushups?" Bruce barked. He was always barking, so it carried less effect.

"Sorry. Got lost for a minute." She dropped down onto the mat and went to work on those pushups as Bruce paced in front of her.

"Next time you get lost, it might mean Gia Malone finds your title. No more getting lost."

Elle paused her progress and glanced up. "Can we not talk about her?"

Bruce wasn't having it. "Why? You scared of her? You should be. She's getting better by the minute while you stare at swirly clouds."

He was the worst kind of drill sergeant, but that's why she paid him what she did. "Tomorrow we take the Jet Ski out and get you some big wave time. For now, I want you eating, drinking, and living Gia Malone. You hear me?"

Unfortunately for Elle, she didn't really foresee that being too big a problem.

Chapter Seven

Gia pushed open the door to the Cat's Pajamas at 7:45 sharp to see that her friends had already beaten her there. Wait. Most of them, anyway. Instead of Autumn behind the counter, she saw that Kate was on register as Steve prepared drinks.

"Well, this is new," Gia said with a grin. "You taking over the business, Carpenter?"

Kate laughed. "No way. Counter help at best. Autumn's extra uncomfortable today, so I told her I'd fill in while she took the morning to rest. I have the next two days off, so I don't mind. And hey, I'm not as bad as I used to be."

"Well, you look sharp back there."

"Thanks," Kate said, and dropped her gaze to the register. She was never one for much attention, always moving out of the spotlight, which Gia found endearing. Kate was good people, and she'd been an amazing partner for Autumn.

"I should check in on her later," Hadley said from her chair at their table. "I could read to her like I do the kiddos at the hospital."

"Autumn would probs love to be read to. Please promise me you'll do that," Isabel said, with a mischievous smile, because in truth, they knew Autumn would have little patience for inactivity and was likely doing everything in her power to claw her way back to her prized coffee roaster.

"On second thought, maybe not such a good idea." Hadley brightened. "I can't help but remember when my dads would read to me when I was sick. We would go through book after book. It's where I developed an appreciation for the written word."

Isabel regarded her. "You really did grow up in a gay fairy tale, didn't you? Two dads with an eye for decorating, copious milkshakes, and probably a damn pet unicorn."

Hadley sipped her mocha. "And proud of it."

"I have to head to work early," Isabel said, standing. "I'm taking Fat Tony to the office with me. He and Raisin have signed a temporary peace treaty and I thought what better way for them to practice their manners than in my place of employment. Sounds like the perfect plan to me."

"Good luck with that," Gia said. "My money's on my man Tony."

"I could take bets," Hadley offered.

Gia looked at her. "Vegas theme night has changed you forever. You know that?"

"Iz, wait!" Kate said, racing over with two to-go cups. "I'm supposed to send these for you and Taylor. It's on the list she gave me."

"You're the best substitute Autumn ever, and I would never just say that to you either, because those stakes are fucking high. *Ms. Pac-Man* tonight?"

"Done."

"Hey!" Gia said. "I'm sitting right here."

"You're invited, too, Surf Queen. You know the invite is standing. All right. Me and my asshole cat are out. Peace, bitches."

Hadley stared after Isabel. "She always has the best exits, wouldn't you say? I need to work on mine." She finished the last bit of her mocha, returned the cup to the counter, and regarded them. "Well, everyone here in the coffee shop, I'm off to take Rodeo Drive by storm." With that, she flipped her blond hair and sauntered to the door. "How was that?" she asked meekly, glancing back.

Kate squinted. "That was pretty good."

Gia nodded at Kate. "I'd give it a solid seven."

"Seven sounds about right," Kate said, nodding back.

"A seven?" Hadley sighed sadly. She shook her head as if she just couldn't quite believe her failure. "I'll work on it."

Once they were on their own, Gia followed Kate back to the counter and kept her company while she took orders. "How's station life?" Gia asked, in between customers. Kate's job as a firefighter had always impressed her, as had Kate herself. To say she had a little bit of hero worship where Kate was concerned wouldn't be inaccurate.

"Nothing to complain about. My ladder's a good one, and there's way more action out here than back home. That's for sure. Handful of vehicle fires and one structure just yesterday alone." Kate had only recently made the move from a small town in Oregon, where she'd been a lieutenant. She'd had to take a lesser role at the larger company, but it was apparently paying off. "Office building went up earlier this week, and we were able to contain the blaze and slow its progress. By nightfall, the burn was totally under control. It's a solid group."

"And I play in the waves all day," Gia said, only half joking. There were times when she wished her job came with a greater good like Kate's. Her life was fun, but that was about it. Shouldn't there be more?

"Don't sell yourself short. I don't have throngs of fans fawning all over me, asking me for autographs. Girls swooning."

"That part's not so bad," Gia said, feeling a hint better. She gestured to the counter Kate was wiping down. "You got this under control? I'm supposed to watch film with my coach before a press junket later today to promote the tour."

"Watching film, how does that work? That's film of you?"

"Unfortunately, yes. So I can see all the ways I suck and hopefully get better. Part of the job. Just the tedious part."

"And you have a coach?"

"Part-time. Katrina McAllister, who was a former pro herself. We met through Billabong, when they used to sponsor her. I was an up-and-coming nobody on the Qualifying Tour, longing to play with the big kids and be like Katrina someday."

Kate took a moment to wait on a customer, passing them her understated but incredibly effective grin and gaze. Gia wouldn't know how to duplicate that kind of quiet charm if she wanted to. She was fairly sure Kate had no clue the effect she had on women, which was probably why it worked.

"Pretty awesome that she's now your coach."

"Sometimes I still can't believe it." Gia finished her drink. "I better head over to her place. You guys got this?" she asked Steve and Kate.

Steven grinned. "Yeah. We have a new employee starting in about an hour, so we'll have extra hands."

"Cool. Say hi to Autumn for me. I'll check in with you guys after the junket about a little *Ms. Pac-Man* action."

"Deal."

When Gia arrived at Katrina's house on the beach, she found her coach already watching the footage of the most recent tournament in Fiji. Katrina didn't take her eyes from the screen when Gia entered.

"Ten tournaments a year and five of them are already gone. What are you going to do about that?"

"Well, hello to you, too."

Katrina relaxed into her leather couch and stared at Gia in that no-nonsense way she had. Her blond hair was cropped short and sun bleached. Retired or not, she still sported a surfer's physique because she hit the waves and the gym daily. Katrina didn't mess around. "We have a lot of work to do. Look at this." She rewound the footage and Gia took a seat. "See the way you overcorrect on that turn? That's what caused you to lose your balance, or that ride would have pulled in a killer score."

Gia shook her head. "I anticipate too much."

"Then stop."

"It's not that easy."

"Well, it is for your competition." Katrina fired up the next clip, only this one was of Elle, tearing into a wave, carving the pocket like she was made to do so. Gia both cringed and applauded the finesse. "Check it. She's not anticipating anything. She's living that wave, and if you want to take number one, you have to learn to do the same."

"If it were that easy, I'd be doing it already."

"You think too much. You need to learn to feel your way through those waves."

Gia laughed. "The only time thinking too much is a bad thing."

"Tons of times it's better not to think," Katrina said, moving to the kitchen and taking out the ingredients for protein shakes for the two of them. "Dancing is one example. Sex is another. Falling in love is best served without a side of overanalyzation."

"If you say so."

"What? You've never fallen head over heels for someone?"

"Nope. I had a girlfriend in my early twenties. We lived together for four months and I started to think it was love. It wasn't. It was more about convenience for both of us." She pointed to the blender. "No strawberries in mine."

Katrina nodded, and tossed the extra strawberries into her own pile. "Interesting glimpse into your sad little love life, Malone."

"Hey!" Gia said, but was drowned out by the sound of the blender roaring to life.

Moments later, the room returned to silence. Katrina studied her. "You know? Maybe this whole in-your-head thing is symptomatic of all aspects of your life, ever thought about it?"

"Of course. I think about everything, remember?"

Katrina laughed. "My bad. Maybe if you worked on thinking a little less, feeling a little more, it would transfer to your surfing."

Gia scrunched up her face. "Seems like a leap."

"Well, consider that leap your homework assignment. Now c'mon. Let's watch some film of you falling on your ass like an idiot and see if we can't find out why."

Gia forced a smile. "My favorite pastime."

❖

"Tell me what's about to take place here," Jordan Tuscana asked. "And remember to direct your answer to me, not the camera."

Elle nodded. She knew the drill. Jordan had been shooting a documentary chronicling the lives of several of the female surfers on the Championship Tour for the past two years now. As one of the subjects, Elle answered questions for Jordan on occasion or allowed cameras to follow her here or there. She was actually thrilled about the project and the attention it would bring to the tour and the sport overall. Plus, Jordan was a fantastic director and made the process easy.

Elle smiled widely at Jordan as the camera rolled. "Today's a pretty standard junket, giving members of the press the opportunity to sit with athletes from the tour and ask whatever questions they have. We do these kinds of things between tournaments, and it's a great way to talk to a variety of media outlets all in one place. The downside? The afternoon always feels ridiculously long, and by the end of it, you're sick of hearing your own voice."

"Talk about what it's like sitting alongside your competitors," Jordan said from off camera.

Elle didn't miss a beat. She liked this question. "I'm one of the surfers who doesn't mind sitting next to a competitor at a press event. It gives me a chance to see them up close and personal for a change, and not just on their board. Call me calculating, but once you know more about them, it's all the easier to take them down." She beamed at Jordan, knowing she'd be able to use that little nugget as a lead into the footage she'd get that day.

"Perfect," Jordan said. "We'll be shooting B-roll of the junket throughout the afternoon, but I'll find you if I need more."

"I'll be around," Elle said. "And say hi to Molly for me. Those truffles you brought last time knocked me over. In a very good way."

Jordan laughed. "I'll be sure to tell her. I'm trying to get her to come out here with me next time. She needs some time off."

"If she does, we're going to dinner on me. I need to meet this chocolate wizard."

"Well, now she definitely has to come. Free dinner."

As Jordan departed, a young man, Andrew, took her place at Elle's side. "Ms. Britton?"

"Elle, please." She extended her hand. "Nice to meet you."

He shook her hand. "Likewise. I'm Andrew. I'll be your escort today. I'm here if you need a break or some water. Just say the word."

"Awesome. We're gonna get along, Andrew. I can just feel it."

He smiled and she knew she'd put him at ease, which was the ultimate goal. "We're going to get you set up in the Jefferson Room. They have you answering questions with Gia Malone today."

She laughed. Oh, of course they did. These organizers were no fools. Not only were the two of them popping up in multiple, and conflicting, headlines together, Gia was rapidly rising in the rankings, and everyone wanted a piece of the rivalry. So be it. "Sounds good." She spotted Gia speaking with a girl who was presumably the assistant assigned to her. "Excuse me a moment, Andrew. I'll meet you in Jefferson in five. Sound okay?"

"Yes, ma'am."

She made her way through the groupings of people and arrived at Gia's elbow. "Can I steal you for a minute?" she said quietly.

Gia turned and met her eyes. "Oh. Hey. Yeah. Just…yeah." She excused herself to the assistant and followed Elle. Once they were a safe distance away and alone, Gia paused their progress. "What's up?"

"We're together today."

"So I've heard."

Elle smiled. "What do you say we have some fun with these people?"

Gia looked perplexed, but really pretty at the same time. Elle took a moment to take in how long her lashes were and how perfectly they accentuated her big brown eyes. That now familiar shiver moved through her.

"And how exactly would we do that?"

"Fodder. Let's give it to them. They're looking for competitive banter, or flirtation, or all-out tension filling the room. If they're gonna make money off us, the least we can do is enjoy ourselves and bolster the Trainers campaign a little."

Gia smiled. "Could liven up a boring day."

"My thoughts exactly."

"All right, then. Let's do it." A pause as a twinkle crept into Gia's eyes. "Have any more dreams about me?"

Elle swallowed hard as she led them in the direction of the Jefferson Room. "No. Can't say that I have. I'm really sorry about that, by the way. What an embarrassing thing to confess to someone." She was speaking way too fast. Gia made her nervous, as did the topic. She still didn't have her hands around it.

"You were drunk and feeling it."

Elle paused them in the hallway and waited for a couple of other athletes to pass. "I was. I would just hate for you to get the wrong idea. I think you're, well, a lot less awful than I did just weeks ago."

Gia inclined her head from side to side as if weighing the statement. "I'm happy with less awful."

"That sounds bad. Let me try again. I genuinely like you. But in terms of any kind of attraction…"

Gia scoffed dejectedly. "Fine, Elle. We'll just be *friends*."

"Ha. Okay. I see. You're joking about it now, which is great. It should be something that we can joke about easily. I'm glad to see that. It means we've moved past it." She paused, and shifted her tone to earnest, feeling the need to continue explaining herself. When would that compulsion end? "I want to make sure you're really okay about it and that I didn't ruin what tiny bud of mutual respect we had going."

Gia held up a hand. "The tiny bud is intact. Honestly, it's cool. I'm a grown-up and not weirded out."

"Great. That's a relief," Elle said, not quite sure if she believed Gia. "You know what? Why don't we get dinner sometime? In fact, we really should. It would be good for us. Do you have plans after this?"

"You're asking me out already? That was quick."

Elle felt the color hit her face and burn her skin at the concept of an honest-to-goodness date with Gia. "No. I just meant a friendly—to chat is all. You know. Restaurants are fun." She'd said stupider sentences, but not many.

"Yes."

"Yes, what?"

Gia grinned. "Yes, restaurants are fun."

She was still teasing Elle and enjoying it. Elle kind of enjoyed it, too. It felt…risky, somehow, the playful interaction with someone she'd fantasized about unconsciously (and a little consciously, too).

Especially since she never fantasized, ever. This was all so new and unexplored.

"So, dinner after?"

Gia stared at her for what felt like forever. It seemed she was weighing the offer. "Sure. We can have dinner together. At a fun restaurant."

"Great," Elle said, her confidence on an upswing as she rounded the corner into the Jefferson Room. Having dinner was a great idea. They'd have a chance to get to know each other better, and that just meant more time scoping out her competition. Which would only help her stay one step ahead in the long run. This was actually a really brilliant plan.

And she wasn't terrified at all.

Nope. Not one little bit. A dinner alone with Gia, just her and Gia staring at each other across a table, was just what she needed to move beyond her current…preoccupation.

❖

Elle looked gorgeous today. She'd done something fancy with her hair, assembled it in a complicated braid that Gia could never begin to understand. Some sort of intricate pattern. Hair had always been something she pushed out of her face, but Elle took her hairstyles very seriously and really put in the time. It had paid off.

"What do you think about that, Gia?"

She blinked. The reporter on the couch across from them had apparently asked her a question and she'd missed the whole thing. What in the world was he referencing?

Elle passed her a smile. "About my steady training in preparation for San Clemente."

"I think training is great. It's what has me winning so much."

"Well, you won the *last* tournament," Elle said, with a big smile. "Everyone gets lucky once in a while."

"Until it keeps happening, negating the luck factor altogether." She met the reporter's eyes. "I'll be taking San Clemente. You can write that down."

"She might take a heat," Elle said. "Let's all hope she takes at least one. Can you imagine the bruised ego if she doesn't?"

"Is that what you were feeling after the final in Fiji?" Gia asked, with a smile.

"No," Elle said, her eyes narrowing. "I was too busy wondering why you cut in on my wave when you had plenty of your own to choose from."

The two reporters exchanged wide-eyed looks and typed away on their laptops like busy little bees. Elle was right. It was kind of fun, playing to their audience. Not that all of it was an act. She honestly planned to take the Swatch Pro at San Clemente, and every tournament left on this year's tour. Sparring with Elle about it had her fired up, and a little...wait. Turned on? No. That couldn't be right. That'd never been a symptom of competition for her, so why would it be now? She glanced over at Elle, that braid, the blue eyes, and perfect face and the curves, and for the first time she acknowledged that she might want to do a little more than just compete with Elle Britton. While her first instinct was to shut that the hell down, she heard Katrina's words in her ear, reminding her to feel her way through, rather than think. Surely she didn't mean a scenario as crazy as this one.

"What do you think about that, Gia?" Dammit. She'd done it again.

"I'm sorry. Can you repeat the question?"

"The rumors that you and Elle have been spending time together outside of the tour."

"Well, we're working together on a campaign. It's inevitable."

"And that's about the end of it," Elle said, with a smile.

"Speaking of the end, I think we've come to the end of our time," Andrew said, stepping forward. Luckily, this was the last interview of the day, and Gia had survived. She stood, shook hands with each of the reporters, and thanked them for their time.

"Where should we go to dinner?" Elle asked Gia.

Both reporters turned back abruptly and stared back at them in surprise. She was fairly certain that Elle had done that on purpose.

"I'll let you choose."

Once the reporters exited the Jefferson Room, Gia addressed Elle. "Are you sure that's wise? They're going to keep shipping us."

Elle passed her a sideways look. "What's shipping?"

"Imagining that we're a couple. Projecting that kind of relationship on us. It's a term my friend Isabel uses when—never mind."

Andrew stepped forward. "My sister ships everybody. The practice is rampant."

Elle marveled. "I had no idea. Shipping, huh?"

Gia pressed on. "Isn't your boyfriend going to be upset if these articles keep hitting the web?"

"I don't have a boyfriend," Elle said, and gathered her bag.

"Okay, but you're *straight*."

Elle's smile faltered noticeably and wrinkles appeared on her forehead. After a moment, she brightened to full Elle wattage again, leaving Gia intrigued as to what had just taken place in her head. "All press is good press, Gia. Good rule of thumb."

"If you say so."

"I do. Let's eat."

The restaurant Elle selected for them was one Gia had heard of. Popular, trendy, and hard as hell to get a table. Well, unless you were Elle, apparently. The host at the front made a huge fuss when he saw her, kissing her cheek and asking about her week.

"Been a little hectic," Elle answered. "Lots of press for the tour. How's your mom?"

"Much better. With that hip replacement, she's good as new."

"Thrilled to hear it. Give her a kiss on the cheek and all my best."

"She would love that," he exclaimed. "You know how she adores you."

"It's mutual, Trevor. It's mutual."

Did Elle literally know everyone in California? Was that a true possibility? As they were guided to their table, right in the center of the restaurant, Gia felt like she'd been dropped in the middle of Europe. The black, white, and red interior was outfitted with a handful of small, round tables leading up to a black and red bar. Wine bottles lined the walls, and the menu contained a handful of tapas dishes Gia couldn't begin to decipher.

"You're a people person," Gia said, as they settled across from each other.

"I think that's accurate. I happen to like people a lot. Don't you? Isn't that what makes the world go 'round?"

"I like the people I know already."

Elle nodded. "But you have friends. I've seen them."

"True. I guess I have a small but close group. But you? You're like the friendship ambassador."

"Some wine?" the sommelier asked.

Gia liked wine but knew very little about it. She gestured for Elle to go right ahead.

"I think we'll take a bottle of your Cakebread Cab. The 2015 if you have it."

Quietly, Gia admired Elle's confidence. Plus, she always smiled and treated people courteously. She remembered how not too long ago, she'd decided that Elle's friendly disposition was 100 percent fake. And while she hadn't bought into it entirely just yet, she was starting to understand that there was room for error in her initial judgment. What did Elle possibly have to gain from being nice to her assistant, Andrew, earlier? It was unlikely she'd see the guy again, but she'd gone out of her way to be warm and inclusive. Gia was willing to admit that she might have pinned a lot of resentment on Elle simply because she was the competition, and was not necessarily an awful person.

"I believe we have the 2015," the sommelier said, with a bow, and disappeared into the nearby wine cellar.

"This can't be good for your training," Gia remarked with a smile.

Elle placed a hand over her heart. "Oh, you're so sweet to look out for me."

"That's me," Gia said, with a laugh. "The sweetest."

They stared at each other as the melody from the nearby Spanish guitar floated past. "So," Elle said.

"So." Another pause. "What made you ask me to dinner?" Gia asked.

"Honestly? It was a spur-of-the-moment decision."

Gia sat back in her chair. "One you're regretting now?"

Elle shook her head, and the music played on. "I wanted to get to know you better, and now I can."

"Scoping out the competition. Nothing wrong with that."

They waited while the sommelier poured the wine. Elle took a sip and basked. "It's really good."

Gia liked the way she savored the taste, the way she pressed her lips together lightly at first and then more firmly. She had good lips. Gia tended to stare at them a lot.

"Tell me, are you from California?" Elle asked.

"No. I moved here when I was nineteen with hopes to make it onto the Qualifying Tour."

Elle seemed puzzled. "Okay, then where did you learn to surf if not here?"

"Hawaii. My mother was a captain in the Air Force and we were stationed at a base there. I had this friend who would come to the islands to visit her family each summer. She talked this huge game about wanting to learn to surf."

"An influencer."

"Big-time. I looked up to her in every way."

"What was her name?"

"Hunter, which I thought was so much cooler than a stupid name like Gia. She was smooth, and put together, and knew she was gay way the hell before I did. Everyone wanted to be around her. Meanwhile, I was just trying to figure out how to string two sentences together around girls I thought were pretty." She laughed. "Still am."

"So, the girl with all the cool moves taught you to surf?"

"Hardly. She was awful at it. But then I gave it a shot, and it's like the world came into color." She shook her head at the still-vivid memory. "When I finally managed to stand up on that board for the first time, it's like I'd found my purpose. Sounds stupid, hearing it out loud."

Elle shook her head, and her eyes held understanding. "It's the furthest thing from stupid I've ever heard. Tell me more."

"I practiced. Mornings before school. Afternoons following school. All summer long. Hunter gave it up after that first summer. Spent her time chatting up girls at the mall while I lived in the ocean with my board."

"And what happened to Hunter? The suspense is killing me."

"Honestly? I'm not sure. We lost touch when my mom was transferred back to the mainland. I'm confident she's still landing more girls than I ever could."

Elle set down her wine. "Oh, I bet you do okay."

"Apparently the dream version of me does." They looked at each other and laughed.

Elle glanced away, a blush firmly in place. "As I may have mentioned before, it was the article about us that caused the whole thing. The one that was *shipping* us." Elle smiled at her own use of the term. "I read it before going to sleep that night."

"Aha. So you find tabloid gossip…inspiring." Gia tilted her head and caught Elle's gaze. "I'm sorry if the dream made you feel awkward or upset you."

"It didn't upset me," Elle said. "Well, it did for a while." A pause. "And then it didn't."

They stared at each other. Gia wondered where all the sound in the room had gone. Her head felt light, like it might float away at any moment. She blinked and reached for her glass of wine. "Good. That's good, then."

Their waiter returned and they ordered food, a combo of different Spanish tapas to sample. Again, she let Elle, who seemed more adept at the menu options, do the choosing. They each went for a second glass of wine as they chatted. Slowly, and with the help of time and alcohol, the mood shifted as they each relaxed.

"What about you?" Gia asked. "When did you first get on a board?"

"Oh. Well, I was a California kid through and through. My parents were beach people, so my brothers and I were in the water from the beginning. Got my first surfboard at seven. Won my first competition at nine."

"You were a surf prodigy. I do remember hearing that part of the story."

Elle had the decency to demur. "I practiced a lot. *Prodigy* is a strong word."

"I don't think it is, in your case. Not that it's going to help you in San Clemente."

"You're ruthless, you know that? And you're not going to win."

"I'm *driven*. And I am, too."

Elle raised her glass and touched Gia's. "To taking each other down. That should be the story of our joint memoir."

"Wow. First, you're dreaming about me, then you're asking me out to dinner, and now we have a joint memoir? You move fast." She watched the recurring pink hit the tops of Elle's cheeks and blossom, enjoying that she inspired it and wanting to inspire more, while at a loss at just how to navigate this new circumstance. *Get out of your own head. Don't overthink.* She exhaled. She was trying.

"I think about you differently since the dream. Is that weird?" Maybe Elle was really feeling the wine, but that comment sent a sweltering wave dissolving over Gia. She was glad they'd taken an Uber to the restaurant. They should definitely take separate ones home.

"Do you have a crush on me, Elle?" She said it as a joke, a deflection, because that was easier, but she honestly had a stake in the answer.

To Gia's surprise, the self-assured smile slid right off Elle's lips. "I mean, I don't think so." A pause as her gaze hit the tablecloth. "I don't know. What if I did?"

Gia laughed it off, and took another sip of her wine. Elle laughed, too, and they both seemed to do their damnedest to downplay the exchange as nothing but lighthearted banter. But there was a weighted charge between them now that was new and as intoxicating as the wine. The comment felt so far out of left field that Gia didn't know which end was up. She was now having impure thoughts about Elle Britton, who in turn kept dropping hints of a possible attraction of her own, all because of a random sex dream? How in the world did they get here? Gia wasn't sure, but she gestured for the check and distantly blamed Isabel. She needed some air, some space, and maybe a therapy session with Hadley, because this whole thing felt catastrophic and thrilling. She couldn't decide which. It was both. It was everything. And the room had way too little air.

"Thanks for inviting me," Gia said, once the waiter returned with her credit card. "I should probably get home. I'm meeting Katrina early tomorrow for a workout."

"You're lucky you scored her."

Gia nodded. "You don't have to tell me. She knows our world and what it takes to survive the big waves."

"My guy, Bruce, is great, but I grew up hero-worshipping Katrina. I had her poster in my room."

"That makes two of us."

"Oh yeah? Did you demand your mother find you those exact same board shorts? The ones with the green and the—"

"Yellow vertical stripes. I hounded her daily. I also taped her finals heats with an actual VCR."

Elle pointed at her. "I still have my tapes."

"Shut up. Truly?"

"I do. I couldn't throw them away if I wanted to. Did you try and spike your hair like hers?"

"I tried, and failed miserably."

"Same."

They stood at the entrance of the restaurant, waiting for rides and grinning at the unexpected common ground. It'd been a while since Gia had met someone who understood how great Katrina was. Is. "You're a cooler girl than I thought, Elle." She held up a hand. "And don't let that go too far to your head. I might deny saying so tomorrow."

"Or maybe you won't."

A moment passed between them, and Gia softened. "Or maybe I won't."

Elle laughed and turned to face the street, the wind lifting the loose strands of blond around her face that had somehow escaped the braid. Gia felt like she'd seen behind the curtain tonight, to a version of Elle she hadn't realized existed. But then again, maybe she hadn't wanted to know. Until now.

Elle's car arrived first, and she turned to Gia. "Thank you for tonight. I had a great time getting to know more about the infamous Gia Malone."

"Next time, I choose the place."

Elle took a step in, a close one, and Gia felt it all over. "There'll be a next time?"

"Yeah. Why not?" Gia asked.

"You're asking me?" She shook her head, and her tongue briefly wet her bottom lip.

Gia's stomach took a wonderful dip.

"I see no reason at all."

Elle slipped into the back seat and Gia stared through the window at her silhouette. The car pulled slowly from the curb and disappeared into the night, right along with everything Gia thought she knew about the world. What was she supposed to do with that glimpse of flirtation and this newfound attraction to someone she didn't even like a month ago? Gia raised her hand to her forehead. She needed an Advil and a sounding board, because her head was pounding with problems.

CHAPTER EIGHT

Something was up with Christopher.

He'd been quiet since they'd sat down for coffee at the quaint little garden table he'd selected for them at the outdoor café. Elle was consistently impressed with his ability to seek out the beautiful spots in the world. Now, if only he seemed to be enjoying their surroundings as much as she was.

"Hey, goober. You're not saying much."

He raised his handsome gaze and furrowed his brow. "Did you just call me a goober?"

"Yes, and it got your attention," she said playfully. "Why so solemn?"

He inhaled quickly as if snapping out of it, and met her eyes. "We have fun together."

She nodded. "We do."

"We talk about things that actually matter, and you're charming and flat-out gorgeous. I think you're very attractive."

She smiled. "I could say all of those same things about you."

"But let me ask you this." He sat forward, scooting to the edge of his chair. "Do you go home and think about me?"

"Of course."

"I don't mean about what we laughed about or what we ate. Do you think about *me*?"

Now, that was a harder question to tackle, and Elle took a moment to figure out what to say next. He didn't give her the chance.

"Because I don't think about you."

The coffee caught in her throat and she found herself sputtering and gasping in attempt not to choke. To his credit, Christopher leapt into action and slid a bottle of water her way. "You okay?" he asked softly, when she regained control. Why were his eyes kind when his words were cruel?

"Other than what you just said to me?"

His eyes widened and he looked genuinely horrified. "Hey, I didn't mean that the way it sounded. It's just...we've clicked, I feel like."

"I thought so, too." She liked him more than any guy she'd dated before.

"I could hang out with you all day and night, but I don't think the romance is there."

"Yeah," she said, reflecting on their time together. They had so much in common, and she truly liked Christopher, but they'd pretty much stepped away from the physical, to a soft and simple peck at the end of their dates. Nothing more. She *didn't* go home and think about him...at least, not like *that*. Maybe she shouldn't be so surprised that he'd noticed. "I guess it's not there."

She watched as relief took shape on his face. "I want you to know that this is in no way your fault. I think you're an amazing woman and I still want us to be friends. To keep doing stuff together. But there's something I need to let you in on, which may not be easy to hear."

"Of course. You can tell me anything."

"I'm gay."

"No."

"Yes."

Elle laughed hesitantly. "No, you're not. There's no way."

"Trust me. I used to think the same thing. Even very recently."

She blinked. She blinked again. A third time. She tried on the statement. "You're gay."

Birds wrestled in the birdbath nearby and he covered his eyes with his hand. "This is new for me, too. I mean, it's not. But it is new for me to say it out loud. I'm thirty years old and I'm finally admitting to myself what's always been there."

"Hey," she said quietly, pulling his hand down from his face. She reminded herself to focus less on her own surprise and more on her friend's feelings. This was a big admission for him. "You don't have to feel embarrassed or nervous in front of me. What do I know about anything? I can't even whistle." That netted a small smile. To help, she gave it a shot, forcing air through her lips in an abysmal display. "See? I'm a wreck of a person."

"No, you're not. You're put together. I've always thought so." He sat back in his chair and drank his coffee like a shot of bourbon.

"Well, I'm glad it looks that way." A new thought descended. She brushed the hair away from her face and inclined her head. "Can I ask if there's something in particular, other than your lack of connection with me, of course, that has led you to this revelation? A someone, perhaps?"

And then it all came tumbling out like a pent-up confession. "More like every man on the planet. Including Dash, and if you tell him that, I'll kill you, friendship or not."

"Aha." She laughed, and used her fingers to lock her lips. "Well. It sounds like the world has opened up for you, Christopher."

He took her hand and gave it a squeeze. "Are we okay?"

"How could we not be? We're too adorable people in a garden that looks like it was heaven sent. My good friend trusted me enough to tell me something important about him."

He smiled and exhaled slowly, as if the relief was a welcome hit. "You're amazing."

"Thank you. Hey, can we still check out that little sushi spot near the Grove next week? We just won't make out afterward."

He touched his cup to hers. "I made the reservations last night."

"Awesome." She beamed. "Yelp says their Seattle roll is worth its weight in gold."

"Then we gotta have it," he said. "Oh, and what about that Harrison Ford cop movie we were waiting for? It opens next week."

"I could do Thursday night," she said, scrolling through the calendar on her phone.

"Thursday works for me."

In only a matter of minutes, their brand-new friendship was a hundred times more comfortable than their romance-that-wasn't. The pressure was gone, and they could just…be. Elle was happy for Christopher and could already detect a lightness about him that she had never noticed before. She wondered what that must feel like.

"Oh, and Elle? You're going to find someone amazing. I have no doubt in my mind."

"You never know." For the first time, after years of feeling that romance was an impossibility for her, the pieces of a long-unrealized puzzle were beginning to assemble themselves slowly. She didn't know what they meant quite yet, but she was starting to have an inkling.

Christopher studied her. "What's the look on your face? You went somewhere just now."

Elle decided that Christopher had been honest with her, which couldn't have been easy, and the least she could do was let her guard down with him. In fact, he was likely the perfect person to talk to about this. She leaned in. "Do you remember the girl from the surf bar I took you to? The brunette across the room with her friends?"

"Your competitor, yeah. You two talked at the bar."

"What if I was starting to feel like I might have a crush on her? A small one. Almost nondetectable, but still a crush."

Christopher didn't balk. He didn't widen his eyes in surprise. He simply nodded as he took in the information. "Do you think she has similar feelings?"

"Definitely not. I mean, she teases me about a sex dream I had about her, which I shared in a drunken moment of idiocy, but I think that's all it is. Just playful fodder."

"You had a sex dream about her? And she knows?"

Elle waved him off. "Yes, but that was so last week. This week, we had dinner, and the thing is, there's so much more to her than I'd realized. I'd always thought of her as this less-than-warm surfer that I was supposed to take down on the tour. But maybe that was a characterization of my own making, because now I find out that she has this personality. She can be funny when she wants to be, and nervous other times, and she comes with this whole childhood in Hawaii, and don't even get me started on the fact that she's really very beautiful and—"

"Hey, Elle?"

"Yeah?" she asked, a little dazed.

"When you're apart, do you think about her?"

The answer was upon her immediately. She nodded. "I do. A lot."

He smiled. "Then I think it's safe to say that you have a crush on your hands. The only question is, what are you prepared to do about it?"

"I honestly don't know. Probably nothing."

"Well, maybe you don't have to know, in this moment. But can I offer a piece of advice?"

"Please. I would very much welcome any guidance or insight, because everything is feeling very out of sorts, and when you're a control freak like me? That's terrifying."

"Here goes. Don't wait fifteen years to admit to yourself what you probably already know. Life is too short, and you're too wonderful a person to lose out on something that *could* be really great if you were open to it."

"But I don't think I'm..." The sentence died on her lips because she couldn't back it up. She flashed on all her failed relationships with men and how they never held her interest. She'd always believed it was because her career took precedence, but maybe that hadn't been it. Now, through an unforeseen series of events, she'd stumbled onto someone she was actually attracted to, who appealed to parts of her she'd previously imagined were broken. Maybe this meant she wasn't broken after all.

Christopher gave her hand a squeeze. "You were saying?"

"That I have some thinking to do."

He nodded knowingly.

They wrapped up their coffee date with some small talk about Holly and Dash, their work schedules, and what plans they were already making for Christmas, a holiday they both loved. As they walked to their respective cars, Christopher turned to her. "Can I say that I might have suspected? It's an awful thing to say, but in this case, it's true."

Her mouth fell open. "I don't think I believe you. No way."

"Well, then I won't say it. Out loud." He wrapped his big arms around her and kissed the side of her head. "See you on Thursday."

"All right, goober."

❖

As Gia stood in the afternoon rush line at Cat's Pajamas, Autumn tossed her the universal look for "get out of line, idiot, I've got your order." She passed back an "Okay, but I don't want you to feel like you have to give me special favors" glance, and received the "you're not doing that, so stop being stupid" stare. Gia dutifully stepped out of line and took a seat at a nearby table. The one they usually sat at was occupied by a group of frat guys in swim trunks and damp T-shirts. She sent them a cool, even "that's my table" gaze as she passed. Unnecessary, yes, but she happened to be in an awful mood.

Her practice session had been rough, and with San Clemente coming up in just a few days, she couldn't afford a rough practice. With nearly two months since the last tournament, it was up to her to stay in peak surfing condition. She and Katrina had taken the Jet Ski out to catch the bigger swells, but she'd been off her game and couldn't seem to engage. She'd wiped out or been swallowed by a wave an embarrassing number of times, and when they'd found the bigger pipe, she just didn't have it in her to go after it and ended the session early in a frustrated huff. She was annoyed at herself and the world.

"Special delivery," Autumn said, and slid Gia an iced coffee, her afternoon beverage of choice. "Uh-oh. That's a rare look. I've seen it on your face maybe twice. What happened?"

Gia rolled her eyes. "Lame training session. All my fault, so I'm yelling at myself in my head."

"That sounds terrifying. Maybe let yourself off with a light lecture? Some extra chores?"

"Nah. Too easy."

Autumn, with a hand on her growing stomach, slid delicately into the chair across from Gia. "Coffee will make it better, though. It makes everything better."

"Thanks," she mumbled halfheartedly, and thumbed the circular lid. Coffee did help, and she was doing everything she could to see value in the little things, because the larger issues were confusing the hell out of her.

"Would it help if I told you that the kids are dancing up a storm today? Probably because they wanted to say hello to you. I told them you might drop in."

Gia sat up, intrigued. "You can really feel them now?" The idea made her surfing issues fade to the background, at least momentarily.

"Mm-hmm. Here. It's getting to the point where others can, too. At least once or twice for Kate." She took Gia's hand and placed it on her stomach, which was surprisingly firm. At first, she didn't feel anything. Autumn looked skyward and moved Gia's hand to the left and pressed it into her stomach as if to wake them up. "Feel that?" Gia sat upright, because there was a noticeable little flutter against Autumn's skin.

She pulled her hand back in surprise and pointed. "Whoa. There are people in there. Moving. You were right."

Autumn laughed. "Can you believe it? I still can't."

Gia grappled. "I know human beings have children every day, but it's different when it's…Autumn. I mean, you. *You're having kids*. You. My best friend."

Autumn nodded with an acceptance Gia didn't have yet. "That's true. This time next year, there will be rug rats around here causing trouble. Real ones, with thoughts and opinions and wants and needs."

Gia felt a surge of panic and glanced around. "We should probably start getting ready. Making lists or something. What list should I make?"

Autumn stood. "Way ahead of you, champ. You should see the storage locker Kate's rented, full of baby supplies. I tried to tell her we're expecting a couple of infants, not the apocalypse. But it makes her feel better to be overprepared. She's turning into a professional baby supply hoarder, though, no doubt about it. An intervention might be forthcoming."

"Kate's hoarding babies?" Gia's goofy neighbor, Barney, asked as he meandered through the shop. His normally bleached-blond hair had a green streak running through it today. Gia couldn't begin to understand the type of life that dude led. He had a different job every time she talked to him. Magazine subscriptions, errand runner, and her favorite, rare coin collector. Mainly, he just wanted to hang out on the beach and play volleyball with his dude friends all day.

"More like supplies," Autumn said, gesturing to her stomach. "She's getting ready for these guys."

"Gnarly. Gonna down some of your delicious coffee now." He offered Autumn a fist bump and continued his half dance, half walk to the counter.

Autumn, used to Barney and unfazed, turned back to Gia. "I was meaning to ask, are you free this weekend? We thought we might do a gender reveal with our close friends."

"Oh, man. I leave for San Clemente on Sunday, but I could do Friday or Saturday."

"Done. Stay tuned for details. We'll all find out together."

Gia was smiling when Autumn returned to work, but that smile came right off her face when she saw public enemy number one walk through the door.

"Hey," Isabel said to Gia. "I took off a little early today, so I thought I would see what everyone was up to."

"No way," Gia said. "You can't walk in here and be friendly. We're not friends right now."

Isabel seemed taken aback, but only mildly. "We're not friends? Was there a memo I missed again? I suck at memos."

"You can't quip your way out of this one with your Izzy-talk."

Isabel took a chair, turned it backward, and sat down. "Gonna have to be more specific."

"You've ruined my life and now my job."

"Yeah, that was a lot clearer." She softened. "Suggestion time. Why don't you just tell me what's actually going on, with details rather than vague suggestions?"

"Fine. There was the Trainers campaign, and the sex dream, and now I'm in this weird place with Elle where I notice her physically, and actually like her, and then the surfing just...sucks. All of it, your fault."

"Riiiight," Isabel said. "That makes a hundred percent sense. All my doing. No one would question that logic."

Gia glared at her. "Don't argue with me when I'm down. Don't you do it."

"Who's arguing? I'm a fucking support system of awesome, worried for your mental well-being. I'm also feeling intrigued and hopeful about your new extracurricular life. Want to talk about it?"

"With you? Not a chance." A pause. Gia dropped the ire from her voice. "I'm waiting for Had."

"The wide-eyed Cinderella of Seven Shores? I'm the one actually *in* a relationship. You realize that, right? I'm fully capable here. In fact, the most capable."

"Ahem," Autumn said from behind the counter, indicating she'd been eavesdropping on every word. Her capacity to hear each conversation in the coffee shop was a mystery Gia had yet to crack. Like when your mom just intuitively knew you'd skipped school. That was Autumn, every damn time.

"Oh! Autumn, who is happily married, can also help," Isabel said in a loud voice. "She's every bit a pro."

Gia stood. "Thanks, guys, but I'm going to wait."

"Unbelievable," Isabel called to Gia's retreating form. "Is this some sort of single person solidarity? I'm feeling rightfully offended."

"What you should feel is guilty as hell," Gia said, whirling on her. "All. Your. Fault. You and your stupid sparks."

Isabel seemed to suppress a smile, which only angered Gia further. "See, you never have fully explained what it is I did wrong, but if something I said helped you along your path to love, or even a little temporary lust, then I will accept your anger in worthy sacrifice to the cause."

Gia heard Autumn chuckle quietly from behind the counter. She glanced from one of them to the other. "You two are awful people who deserve each other's friendship."

Isabel blew her a loud kiss and Autumn followed suit. She would forgive them both in around ten minutes. For now, it felt really good to focus her anger. She stomped down the sidewalk to Seven Shores and took in the empty courtyard. Hadley was working the afternoon to evening shift at Silhouette, and if she was quick, maybe she could catch her before she left for work. Hadley would understand. She'd help her figure this out.

"My dear goodness. Sounds like things have escalated," Hadley said from in front of her dressing table fifteen minutes later. She stared at Gia through the mirror as she transformed into the sophisticated version of herself suited for the posh boutique on Rodeo Drive. A little blush, a little mascara, and an updo, and Hadley went from endearing to impressive.

"I don't know that I'd say *escalated*," Gia offered, as nonchalantly as possible. "But the whole Elle thing has me wigged out and distracted. It's starting to affect my surfing, and that can't happen. You get me?"

Hadley swiveled on her stool and faced Gia, who sat on the sage comforter atop Hadley's bed. "You realize that this is the same Elle Britton that you've seethed over for the past several years, who you've made me despise right alongside you. While it was fun to tease you about the chemistry and all, I never actually thought anything real would come of it. This has taken a turn, I say. A *turn*. Hand me the hairspray. I'm short on time."

Gia passed Hadley the bottle. "Nothing will come of it. It's just a blip."

Hadley deflated. "Why is that? Why are you so quick to decide?" She sprayed her hair and surveyed the results in the mirror.

"It's impractical." Gia stood because she was far too fired up not to. "It's a phase. I'm sure I'll be back to hating her next week, and the attraction will be gone."

"You're gesturing a lot."

"So?"

"It's what you do when something is really bothering you. Tells me this is major. And so what if the attraction fades? If it fizzles, it fizzles. Can't hurt to enjoy it a little in the meantime."

That last sentence snagged her attention. She didn't allow much time to enjoy things. There was surfing, which was her main focus, her job. For fun, she really just turned to her friends and maybe retro video games. But that was about it, all she allowed herself time for. *Can't hurt to enjoy it a little.* She nodded, finding the parallel to the homework Katrina had given her. "I guess that's not horrible advice."

"Of course it's not horrible advice," Hadley said, standing and crushing Gia's face into her stomach in a commanding hug. "It's from me."

"Ow. You're smashing my face."

"You love me." Hadley released her and went in search of her bag with Gia hot on her heels, not quite finished with the discussion.

"Katrina says I get in my own head too much."

"You do. So maybe don't overthink as far as Elle is concerned. Follow"—she smiled—"other parts of you."

Gia sighed. "I thought for sure you'd understand. Tell me to proceed with caution."

"I do understand. But it is my sincere hope that you allow yourself to be open and receptive to the ways of love."

She shook her head. "Only you would say a lame sentence like that."

"Make fun of me all you want, but I'm not the one daydreaming about my number one rival without any clothes on. Don't deny it either. I know you."

"You and Izzy and Autumn are ridiculous, you know that?"

Hadley ushered them out of the apartment. "You're probably right. We're the ridiculous ones. Call me later. I'm off to take the design world by storm." Hadley sashayed to the top of the outdoors stairs and struck a pose.

Gia squinted in confusion. "What are you doing?"

"Trying to make an exit. Did it work?"

"I don't think so."

"Well, tomorrow is another day. Be good, Gia, and by good, I mean carefree."

"Yeah, yeah." Gia stood on the outdoor walkway in front of Hadley's apartment and walked the few steps to the door to her own. She could see the ocean over the top of the complex across from her. She watched the waves a moment, a trick that had always calmed her in the past and set her at peace. It wasn't working. She took out her phone and did something even she couldn't fathom: she texted Elle.

Training today? It was doubtful she'd get a reply. She wasn't even sure why'd she done it, other than the fact that she was restless and out of sorts and couldn't help herself, flashing on the good time they'd had at dinner. She turned to enter her apartment when her phone chimed. Whoa. Her heart sped up and she clenched one fist before glancing at the readout.

Morning session complete. What are you up to?

Panic hit and her mind raced. Not sure what to do, she moved to the railing, then away from it again, and then back. She was tempted to toss the phone over the balcony, the stupid device! What the hell was she supposed to do now? Finally, she took a seat on the top of the stairs and typed a response.

Wanna join forces this afternoon? She hit Send before logic could interfere.

Elle's response was faster this time. *Well, that could make for an interesting workout.*

The blush hit and although no one was around to see it, the mortification followed anyway. Gia didn't casually blush. She was an athlete, and a stoic one at that. She stomped on feelings, ate them for breakfast, and pushed forward to the win at every turn. Who was this new chick taking residence in her body? She started to type that she'd only been kidding when a second message from Elle hit.

Come to Hermosa Beach. My turf. 3 pm.

Deep breath. *Don't think.* She typed, *You're on.*

This could get interesting.

CHAPTER NINE

After lunch and a short rest for her muscles, Gia did some stretches, put on a sky-blue bikini top and board shorts, hopped in her Jeep, and headed for South Bay, home of Hermosa Beach. The twelve-mile drive took close to half an hour in traffic, giving her plenty of time to second-guess what was probably a horrible idea. Who trained with their competition? No one did, because it was stupid. Something else was driving her, and it had little to do with surfing. *Don't think. Don't overanalyze.* But she knew exactly what it was. She craved time with Elle. Craved being in her presence, staring at her, talking to her. It was becoming all too familiar, that want, and it came with a power like nothing she'd ever experienced.

In fact, she was beginning to wonder if she could fight it if she tried.

Elle's directions were perfect, and when she arrived, Gia found her on a stretch of quiet beach. Some dudes tossed a football down the shore. A couple walked their schnauzer. Meanwhile, music blared from a radio propped up in the sand (something current and poppy that you'd hear on the radio) as Elle did lower abdominal crunches on an exercise mat in her red sports bikini. Gia blinked at the skin on display. She'd seen it all before, a million times. Yet things seemed very different now. She swallowed back the desire that enveloped her.

"What's up, Two?" Elle asked, not so much as pausing her crunches. At least she offered a bright smile.

Gia stared down at Elle. "If that's my cue to call you One, it's not gonna happen."

Elle sat up and draped her forearms across her knees. The sun caught her eyes just perfectly, highlighting the light blue. She had a thin sheen of perspiration on her forehead, and her smile, as always, could light up even the darkest of rooms. She met Gia's gaze. "I'm willing to let you call me whatever you want. Within reason. Count for me?"

Gia grinned and took her spot at Elle's feet as Beyoncé empowered them both from the radio in the sand. She began counting off the crunches. "Two, four, six, eight, ten." Every time Elle raised up, her gaze met Gia's and held for a fleeting moment. "Twenty-two, twenty-four, twenty-six." Her first instinct was to look away, to deflect, or make a joke. But, no, not this time. She held on, relishing the way their locked eyes made her feel. She felt connected to Elle and loved every second of it. When they hit a hundred, Gia took charge. "Sit-ups. Fifty."

"You're a demanding trainer. You sure you want me in tip-top shape? Could be consequences. Swatch Pro is just under a week away."

"Yeah, well, I happen to know how good your competition is, so I think we're okay." They traded off counting for each other, and as they worked out under the hot sun, Gia felt herself relax more and more and truly relish the afternoon and how much fun the two of them were having together. Competition banter and all.

They decided to end with a run along the beach before hitting the waves. She allowed Elle to set their pace, and it wasn't an easy one. "Are you showing off?" she asked.

"Maybe a little." They ran on, and Elle tossed her a glance. "I'm glad you came by. Got my ass moving more than I have all week."

"Same. Maybe we should have been training alongside our competitors this whole time."

"Well, the pretty ones at least." Elle pulled ahead and Gia turned up the gas, hot on her heels with a broad smile on her face. The exertion, the endorphins, or maybe the fact that she didn't have to look Elle in the eye had Gia feeling lighthearted and courageous.

"Are you flirting with me?" she asked.

A pause. "Maybe."

Maybe. Wow. Gia wasn't inventing things. And if Elle was flirting, what exactly would all of that mean? Did it change anything for Gia? Would she suddenly want to pursue Elle Britton officially? Sounded like a dumb idea in the larger scheme of things, but for a minute she allowed herself to enjoy the unravel. The idea.

"Were you flirting with *me* at the restaurant the other night?" Elle asked. Her tone was playful, but Gia saw through it. Maybe Elle was just as intrigued by their newfound dynamic as Gia was.

What the hell. She decided to go for it. "Yeah, I'd say I was. Just in fun, though."

"Okay. Good to know."

They ran on as the sun continued its descent in the sky and the waves rolled in not far from their feet. The sound of the water and distant seagulls served as their soundtrack while they each seemed to retreat to the quietness of their own thoughts.

"What about you?" Gia asked. "Were you flirting with *me* at the restaurant the other night?"

"I think so."

Another pause, as Gia processed this. She'd guessed as much, but hearing it out loud was something else entirely. It also brought up a lot of questions. "But you're straight." The words had tumbled from her mouth. Unfortunately, Gia didn't come with a ton of finesse and pretty much just said things as they occurred to her. Hearing that sentence out loud, however, had her wishing she had employed some of Hadley's sensitivity.

Elle stopped running, which also brought Gia to a stop. She placed her hands on her hips and took a moment as her breathing slowed. She stared at Gia. "I never said that."

"Oh." Gia didn't know what to say to that, but she had to say something. She stared briefly at a seagull splashing in the surf. "I just thought so, because you've always dated men."

"Well, everyone's straight until they're not, right?"

Elle ran on, leaving Gia staring after her, shocked, encouraged, and shocked again. She caught up and they ran for another ten minutes with only the sounds of the beach accompanying them.

"You should stick around after we surf. We can have some food." A pause. "I should have just said we can have dinner. That would have been better."

Gia laughed. "Either works for me. I'm pretty simple that way."

"Are you, though?" Elle asked, which made Gia stop and think. She'd always considered herself a fairly what-you-see-is-what-you-get person.

"I think so, yeah. My needs are basic. Food, waves, and friends."

"And nothing else?"

God, why did Elle have to say that? Because now Gia had that low pull in her stomach and thought acutely of other needs. "There's more. Those are just my generals."

Elle nodded, and they reversed their direction, heading back up the shoreline toward where they'd begun. "I guess I've just been giving the subject a lot of thought lately. The something else."

"And?"

"It has me intrigued, and thoughtful, and examining my life in the most unexpected of ways."

Aha. Now they were getting somewhere. "Like flirting with women?"

"Yeah, I guess that's part of it." The thing about having a conversation in the midst of a run was you didn't have to look the other person in the eye. Somehow that helped grease the wheels.

"Any idea what brought this on?"

She could see Elle nodding out of the corner of her eye. "I think it was you. The dream and then us spending time together. We click way more than I ever would have predicted. I think about you sometimes now. I don't know." A pause. "We should surf."

Must have been some dream. She'd give anything to have experienced it firsthand.

As they swam out to the larger swells, Elle in front and Gia trailing behind her, it felt as though they were heading toward something bigger, something inevitable that had nothing to do with waves. While Gia felt terrified, unsure, and adrift, she also couldn't pull them off the track they were on now if she tried. This thing between them was like a runaway boulder, and all she could do was get herself out of the damn way.

They surfed together but not. Gia would take a wave, ride it in, as Elle did the same. They also didn't communicate much out there on the water, other than a few encouraging calls.

But they did notice each other.

Wherever Elle was, Gia was aware. She watched her form, her speed, her power, and flow. Beyond those things, she watched Elle. The look on her face as she drove hard to the pocket. She pulled her bottom lip in, and her right eyebrow dipped down in concentration. The swells were small for what they were used to on tour, allowing Elle to stay upright, tackling one wave after another like the pro that she was. But these were beach breaks they were surfing, waves moving over shifting sand, each one a little different from the next—which kept things interesting. But that wasn't all that was interesting. Gia felt Elle's eyes on her, too, moving across her skin, watching her technique, her body, making the whole experience take on an…erotic undertone.

They surfed until late in the day when their energy ran dry and their hunger took over. As they paddled their way back to the shore,

Elle looked over at Gia. "I will admit, I didn't know what it would be like surfing with you outside of a competition."

Gia smiled. "And?"

"I'm surprised how much I enjoyed it. It wasn't nearly as stressful as I imagined."

She laughed, not sure if that was a compliment or not. "I had fun, too. Not going on record or anything, but maybe you're a great surfer." Gia never in a million years would imagine those words coming from her lips just three months ago, but she wanted Elle to know that about herself.

"Yeah, well, you happen to be good at it, as well."

Gia turned to Elle, her mouth hanging open in shock. "Really? Good? You're going with good? I gave you great."

"Fine. Maybe you're better than good. But we're still off the record."

"Thank you."

They hit the shore and dragged their boards in. Elle glanced back out at the water. "Did you see the clean walls out there? I was loving it. Just big enough."

"I could tell, wave hog. You were all over them."

"Says the final heat interloper."

Gia shook her head. "You're *never* going to let that one go, are you?"

"Would you?"

"No," Gia said automatically. They laughed at her candor. "You gotta do what you gotta do."

"All in the name of surfing. Hungry yet?"

"Starving."

"Thought so. Follow me." Elle didn't live far from their spot on the beach. She led Gia down a windy path to the back of a one-story blue house, where they deposited their boards and bags just beyond a wooden gate that came to Gia's waist.

She stared at the house. "This is you?"

"For the past six years."

She took a moment for the appropriate amount of jealousy. "Cool beach access."

"My thoughts exactly when I paid too much for the place." Elle led Gia up the steps to a back deck accessorized with two comfortable-looking patio chairs facing the shore with a table between them. She imagined Elle sitting outside, salt water drying on her skin, watching the sun go down. Didn't sound awful at all.

Elle unlocked the back door and tossed Gia a look over her shoulder. "Hey, remember when you were distant and unfriendly?"

Gia nodded. "Remember when you were fake and attention seeking?"

"Hopefully, we've eliminated 'fake' from that sentence."

Gia chuckled and followed Elle inside. She took a moment to orient herself to the space. Everything about the interior of Elle's house said soft. The colors, a variety of whites and beiges, the shape of the furniture, all rounded and cloud-like. It was the perfect place to collapse after a long day's workout. Every aspect of Elle's home screamed "fall down right here." Gia wanted to. Even the art on the wall communicated serenity. "You have a very chill house. I don't know how else to say it."

"Chill, huh?" Elle laughed. "I don't think I've ever heard it described quite like that, but yes, it's very *chill*. I happen to need chill in my life. What's your place like?"

Gia paused. "It feels significantly less adult than this. Also less comfortable."

"Let me guess. All wall-to-wall neon surfboards?"

"Nooo," Gia said, drawing out the lie. "I have a couch, too."

"Wow," Elle said, in mock appreciation. But as Gia perused the place further, Elle did have nods to their shared profession on display, just not as in-your-face as Gia did. A framed news article on the wall from a big tournament win from Elle's teenage years. A color photo of her on the day she took the world championship. There were also photos of her with her parents, her younger brothers, and people Gia presumed were her friends. Elle's life seemed vibrant and happy, warm even. As she took in the personal touches and got to know Elle a little better, she noticed herself smiling.

"You are a person," she said, in teasing fashion, to Elle.

"As much as possible, yes," Elle said over her shoulder. Her breath tickled Gia's skin, sending a shiver inching through her. "How about a shower before dinner?"

Gia turned around and raised an eyebrow in the quiet of Elle's living room.

The insinuation prompted Elle to falter, and the perfect smile fell from her face. "No. I didn't mean it like that."

Gia didn't mind seeing Elle on defense. It was too rare an occurrence for her not to enjoy it. She couldn't stop herself from pushing back. "Because that's what it sounded like. So, not an invitation, then?" Gia asked, with a raised eyebrow.

Elle exhaled, understanding that she was being teased. "The eyebrow again, huh? You can use the guest bathroom, through there."

Gia followed Elle's gaze and grabbed her bag. "Thanks. I'll be quick." The hall bathroom had Gia captivated. Matching light blue hand towels, and little soaps carved into different shapes. Seashells, anchors, and starfish. Foaming hand soap, and the thick kind of tissues you find in all the good hotels. Elle had her life together, that was for sure.

Gia took a quick shower, dried off with the fluffiest towel she'd experienced in a quite a while, slid into her jeans and white slouchy top, and headed to the kitchen, where she found Elle already showered and unpacking a delivery bag.

"Food's here."

Gia glanced at the front door and back to Elle. "How is that possible? I took a ten-minute shower. Are you capable of stopping time?"

Elle smiled. "It's from an all-natural restaurant around the corner. I have a delivery service already scheduled several times a week. Just asked them to make it two tonight."

"That easy, huh?" Gia joined Elle in the kitchen, glancing up at the copper pots and pans that hung from above the center island. More adulting. "So, what are we having?"

"Lots of baked chicken, broccoli, twelve-grain bread, and jalapeno corn which, trust me, will blow your mind." Elle tucked a strand of wet hair behind her ear, and Gia attempted to stay focused on the conversation.

"Mind-blowing corn? I'm in." Good save.

At Elle's suggestion, they skipped the kitchen table in favor of the coffee table, and sat on the floor of her living room, which wasn't a problem because wouldn't you know it, the accent rug was fluffy and awesome. It wasn't the most exciting meal in the world, but in the middle of the season, it was definitely the kind of food Gia should be eating. Well, they both should.

Elle regarded Gia thoughtfully, spoon in hand. "I can't believe you thought I was fake. I happen to be a really friendly person."

Gia considered this as she finished chewing. "You are. But you have to admit that you lay it on a little thick when in the limelight." But even Gia was starting to backpedal from the theory. Elle was actually a pretty bubbly person in front of the media and away from it. That's apparently just who she was.

"It's true that I can schmooze." She sparkled even as she said the word, as if the thought took her there. "But that's part of the game, unfortunately. Do you know that there are women on the tour, the top professional surfing tour in the world, that don't have sponsorship?"

Gia nodded. She didn't understand how they managed it. Travel alone could run past the $50,000 mark.

"Sasha Christianson, from Australia?"

"Yeah?"

Elle raised a hand in punctuation. "Number thirteen in the world and isn't sponsored. Not by choice either, and that makes no sense. She pays for everything out of pocket. If she doesn't win, she operates at a loss by the end of the season."

"I know. It sucks."

"Which means she's probably going to be off the tour soon. How long can one person sustain that kind of financial hit? She has to eat. Pay rent."

Elle had a valid point. The surfing world was just as sexist as any other sport out there. The women were rewarded for their appearances with ads, sponsorships, and endorsement deals. Others used their charisma to pull in the necessary cash to compete. But if you were a less-than-attractive or shy person, the going was rough, if not impossible. Didn't matter how great a surfer you were. Your only hope was to have been born independently wealthy and bankroll your travel and tournament fees personally. It didn't make sense.

"So, I was fourteen years old, trying to figure out how in the world I was going to make it to the next tournament, and then the next," Elle said. "We were a middle-class family. My parents did everything for me that they could, but I was going to have to figure something else out long term. It was clear to me that sponsorship was the only way I was going to be able to make a go of surfing from a career standpoint."

Gia started to understand. "You learned to court the media."

"Big-time. I had to. And I got good at it." Elle paused to bask in the glory of the corn. She pointed at Gia's plate. "Right?"

Gia grinned. "It's pretty good."

"The more press I did, the more doors I noticed opening for me. Listen, all I wanted to do was surf, and I had found a way in. If we're being honest, I didn't mind that part of the job that much. It was fun. Still can be."

"It's shocking you were able to figure that out so young."

"I'm not alone. You're sponsored up yourself."

"I just do my thing," Gia said. "Been lucky, I guess. I don't play the media game as well."

Elle nodded. "Yeah, but the whole mysterious allure you have going doesn't hurt. Even I was curious about you from the beginning."

"I'm not as talkative as some of the other surfers. That part is true. What's the name of this restaurant again? This chicken isn't bad."

"The Salt and Herb. It also doesn't hurt that you're beautiful. It's why you're in all the gossip columns. People want to know what's going on with you."

Gia filed away the compliment to think about later. "They want to know a lot more since we started working on the Trainers deal together."

Elle held her gaze. "I guess we're giving them something to talk about. They just don't know whether we're ready to kill each other or climb into bed."

This was an opening if Gia had ever seen one. She swallowed her bite of bread, took a sip of water, and went for it. "So how are things going with that guy you were seeing? What was his name?"

"Christopher, and we ended things. The spark wasn't there."

There was that damn word again. "Oh. I'm sorry."

"You don't have to be. Really. Sometimes things work out the way they do for a reason. Can I take your plate?"

"Thank you." Gia watched Elle's journey to the kitchen. Her bare feet. The slight sway of her hips that filled out those yoga pants perfectly. Her hair that had been wet from the shower was now mostly dry and blond again. "Does it feel to you that things are happening for a reason a lot lately?"

Elle took a moment from where she stood at the sink. Her voice carried sincerity when she answered. "Actually, it does feel that way."

Gia followed Elle into the kitchen. "Should I go? I feel like we're treading on unstable ground here."

Elle dried her hands and sighed. "I don't want you to. There. I said it."

And with those simple words, Elle had communicated a lot. For once, Gia didn't have to get out of her own head because she wasn't in it. She knew what she wanted, what she'd been craving. She stepped into Elle's space, briefly met her searching blue eyes, and caught her mouth in a kiss. But it wasn't just any kiss. Elle received her right away, her mouth soft as it moved slowly against Gia's. The feeling that came over Gia as they kissed was so new and unexpected and wonderful that she wasn't sure what to do except to keep going. At the touch of Elle's tongue against her lips, Gia opened her mouth, shocked by the pure heat that shot through her at the feel of Elle's tongue in her mouth. She was backed against the counter, and Elle was up on her toes, having taken control. So unexpected, but beyond okay. Elle moaned quietly when Gia's hands found her waist and hauled her in. It was the most wonderful sound. Did people really fit together the way they did in this moment?

"Ahem," a voice behind them said, and then erupted into a sputtering cough. They broke apart and turned to find a very surprised and apologetic-looking woman standing in the entryway of Elle's home. She held a key in the air.

"Sorry. You didn't pick up your phone, so I just popped by to pick up the red dress you borrowed. I was gonna sneak out with it, but that would be creepy and you'd probably hear me because I'm a klutz. Hi," the woman said to Gia, with a wave. "Holly. The best friend."

Gia nodded back, her hands still on Elle's body. "Gia. The—"

"Number two surfer in the world. In Elle's kitchen. Kissing her. Yeah, I gathered that part. Nice to meet you."

Elle still hadn't said anything. Whether she was shocked, regretful, or embarrassed remained unclear. Regardless, Gia took that cue, understanding that her presence was most likely complicating things. "I was actually just getting ready to head out. That's what was happening. I'll let you two—yeah."

"You don't have to go," Elle said quietly. She was meeker sounding now, less confident than her usual self, which told Gia that getting out of the way was the right thing to do here. This was, after all, a new and delicate situation for Elle.

"I do, though," Gia said. "Lots on my agenda." She met Elle's gaze briefly, and gave her hand a squeeze. "I'm sure I'll see you around soon."

Elle nodded, still not using too many words. As Gia headed to the door, she nodded to Holly, who returned the gesture with a four-finger wave. No one said a word as she exited the house in what was probably the most confusing and awkward moment of her life. She hit the sidewalk and realized one thing. Didn't matter. The kiss back there, of earthshaking magnitude, topped any and all awkward exits for the rest of time. That kiss would go down in Gia's history books as the most electric, the most satisfying, and maybe the most perplexing exchange of her lifetime. She could analyze the clunky ending, or revel in the captivating kiss.

She exhaled slowly and closed her eyes. It was a no-brainer.

❖

"Might just be me, but it seems we might have some things to discuss," Holly said, breaking the silence in Elle's kitchen.

Elle blinked several times, nodded. Blinked again. "Probably," she said, still trying to regroup and move out of the haze she found herself in. It was a pretty nice haze, though. Why hurry?

Holly dropped her keys on the counter, set down her bag, and moved purposefully to Elle's living room, where she took a seat expectantly on the sofa and crossed one leg over the other. "Ready when you are." She smiled, signaling her enjoyment of this newly discovered dynamic.

Elle followed her into the living room and took a seat in the chair across from Holly. Her lips buzzed pleasantly and her stomach was fully occupied by hyperactive butterflies. Lustful ones. Her skin tingled where Gia's hands had been, and her mind was still stuck on a loop of the moment Gia kissed her. *Gia kissed her.* That had actually happened, and she wasn't able to get the world to go back to normal. Not after that.

"I can see that I'm going to have to take the lead here," Holly said. "True or false. You were just kissing Gia Malone, your rival, your former nemesis, and a *woman*."

Elle could answer that one easily enough. "True."

"Great. We're making mind-blowing progress. Can you expand on how this romance went from tabloid gossip to a real life make-out session in the middle of your kitchen? Inquiring minds want to know." Holly leaned in.

"That part's a lot more complicated."

"Step one?"

"A sex dream. Mine. About her. I told you about it. Then I told her about it. Then mild flirting. Then not so mild." Her mind was slowly coming around and moving through the series of events, as much for herself as for Holly. "The eye contact during our ab workout earlier today was more killer than the workout itself. I think I wanted her to kiss me, Hol. I did. But I wasn't prepared for it. Christopher was right."

Holly's eyes went wide. "Christopher is in on this? What the hell?"

"We're not dating anymore. He's gay and thinks I might be."

She covered her mouth. "Oh no! I just outed him. That's awful. I'm a horrible friend. God."

Holly held up a hand. "Don't worry. He spent the weekend conga dancing from one gay club to another. The cat's out of the bag. Big-time. I just didn't realize he was your wingman. I'm the wingman!"

"Don't worry. You're still my number one." She smiled in relief at the news about Christopher. "He did all that? That's nice. I'm glad he's living it up."

"Apparently, he's not the only one," Holly said, by way of reminder. "Let's get back to you, you minx on a surfboard. Who knew you had this in you?"

"Not me. That's for sure. I wish I'd known sooner."

"That good?" Holly asked quietly.

Elle nodded numbly. It was all she could do. She held out her hands as if searching for words and dropped them. "Now what do I do?"

"Well, I think we've figured out why your relationships don't last."

Elle had to laugh. "How pathetic of me not to get it. How dumb can I be?"

"Can I ask a more serious question now?"

Elle extended her arm, giving Holly permission and the floor.

"Do you think this revelation is about women, or just Gia?"

"Both," Elle said without hesitation. "I notice women now. In a way I never have before. I didn't *know* to notice them before." She paused. "But more specifically, this is about her. She's the one I think about. No one compares."

Holly nodded, and considered Elle's answer. "If you were to complete the following sentence, what would it be: 'As far as Gia goes, I want…'?"

Elle squinted. "Did you learn this from your therapist?"

"Shut up. Just try it."

"Fine." Elle gave her body a shake and kept an open mind. "Here goes. I want…to know more about Gia. I want to talk to her for hours until I learn as much as possible. I want to kiss her again. Big exclamation point over that one."

"And more?"

"I think so," Elle answered meekly. "Is that crazy? I mean, coming from me? You can be honest. Give it to me straight."

Holly passed her a look.

"Tell it like it is," Elle said, in amendment.

Holly got up and squeezed herself into the oversized chair next to Elle, linking their arms. "Nope. Not crazy. While I didn't see this coming, I've never been prouder of you. You saw something in yourself and tackled it head-on. You're brave and doing the right thing. I love you for it."

Elle dropped her head onto Holly's shoulder. "Thanks, Hol. I needed to hear that." A pause. "Am I going to survive this?"

"I guess we're about to find out."

Elle looked up at the ceiling as if it would have the answers. "She left here like the house was on fire."

"Maybe *her house* was on fire, if you know what I mean." Holly bounced her eyebrows.

"I don't, but I think you're using a euphemism."

"I am. You've been out of the sex game for...well, your whole life, so you're going to have to work on picking up on euphemisms, innuendo, sexy talk, all of it. Just think, Elle, a whole new world is about to open up to you."

Elle held up a hand, feeling excited but also a touch panicked. "Let's not get ahead of ourselves, okay? It was one kiss. One very enjoyable kiss, but still just a single moment in time."

"Too late. I have to enjoy this. A major breakthrough has happened. So many questions have been answered." She sat taller. "Oh! Wait till the surf rags get ahold of this."

"There's not anything to get ahold of yet. And if there is, they're not getting it. It was one thing to have fun with us when it wasn't real, but it feels different now somehow. I feel the need to protect it. Protect *her.*"

Holly nodded. "Did you hear yourself?"

Elle shifted in the chair to so she could see Holly. "What?"

"You just said it was real."

Elle nodded, and felt herself drift back to a stolen moment in her kitchen when the world felt right for the first time. "I guess time will tell."

CHAPTER TEN

Gia loved the way the small fire on the beach danced in an unpredictable pattern. She glanced across it at the smiling faces of her friends, all gathered for Autumn's big reveal in a jumble of anticipation and excitement. And what better way for them to celebrate the news than with a beach fire? One of their favorite longstanding traditions. First, as always, they'd dined on steak à la Hadley, straight from her trusty hibachi grill, and chatted as the sun disappeared beyond the water line. Between the grill and the beach fire, they were breaking all the important Venice Beach rules. But they were careful enough with the fire, and it didn't hurt that Gia had made friends with the local cops, who happened to be fans and generally looked the other way.

Wrapped in a blue hoodie and cradling a beer in both hands, Gia couldn't wait to find out what kind of small folks they'd be meeting in just a handful of months. In fact, she'd been counting the hours until they found out, a detail she didn't admit freely, because those kinds of bursts of emotion were best left to Hadley. However, the energy that floated playfully in the salty air around them had Gia's spirits high and her heart full. This was her family, and it was growing! This made it a big night for all of them.

"Are we taking bets?" Taylor asked with a grin, snuggling farther beneath the blanket around her shoulders. "Because I've been feeling like this is a pair of boys from the beginning, and I'm known for killer intuition."

Hadley's eyes lit up. "Two little boys in caps and bowties will cause my heart to burst. I won't be able to take it."

"We wouldn't blame you," Isabel said.

Autumn placed a hand on her tummy, from where she sat cross-legged near the fire for optimum warmth. "I don't know, guys. We might be dealing with one of each. Remember they're likely not identical. We transferred two embryos."

Taylor hugged herself. "I love that you guys don't know, either."

"Nope," Autumn said. "I handed over the sealed envelope the doctor gave us. Only the bakery knows what was inside. I get that pink cake and blue cake is clichéd, but for clarity, that's what we're dealing with today. I considered going with green and yellow to be politically correct, but with pregnancy brain, I didn't want to confuse myself."

Gia waved her off. "No judgment here."

"Girls," Kate said. "Just to break our hearts, and make us worry for them. They're gonna be girls. Just wait."

"Now I'm picking out their swimsuits," Hadley said, staring up at the stars. "You guys are killing me!"

Gia laughed. "I think we have to know already or risk losing Had. Where are the clichéd cupcakes? Is it time?"

Kate picked up a foil-covered tray prepared by the bakery up the street. "Yep. I think we're there." She moved around the outside of the circle, handing out little cupcakes with chocolate frosting. "Two for everybody. One with chocolate icing, one with vanilla."

"I'm going to die," Hadley said. "We're moments away, but I'm going to die before we get there."

"You won't die." Autumn laughed as Hadley fanned the side of her face even though it was freezing out. "How are you more nervous than me?"

"Because she's Hadley," Isabel supplied. "I'm pretty sure she might shoot up into the stars at any moment, which is why I'm staying the hell over here."

"Mock me all you want," Hadley said, gleefully raising a cupcake in each hand. "This is a huge moment!"

"Okay, ready?" Kate asked the group, who nodded back. "Chocolate first. On the count of three, take a bite. One, two, two and a half…"

"Hurry," Autumn called out.

"Three!"

In unison, six women bit into their chocolate cupcakes and began screaming through mouthfuls of pink cake.

"It's a girl!" Hadley squealed, leaping to her feet and turning in a circle, as if not quite sure how else to express herself.

Autumn laughed through sentimental tears, meeting Kate's gaze. "We're going to have a daughter." Kate kissed her in response.

"Oh, man," Gia said, shaking her head in disbelief. "A tiny surfer chick."

"Congratulations!" Isabel and Taylor yelled in unison, still scarfing the cupcake. As the chatter picked up, and they all talked over one another in a celebratory flutter, Autumn held up her hands.

"Wait. Don't forget, we have one more."

As if programmed, everyone fell into silence and focused on the vanilla iced cupcakes. "You ready?" Autumn asked Kate, who nodded happily back.

Autumn turned to the group. "One, two, and three!"

A burst of blue greeted Gia as she took a tentative bite. Her heart filled and she grinned at her friends.

"Oh my God!" Hadley said to her cupcake. "You're a boy. You're a little baby boy."

"One of each," Kate said, in mystification. "Now I feel like the one about to shoot off into the stars. Was not expecting this."

Autumn smiled knowingly. "I just had this feeling."

"Did you peek?" Isabel asked. "Honestly. Did you?"

Autumn shook her head and touched her stomach, which seemed to have grown since even the day before. "Didn't have to."

It had been an evening Gia would never forget, filled with warmth and friendship and the excitement of things to come, of *people* to come. As the formality of the evening shifted, the group relaxed into side conversations, flanked by the tunes from Autumn's radio. Gia's thoughts drifted off on their own as she drank her beer and wondered what Elle was doing tonight, what she was wearing, how she was feeling.

"Did you hear anything we just said?" Autumn asked, knocking her in the arm.

Gia blinked and played back Autumn's words. "Yeah, you just asked if I heard you."

Isabel laughed. "And did you?"

"No." She tossed a stray woodchip into the fire. "I was somewhere else for a minute."

"Anywhere good?" Isabel asked.

"Maybe." Gia smiled into the fire.

"What's Elle up to tonight?" Isabel asked boldly. Hadley smiled knowingly at Gia across the fire. Gia hadn't divulged the fact that she and Elle had shared a kiss to anyone, wanting to hold on to that information for herself a little while longer. But her friends knew her well enough to pick up on a change.

"What makes you think I would know?" Gia challenged, but the smile crept onto her face against her will.

Isabel's eyes danced, and though that would have irritated Gia just last week, tonight she didn't mind the insinuation. "Just a hunch."

Hadley was on her feet and moving around the fire until she landed next to Gia. In fact, it seemed as if everyone inched in until they were sitting in a tight little group. "Any developments on the Elle front?" Hadley asked, as if the most natural of news reporters. "There are, aren't there? Don't you dare hold this back. Do you remember Isabel when she first started up with Taylor? Do not be like Isabel."

"Hey!" Isabel said. "I didn't know the friend rules back then."

"We forgive you," Hadley rattled off before scrambling to refocus on Gia.

Gia took a deep breath, because what she was about to say was new for her. "I do have a confession."

"Here we go," Autumn said happily, as she popped the last of a pink cupcake into her mouth and leaned in.

Gia decided to just say it. "I think maybe I've misjudged Elle in the past or whatever. Maybe. Probably." She'd come to terms with that concept internally but had never articulated it out loud before. In front of *people*, no less. The words were not her most eloquent, but they were all she had. Her declaration was met with five people exchanging knowing smiles with each other, understanding what a big moment this was for Gia.

"What do you mean by misjudged?" Taylor asked, delicately. She held out a hand. "And if I'm prying with that question, I respectfully withdraw it."

"Nah, you're good," Gia told her, and considered the question. She appreciated Taylor's sensitivity. "I guess I don't think Elle's the fake and plastic Barbie Doll I always thought she was. I've gotten to know her better, and she doesn't seem fake at all. I think that's just how she is. Bubbly, I guess. And nice."

"I've been working on unhating her. I should keep at that, then?" Hadley asked, very seriously.

Gia smiled at her. "Probably should."

"Okay, I can do that. Hating takes too much work anyway. Such a chore."

And almost like Isabel couldn't resist, she asked the question they all seemed to want to ask. "And are you two firmly living in the friends column, as in now and forever, or are we tiptoeing through the tulips to the avenue of hot and heavy?"

Taylor passed Isabel a look that didn't seem to deter her one damn bit.

"I think we're friends," Gia said conservatively. "Who are maybe attracted to each other. But that's about it. Nothing major." She could try to downplay this all she wanted, but she knew these women, and now that she'd given them this much, they would be desperate for more.

"I knew it!" Isabel practically shouted.

"This is pretty big news," she heard Autumn murmur to Kate.

Hadley sat there beaming, no words necessary, while Taylor brought them all back to the fold of the conversation the way only Taylor could. "That's great, Gia. Take your time. Don't let these guys rush you."

Gia met Taylor's gaze and nodded once in appreciation. "Thank you, Taylor. I won't." She addressed her friends. "No biggie. Elle's a better person than I thought originally. Not a bad discovery."

"Not at all," Kate said, with a smile of support. She could always count on Kate, who never overreacted—probably a skill that helped her when fighting fires.

"I'm just bummed we're losing you to the road again soon," Autumn said. "How long this time?"

"About eight days," Gia told her. "I'll get there in advance of my first heat, and we'll take it from there. If I'm knocked out early, which I won't be, I'll be home even sooner."

Isabel raised her beer. "Here's to not getting knocked out early."

"And to the tiny boy and adorable little girl we're going to meet soon," Hadley added.

Gia thought on the week ahead with a mixture of enthusiasm and trepidation. She needed to win this tournament in order to strengthen her ranking and take down the one person who could get in the way of a head-to-head battle with Elle: Lindy Ives, the powerhouse from Australia who was hot on Gia's heels. She was ready to go hard and land the points she needed.

Beyond surfing, it hadn't eluded her that the Swatch Pro would afford her the opportunity to see Elle again, and God, did she want to. But honestly? She wasn't sure she could wait that long. She felt uneasy with the way they'd left things, and that night at Elle's house was never far from her mind, her daydreams, her…fantasies. Had the kiss been a fluke, as amazing as it was? Quite possibly.

But then again, maybe not, and she had to explore that option. Every part of her wanted to. She understood that with no call, no text, no word from Elle at all, maybe she didn't want to see Gia.

But it was a risk she was willing to assume.

"Another beer, Gia-Pet?" Autumn asked.

"You know, I think I might head out. I have an errand to run."

"Must be important for a Friday night."

Gia nodded. "Yeah, it really can't wait."

❖

"I don't think you properly appreciate the music," Christopher said to Elle as they turned the corner into her neighborhood. They'd hit up the little jazz place, the one that had snagged all the rave reviews, only to find that they were at complete odds over the music.

"I love jazz," Elle explained. "But that music tonight had no identifiable melody. It was a series of random notes. I couldn't get into it."

He shook his head. "I think you're missing the point. Jazz is supposed to be unpredictable."

"Then call me crazy, but it was *too* jazzy. I need beginner's jazz. That was advanced placement."

"Who's that?" Christopher asked, ducking his head and peering through the windshield as they approached Elle's house.

She followed his gaze and her breath caught. Seconds later, a smile took shape on her lips. Sitting on her curb, headphones in her ears, sat Gia in jeans and cozy blue hoodie. A chill moved through Elle and she shimmied against it. "That's Gia."

He nodded. "Her photos don't do her justice."

Elle sighed, knowing that was the damn truth. "She a knockout, isn't she?"

"I see why you're dreaming about her." He reached for the door handle. "I'm gonna say hello."

She froze. "Do not say anything embarrassing. Or that I don't understand jazz."

He balked. "I'm a gentleman."

As the car pulled into the driveway, Gia stood and pulled the headphones from her ears. She smiled tentatively as they exited the car. Elle had wondered how she'd feel when she saw Gia again. If she'd get the same butterflies, if she'd be happy to see her or awkwardly trying to find her footing after that kiss. But once her eyes landed on Gia's chocolate brown ones, any worry she had flew straight out the window. Her heart thudded out of happiness, not concern.

"Hey," Gia said as she approached the car. "You weren't home, so I thought I'd wait a little while. See if I could catch you." She turned to Christopher. "Hey. Gia Malone."

"Christopher VanCamp. Elle's date tonight."

Gia's eyebrows rose and Elle passed Christopher a pointed look.

"Her very platonic date."

She watched as Gia's features relaxed once understanding took hold.

"Nice to meet you," Gia said. "Elle speaks well of you."

He turned to Elle with a grin. "I'm flattered. Well, if your intentions are honorable, I'll leave the two of you to whatever you have going. Are your intentions honorable?"

"Christopher," Elle said flatly, in warning.

Gia smiled. "Intentions of gold."

Christopher backed up toward his car, still in big brother mode. "Great. Holding you to it. You guys have a nice night. Play her a little jazz," he said to Gia.

"I'll call you tomorrow," Elle said through gritted teeth. While annoyed by his protective act, she couldn't help being touched by the sentiment. He cared, which mattered to her.

They waited as Christopher pulled out of her driveway and headed off into the night. Alone in front of her house at close to eleven p.m., Elle stared at Gia and Gia stared at Elle.

"Hi," she said, finally, after drinking Gia in.

"Sorry I crashed the end of your night. I didn't mean to—"

"I'm not upset."

"Good."

Another pause, but not the uncomfortable kind. No, this silence came laced with something light and important. That didn't make sense, but then not much did lately. "I've been meaning to call you," Elle said. "I should have. Called you. Or sent a text."

"It's okay. I don't think there's a hard and fast rule. I just…wanted to see you." Wow, that made her stomach tighten pleasantly. "Once the tournament hits, who knows where our heads will be."

Elle nodded. "The calm before the storm." She glanced around, acutely aware that they were still standing outside and she'd completely lost the manners her mother had instilled in her. "Why don't you come inside? I need to pack, but we can talk."

Gia nodded and followed her up the walk. Once inside, Elle moved about the house flipping on lights. An overabundance of them, she now realized. She flipped off a couple for good measure. All the while, Gia watched as amusement crept onto her features.

"Lighting schemes are important to you," she said, from where she stood in the entryway. That blue hoodie sure did look soft. She imagined gripping it and pulling Gia toward her.

"I'm a details girl. A micromanager."

"Let me guess. You have a packing list and organizational gadgets to keep all your stuff color-separated and tidy for any and all tournament travel."

"Follow me and find out," Elle said, with a proud smile. She led the way down the short hallway off the living room to her bedroom, where her suitcase was already laid out and halfway packed. She turned to Gia and found her studying the room. "What's that look mean? I'm afraid I don't know all of your looks yet."

"Yet?" Gia asked, with a slight raise of her eyebrow.

Elle felt the color rush to her cheeks. "Yet," she repeated quietly, owning the statement.

"I was just thinking that every room in your house is the epitome of comfort. Look at this place. You have like twelve amazing pillows on this bed, all fluffy and soft looking."

Elle shrugged. "I work hard physically. I like to be comfortable when I'm off the clock, and I go out of my way to make sure I am."

"More planning," Gia said. "I'm learning more and more how important control is to you."

On that cue, Elle flipped open the suitcase on her bed.

"Holy hell," Gia said. "You have sections to your suitcase? It's like a grid system in there."

Elle turned to her innocently. "Bedtime clothes, swimsuits, regular clothes, nicer evening wear. These things need their own space."

"To do what?" Gia asked, her voice louder than before.

"I don't know. Be who they want to be."

"That's some separatist clothes bullshit right there. Let them mingle."

"No way. Not on my watch." Elle's eyes went wide. "Let me

guess. You just toss your clothes in all together in a jumble and head for the airport?"

"Yep, literally an hour before I leave."

"Were you raised by wolves?" Elle asked in outrage, unable to imagine such a fly-by-night existence. Elle moved to her dresser, pulled out the remaining clothes she'd need for the Swatch Pro, and began rolling them into neat little bundles for optimum space. "How do you live like that?"

"It's easy. I get up and pull out what I need for the day."

"That makes no sense to me. Do you even unpack once you're there?"

"What's the point?"

Elle stared at her, her heart rate escalating. "You're killing me."

Gia pointed at the suitcase in exasperation. "Same."

That did it. Without thinking any further, Elle grabbed the fabric of the damn hoodie and pulled Gia's lips to hers, where she kissed her with the pent-up tension brought on by their ferociously defended packing philosophies. Good Lord. How could one person be so frustrating and so sexy at the same time? And the kiss. Don't get her started on the kiss that was more—way more—intense than the first. Warm and shimmy-shake worthy. That kiss eased its way into Elle's system, up her spine, carrying heat through her limbs with startling intensity. She'd never responded to any other partner the way she responded to Gia in just a matter of seconds. She was hot and bothered and without the control she was so used to maintaining. Yep, those were her hands abandoning the hoodie and sliding into Gia's hair without her permission, and the traitorous tiptoes she was up on for better access to Gia's mouth, evening out the slight height difference nicely.

Had it been Gia or Elle who'd guided them onto the bed alongside her suitcase? Regardless, they'd landed there with a bounce before finding each other again in a flurry of breathless gasps. Who really cared who'd taken them there, because lying alongside Gia as they kissed opened up all kinds of access Elle was eager to put to use. She slid her hands inside the hoodie (which was just as soft as it looked) and slipped them up the back of Gia's white T-shirt to the warm skin of her back, which was, oh God, so soft. Too soft to be believed. She heard herself groan and push her body firmly against Gia's as their mouths danced, their tongues tasted, and the room went up in flames around them.

Gia pulled her mouth from Elle's and met her gaze. A check-in of sorts in the midst of the search for air. "Is this okay? Should we—"

"Don't stop," Elle managed, silencing Gia with another kiss, her tongue pushing its way into Gia's mouth, and pulling the most delicious sound from Gia. She could really get used to contented sounds like that. The thought was silenced when Gia rolled on top of Elle, the weight of her body the most welcome sensation Elle could remember experiencing. She took the briefest moment to steady herself, to revel in the full-on body-to-body connection. This was exactly what she'd been missing her whole life. She instinctually parted her legs, allowing room for Gia's thigh between them. "Sweet heaven," she murmured, as her desire quadrupled.

Gia laughed and looked down at her. "Sweet heaven?"

Elle nodded. "Sweet heaven."

"I've never met anyone like you," Gia said, and stole a quick kiss. "You pack weird and have catchphrases like that one."

"Yeah, well. You brood and steal waves, so we're even on that count."

"Whatever you say." Gia slowly made her way to Elle's mouth, once again sending an urgent shot of arousal straight to Elle's center. She moved her hips against Gia's thigh because it gave her relief. Not enough, but some. She felt the pressure between her legs climb with each roll of her hips. Her hands were still underneath the back of Gia's shirt, which was in her way. Elle pushed it up, feeling the back of Gia's bra. The thought of taking it off entirely made her mind shift into overdrive, almost unable to handle the idea of Gia's breasts tumbling into her waiting hands. She'd likely explode.

Gia sucked in a ragged breath and fell to the side.

Elle blinked, summoning her brain but not finding it available. Every part of her body ached for more. Craved it. But the contact was gone. "What's wrong?" she asked through her haze.

Gia touched her cheek softly. "Maybe we shouldn't just yet."

Elle nodded, understanding. It was too soon. She hated that she agreed. *Hated. It.* But Gia was right. This was all very new and happening very fast, and she should probably proceed at a slower pace. She wasn't sure she'd have been able to stop them just two minutes ago but felt grateful to Gia for making the call. "How are we supposed to go back to business as usual now?" she asked quietly, facing Gia on the bed.

"I'm not sure we could."

Elle shook her head, tugging at the hem of Gia's shirt absently. "I wouldn't want to. When I'm around you I feel different, unlike myself, and I suppose I haven't figured out how to navigate that quite yet."

"Different how?"

She studied Gia's dark eyebrows, how perfectly formed they were. She'd be willing to bet a million dollars they were naturally shaped that way. "You have the ability to make me feel everything in… exponentials."

Gia furrowed her brow and wrapped her arm around Elle's waist. "Exponentials, huh?"

"Exponentially happy, or exponentially annoyed." She paused and smiled sheepishly up at the ceiling. "Exponentially turned on."

Gia chuckled. "Now that's a title I can live with. But I get it. You do the same to me. It's turning into an addiction."

"Come here," Elle said, not able to resist another kiss or those dreamy brown eyes. She sank into the wonder of Gia's lips and wasn't sure she ever wanted to leave. She kissed her slowly, savoring each second. Now that they'd set out on this new physical aspect of their relationship, it was like there was no stopping them from touching. Elle could imagine this getting in the way of, well…everything, which in this particular moment didn't sound so bad. "You sure we should stop?" she mumbled against Gia's lips. "Because I could keep doing this for a long time." She eased her tongue lightly into Gia's mouth and out again.

Gia caught Elle's wrists as her hands slipped beneath her shirt once again. "Nope. Not at all sure, which is why I should go. In about two point five seconds, it's not going to be within my power."

Elle sighed and watched as Gia pushed herself into a seated position.

"When do you travel?" Gia asked.

"In the morning. I've got some promo shoots set up with Rip Curl before the tournament kicks off."

"Of course you do," Gia said, with a knowing smirk. "You have more sponsors than God."

"At least *he* gets to duck the photo shoots."

"Like you'd give them up, even if you could."

Elle took a moment. "Honestly, all the extra commitments have become exhausting. Plus, there are other ways I'd like to spend my time." She met Gia's eyes briefly before pulling her gaze away. The confession made her feel vulnerable in a way she wasn't used to. She didn't do vulnerable when it came to other people. Never had. "What about you? When do you leave?" she asked, moving them away from it, nervous about how it made her feel.

"Day after tomorrow." Gia stood and readjusted her hoodie. "No Rip Curl photo shoots on my schedule."

"That's because GoPro is the sticker on the nose of your board."

Gia laughed. "Yes, it's possible I have a few GoPro responsibilities once I'm in San Clemente."

"Will I see you there?"

"Accepting the trophy?" Gia said with a grin. "Yes, most definitely."

Elle chuckled. "Cocky for number two. Don't you think?"

"You forget I have nothing to lose." Gia's eyes flashed playfully, but there was a nugget of truth in what she said.

Elle's smile dimmed, because for her, there was everything to lose. There was nowhere to go but down from her top spot, and she had no intention of doing anything but finishing off the year as world champion. It was great fun to get lost with Gia and explore her newfound freedom, but she couldn't lose sight of who she was and what she'd set out to accomplish. The stakes were too high.

"Then I guess we'll sort it out in San Clemente."

Gia winked. "See you on the beach."

They stole another kiss just beyond Elle's front door.

Everything would be different the next time she saw Gia. They'd each have their game faces on and would focus everything they had on the tournament. For Elle, it wasn't just money on the line, it was her legacy.

She would be good to remember that.

CHAPTER ELEVEN

The sting of the saltwater spray in her eyes welcomed Gia home, to the place she loved most. Competition. She'd shredded her way easily through round one of the Swatch Pro, pulling in a solid 8.67 on her best wave and taking the heat from the two other competitors.

The late spring conditions couldn't have been more exciting and definitely helped her pull out the win. Excellent wave height, swells that let her work her magic, and large crowds that fueled the always present adrenaline. She'd advanced easily against a wildcard surfer out of Hawaii and would move forward to round two with the heat's third competitor, Heather Macaulay, number seven on the tour leaderboard. But it was the kid, the wildcard, who had snagged her attention and showed herself to be more of a badass out there than Gia was expecting. She had gutsy moves and great flow. Both pulled Gia's respect.

Gia knocked Heather on the shoulder as they came in, but Heather didn't seem to be in the mood for niceties, not that Gia blamed her. She'd taken second in the heat and probably wasn't thrilled about it, regardless of the fact that she was still moving forward in the tournament.

"Very cool to be out there with you," the wildcard told Gia, once their heat concluded. "I've been a big fan of yours for a while." She must have been nineteen at most. Gia shook the hand she offered as they toweled off on the beach.

"Now I'm a fan of yours," Gia said. "Malia, right?"

"Yeah. Malia Moore."

"Killer surfing out there. Not just blowing smoke."

Malia grinned but shrugged it off. "Just trying to pull in points. Maybe score a sponsor, you know?"

"Been there. Keep surfing like that, and you'll find what you're looking for."

They approached the roped-off pathway for competitors that was always lined with autograph seekers who went nuts when they saw Gia approach, thrusting programs, notepads, and photos her way. "I'll let you get to work," she told Gia, and gestured with her chin to the fans.

"You guys meet Malia yet?" Gia asked the enthusiastic group. They nodded eagerly at Gia and several thrust their tournament programs Malia's way. She lit up at the attention and got to signing. Gia remembered all too well what it was like to be an up-and-comer, and she did what she could to make it easier for those coming up behind her. With a final nod to Malia and the fans, Gia headed inside where she'd change, clean up, and return to the beach to watch the remaining heats. It wasn't a normal practice for her, but Elle would be surfing later that day and she couldn't stop herself from being there to watch. Though it felt strange to say "root her on," it was a little of that, too.

She was becoming entirely too soft for her own liking.

Two hours later, sitting in the reserved competitors' section, Gia waited for Elle's heat to begin. She was up against Martina Conway, number twelve on the leaderboard, and Gidget So, number five, in what would be heat six that day. While Elle would pull out the win, Conway and So would give her a run for her money. Gidget So, especially, was tenacious and didn't shy away from the big barrel rides. The heat began with Elle drawing first priority. She paddled out aggressively and got to work as the crowd went wild for their number one, easily identifiable in the leader's yellow jersey, always worn by number one. Gia dreamed of wearing that jersey one day in the not-too-distant future. For now, she couldn't seem to stop herself from feeling proud of Elle in it, stupid as that might be.

And Elle was off.

Gia watched with interest.

Nice cut back into the power source. Good. Elle came around with a beautiful turn and looked for the barrel, found it easily. Beautiful position in the eye of the wave. Gia's breath caught and she waited to see if Elle would emerge upright, as that exit looked tricky. To no one's surprise, she nailed it, coasted out of the bottom, and hopped off the board for a nice start to the heat. Gia clapped conservatively, a small but proud smile on her lips while the larger crowd cheered and screamed. "That's how you do it," she said quietly.

The rest of the heat was full of ups and downs. Elle faltered on waves three and four but pulled in big enough numbers on her other waves to turn in two decent numbers for a combined score of 15.37. Elle was headed into round two right alongside Gia.

"You two getting along better these days?" a voice asked. She turned to see Jordan and her all-access pass standing just outside the roped-off competitors' section. She looked beachy and happy with her dark hair pulled into a ponytail, a compact video camera hanging at her side.

"We do okay," Gia said hesitantly. Jordan was a friend, but Gia had to remember that she was also making a documentary and would certainly devour the new turn Gia's relationship had taken with Elle. Since she didn't have a full understanding of what was going on herself, there was no way she could attempt to explain it to Jordan, on camera or off. Nor would it be wise.

Jordan studied her knowingly. "Just don't remember you watching early heats in the past."

"Scoping out the competition is not a bad idea, right?"

Jordan stepped in and dropped her voice. "I'm not busting your balls or anything, but maybe that's not all you're scoping. Off the record, of course."

"Don't know what you're talking about," Gia said.

"Really? Because I've gotten to know you pretty well, and I've never seen *that* expression on your face before where Elle Britton is concerned."

"Listen, I don't know what you think you're picking up on, but she's on her way to being world champion and it's my mission in life to take her down. That's about all there is here."

Right then, Elle passed their section, a towel en route to her hair. She paused when she saw Gia, smiled, and met her gaze briefly before continuing on her way. The exchange had been quick but meaningful. It was clear when Gia turned back to Jordan that she wasn't the only one who had noticed.

"Really? You have nothing to say on the subject?" Jordan asked, enjoying this way too much. "That look you two just shared was… wow."

"Was it?" Gia asked, feigning confusion.

"Please." Jordan shook her head. "Catch you later, Gia. We'll be covering round two tomorrow, so don't, you know, screw it up."

Gia laughed. "Best advice of the day. Thanks, Jordan."

"Don't have too much fun tonight. Or do. Your call."

Gia shook her head and headed back to the resort to roll out her muscles and rest up for the next day. Her hotel room was spacious and bright with a balcony facing the beach. She could see the day's competition happening in the distance. If she sat outside, she could hear the crowd.

As the afternoon shifted into evening, she headed out in search of food, finding several friends from the tour at the restaurant and joining the group. She had trouble focusing on the trajectory of the conversation, mainly about the happenings of round one, who was struggling to hold on to their spot and who was vying to move up the leaderboard. Shop talk didn't interest her tonight. Nope. She couldn't seem to stop thinking about Elle. What she was up to, how her day had been. Their brief encounter on the beach had been their only contact in San Clemente, which was probably a good thing, as Gia needed her head in the game, not in a lust-filled cloud. It was apparent, however, that even without face-to-face time with Elle, she had a way of… distracting Gia.

Ready to relax for the rest of the evening and get a good night's rest before round two, Gia headed back up to her room for some decompression time. Katrina would be joining her the next day, which came with a certain comfort. Katrina always kept her on track, and this tournament would be no different.

"Whoa," she said, as she exited the elevator and rounded the corner to her hallway, nearly smacking into a woman coming the other way. She gave her head a shake. "Sorry about that."

"Trying to put me out of commission before tomorrow?"

It was Elle. She was wearing leggings that came to mid-calf and a red warm-up sweatshirt that said *Boss* across the front. Gia laughed at the near collision, and realized in a burst just how happy she was to see her. "I didn't even realize it was you. I'm so sorry." They took a moment to stare at each other, both smiling. Gia glanced around. "So, you're on twelve, too? Which room is yours?"

Elle hesitated. "No, not exactly. I was just…"

"Just…?"

She sighed, changing trajectory. "Stopping by to say hi to you. That's the truth of it."

Another long stare.

"How did you know my room number?" Gia asked.

"I have my ways." She shrugged it off. "People tend to bend rules for me when I'm really nice to them."

"I don't know," Gia said, taking Elle's hand and dragging her down the hallway toward her room. "Sounds shady."

Elle held up a finger. "I am most certainly not shady. In fact, the opposite." The insinuation had ruffled Elle enough for her to rush to correct the misconception, which just encouraged Gia's playful side further.

"Yeah, but you're creeping around my room. Shady."

But apparently Elle could play the game, too. "You know what? Maybe I should just go, then. I'll let you spend the evening on your own."

Gia paused, liking the pout way too much. Elle was cute tonight. "You don't like to be teased. At all."

"Yes, I do."

Gia laughed. "You get a tiny bit defensive. Look at your outraged lower lip." They stared at each other, and Gia found herself more attracted to Elle in this moment than ever before. Her body hummed just being near her. "Are you coming in?" She prayed the answer was yes. Even if it was only for a few minutes. She could think of a lot of ways to spend a few well-planned minutes.

"Should I? I was just going to say hi. I don't want to disrupt any evening plans you may have."

"Stop being Elle and come inside."

She broke into the kind of radiant smile Elle alone could manage. "Only because you insist." She strolled into the room and gave it a thorough browse.

"Let me guess? You scored a better room?" Gia asked.

Elle turned. "I'm not *that* competitive."

Gia held up her hands. "Just checking." She sat cross-legged on the bed. "You gave 'em a good run today. You had me nervous on that first wave. The exit was a close call, you have to admit."

"Yeah. I got a little tenacious. Probably should have dropped out of the barrel sooner. Wouldn't have scored as high, though. What about you? Schooling Heather Macaulay. You looked good out there."

Gia took a moment, surprised. "You saw?" She imagined Elle would have been prepping for her own heat, keeping her head in the game.

"Well, I wasn't going to miss your first round," Elle said quietly. Sincerely, even. Gia pulled in a steadying breath. She wasn't the only one who was beginning to care, and that knowledge humbled her. How had they gotten here? Who were they? She was starting to understand that this was the tip of a much larger iceberg. Something important was taking place in her life. Fate had flipped everything she thought she knew on its head, and she damn well better find a way to keep up. She wanted to.

Elle came to stand in front of where Gia sat on the bed, and laced her arms loosely around Gia's shoulders. She could smell Elle's tangerine shampoo, and it took her places much sexier than they were just moments before. "It's weird. You and me being here at the same time, around everyone we know, and acting like life is status quo when I'm secretly making out with you back home. Dreaming about it the rest of the day."

Gia nodded. "Not sure I have the rules figured out. Not sure I care."

"It feels…salacious, in a way."

"Big word."

"How about scandalous?" Elle asked with an appeasing smile.

Gia inclined her head, side to side. "That one sounds about right. Maybe I'm your scandal."

"Pshh, you're way more than that."

"Really? And you don't think I'm becoming pathetic?" Gia asked.

Elle looked skyward. "I've never once thought of you that way. Why do you think so?"

"Because when I ran into you earlier, I noticed that I lit up like some goofy puppy. I don't do that. I'm solid."

"So solid," Elle said seriously. "Never one to feel anything at all. Dead inside."

Gia stared at her. "I think you're trying to make a point."

"I am." Elle smiled. "You're human, you know. I like that you're happy when you see me. If you weren't, what's the point?"

"Are we dating?" Gia flat out asked. Had to. "Or just fooling around?"

Elle pursed her lips. "I think I'd go with dating."

"Except we've never been on a date."

"This is kind of a date. A private one."

And that was about all she could take. Gia pulled Elle's face down and kissed her languidly, losing herself in the warmth of Elle's mouth. She kissed as well as she surfed. Before she knew it, they were lying on the bed making out. She pushed her tongue into Elle's mouth and pulled a moan. Hands were now in the mix. Hers. In Elle's hair. At the hem of Elle's sweatshirt, the back of her thighs. God, she loved her body.

Elle came up breathless, her blue eyes dark. "It could get *more* private, you know," she said quietly. At her own words, her cheeks colored and she glanced away, seeming embarrassed. That was a new one.

"What's all that about? Come back," Gia said gently.

"I've never been that into sex," Elle said.

Gia raised an eyebrow.

"But I think about it a lot now. Too much."

"Is there a too much?" Gia asked, trying to keep the mood light for Elle's benefit.

"I'm beginning to wonder." She looked down at Gia. "This is all new for me."

"I know." A pause. "Tell me what you're thinking about."

"You and me, together. In bed. What that would be like. How much I want to find out."

The words alone had Gia affected all over and acutely aware of Elle's body pressed to hers. She shifted uncomfortably. She longed to touch Elle, to be touched. The need, ignited by their kissing and accelerated with Elle's declaration, was near-painful throbbing. "I don't want to rush you. Like you said, this is new. Maybe we take our time. Go slow." Gia hated herself for saying those words. Her body had been betrayed by the damn high ground.

Elle sighed. "I knew you were going to say that." A kiss.

"Am I wrong?"

"No." Another kiss. "I hate that you're right, but you probably are. But we can still fool around."

Gia smiled against Elle's lips and pulled her hips in closer. One of Elle's thighs pushed between Gia's legs, leaving her moaning at the pressure and tiny hits of gratification that came with it. They were like a couple of teenagers, groping and making out on that bed. Five minutes of kissing later and Elle pushed up Gia's T-shirt, taking them firmly to second base.

"Don't chastise me," Elle said breathlessly, staring down at Gia's black bra in rapture. Her fingers traced the tops of Gia's breasts and followed the line of cleavage that dipped into her bra. "Just for a minute."

Gia didn't argue. In fact, she couldn't speak. Elle lightly ran her fingers across the front of Gia's bra, moving lightly over the portion of fabric that covered her nipples. Gia's eyes fluttered closed and her hips rolled. She swallowed, and a sharp surge of arousal slammed hot and hard right between her legs. The throbbing was out of control. "I can't take any more of that," she said, pushing herself into a sitting position and taking Elle right along with her. Her T-shirt fell back into place, and their new arrangement had Elle straddling her lap with a proud look on her face.

"You have amazing breasts," Elle told her. "I know that without even seeing them fully. I can't wait until I do."

Gia laughed ruefully, her arms wrapped fully around Elle's waist. "You're gonna kill me, you know that?"

"Not before I get to enjoy you." Elle tucked a strand of hair behind Gia's ear. "But you have my word. No more of that…for tonight." She climbed off Gia's lap and lay back on the bed. "I don't know about you, but I'm exhausted. We could just relax."

Gia sighed, not entirely trusting that invitation but feeling the weight of the day herself. She joined Elle and laid her head down on the pillow as her adrenaline slowly subsided and her heart rate returned to normal.

"Have you been with a lot of women?" Elle asked, staring at the ceiling. "You don't have to answer that question if you'd rather not."

Gia opened her mouth and closed it again. "I don't know. I haven't exactly kept a list."

"So, a lot?" She glanced over at Gia. "Definitely no judgment."

Gia turned to face Elle, her cheek on the pillow. "Not as many as you think. Trust me. An occasional tour hook-up. And that's only once in a great while."

"That's fair. And girlfriends?"

Gia laughed. "Even worse. There have been exactly two. One broke my heart when I was twenty-three, but it was for the best. She was a surf instructor and older than me. I guess you could say that we were at different places in life. The other was a blip. Since then I've concentrated on my job."

Elle nodded and snuggled into the crook of Gia's arm, fitting there perfectly, like the spot was made for her. Gia felt herself let go and sink into the mattress, releasing the stress of the day. How could the same person who had excited her so thoroughly in one moment help her relax in the next? It was the last thing she remembered before opening her eyes the next morning and staring at the most beautiful girl in the world, still curled into her side and radiating warmth. Elle's fist was tucked under her chin, and her blond hair pooled at her shoulders. She looked like an angel when she slept.

That serenity was shattered when she caught sight of the clock. She sat up, still gathering her wits but knowing this was bad. Really bad.

"Elle! Wake up. We overslept."

Chapter Twelve

Time seemed to move at warp speed as Elle raced from Gia's room in a blind fury. She made a mental list of all she had to accomplish in the next thirty minutes, noting it would be nearly impossible to prep for her heat the way she normally would. Somehow, she had to calm the hell down and regain control, her focus. Wasn't working.

How had this happened? She was never late, and she certainly didn't oversleep.

It was close to nine a.m. when the first heat of round two was scheduled to start. While she wasn't scheduled to compete, Gia was. She'd be in worse shape than Elle in terms of time, lucky to even make it there before disqualification. But she couldn't focus on Gia right now. She had her own problems.

"Everything okay, Elle?" one of the other surfers asked as she barreled to the elevator.

"Yep," she said, hitting the button four times and opting for the stairs when the car didn't immediately arrive.

"Gia okay?" the woman called. "That's her room, right?"

"She's fine," Elle answered over her shoulder. Last Elle saw of her, she was climbing all over the room, looking for her suit and jersey. She distantly hoped Gia would get something quick to eat before the opening heat, knowing it was a luxury at this point and unlikely.

She checked in for the heat and scurried over to Bruce, who stared at her like she'd lost her damn mind, which, apparently, she had. He had her board waiting and waxed, which she owed him for, big-time. This was honestly all her fault. She let herself get lost in the new and exciting world of Gia and forgot the rest entirely. She couldn't let that happen again.

"I'm sorry," she told him. "I don't know how this happened."

"Doesn't matter," Bruce said, hitting her with a hard stare. "Think about what's ahead of you. Get your mind on the heat. Nothing else."

Elle nodded and worked on doing just that. Her eyes caught the tournament standings on display near check-in. Her heart leapt into her throat.

"That's right," Bruce said, following her stare. "You lucked out. Malone went down in the first heat. She's out."

Elle didn't know what to say. She stammered and changed the direction of her sentence, finally settling on, "Did she surf?"

He looked at her strangely. "'Course she surfed. Turned in two sorry scores, and now she's out of your way. Celebrate later, though, you're up."

Elle nodded, scanning the beach for any sign of Gia, all the while battling her warring emotions. Her top competitor, the one with the power to take what was hers, was out of the tournament and now had zero chance of taking home the points needed to close the gap between them on the tour's leaderboard...at least for now.

On the other hand, Gia was out. *Gia.* She hurt for her, and wanted to have a moment to say she was sorry. Without that opportunity, she carried her board to the shoreline for her own heat, in which she'd have to take down the number four surfer, Alia Foz, to advance in the tournament.

The morning conditions were ideal and there seemed to be some killer pipe out there. Now all she had to do was make it hers.

She set to paddling.

Heat two was just her and Foz, head-to-head. The best two waves would take it. One would move forward, one would not. Foz drew first priority and headed out to catch the first wave, but it fizzled before she could capitalize on anything worthwhile. Elle waited, watching, not in any hurry. She licked her lips, tasting the salt that reminded her of where she was and what she was here to do.

There it was, a big sucker, rising like a beast.

She set out for it, paddling like a maniac, monitoring the way the wave shifted as she rose to her feet, catching the ride, taking the first curve with acute agility. She drew to the bottom of the wave, which slowed her speed and took a two phase turn just to get the board moving again. Damn it. She bit her bottom lip and rode loose, trying to take back her power. But every wave had a different personality and broke in different directions for reasons Elle would never fully understand. This wave had a mind of its own and shifted on her, the force of the surge knocking her breathless and off the board. Total wipeout. She caught a mouthful of water and struggled her way to the surface against the forceful current. No go.

Foz turned in a clean ride that would yield her a conservative 5.7. Elle knew she could top it and refused to let her first effort mess with her head. Not today. She set out again, on her feet early, taking a big whip off the top of the wave, power hook off the open face sending a ton of spray. This was it. This was what she needed. She slithered her way to the inside wall, closed it out off the top for a finishing move, and rode her way out.

That's how you did it. She was scored at 7.8.

Foz offered her a nod and the game was on.

They went back and forth, trading waves. With each outing, Elle bettered her score, taking the heat easily in the end with a combined score of 16.9. The crowd, as always, was supportive, and she waved to them in gratitude. She consulted with Bruce, who agreed with her more aggressive approach as the heat progressed, snagged information about her next round, and headed back to the Reebok-sponsored locker room for recovery. A sauna didn't sound so bad about now. She threw a glance to the competitors' box and paused right there in her tracks. Gia smiled back at her. The smile was conservative, yes, but that wasn't the point. Gia had stayed behind and watched her heat, despite what must have been an unexpected and devastating defeat in only round two of the tournament. Elle shook her head slightly and felt the smile grow on her face. Gia was there for *her*. She'd shoved aside her own disappointment and had showed up.

Elle crossed the small expanse of beach between them, leaned across the rope to Gia, took her face in her hands, and kissed her square on the lips. Gia didn't balk or so much as pull away as long-lensed cameras turned from the water to the competitors' box in a clicking flurry. "It sucks. I'm sorry," Elle whispered to Gia, who nodded in response. "Find me later?"

"I will," Gia said, and gave her hand a squeeze.

Jordan Tuscana, with a camera of her own a few feet away, turned to Gia. "You have so much explaining to do."

CHAPTER THIRTEEN

You've been sensationalized!" Hadley proclaimed, from her spot at Breakfast Club. She stared in awe at the laptop showcasing the photo of Elle kissing Gia at Swatch Pro. "You're a real life love scandal sitting in the Cat's Pajamas. And I *know* you! I'm famous by default."

Gia sipped her coffee. "It's definitely getting a lot of play. The photo's on every blog, website, and sports news outlet there is. My phone won't stop blowing up. People want to know everything."

"Well, let's think about it," Isabel said, tapping the table. "Two really attractive women, who've been pitted against each other for years, are making out on a beach in front of thousands. Oh! And one of them is wearing a swimsuit at the time." She shook her head as if stumped. "Nope. Can't imagine why anyone would be interested in that."

Her friends laughed.

"I was shocked she did it." Gia shook her head, but a smile crept onto her face. "She's apologized several times for the impulsive decision, but since when have I cared what the press has to say? Elle's the one with fallout. Until now, she was the All-American girl who would likely fall in love with the All-American boy and have babies photographed by *People* Magazine."

Autumn winced. "She *did* out herself to, well, the world in one giant gesture. That's gotta be a lot to wrap her mind around."

"And do we know how she's doing with that? Does she need support?" Hadley asked. "We can go to her place and be her friends. Maybe she needs friends about now, you know? I could make brownies." She studied the faces of her own friends for feedback.

Gia placed a hand on Hadley's shoulder. "You're a nice person, Hadley. But she won't be home from San Clemente until tonight, so you'll have to put your friendship on pause until then. She said she had a productive chat with her parents, who were surprised but supportive."

Hadley nodded. "Cool, cool. I can wait. But let her know we're here if she wants to talk or have coffee or eat food. It can be terrifying, coming out. And she did it on such a huge stage."

"I can't even imagine," Autumn said. "I told one person at a time over the course of nearly two years, building my courage."

Gia smiled proudly as she thought on Elle's big gesture. "She's pretty tough. I think she'll be okay."

"And you?" Isabel asked. "I know you're bummed about your finish."

Gia nodded, still not over how poorly she'd performed at the Swatch Pro. She didn't understand quite what went wrong. She'd overslept, yeah, and had to race to her heat like a bat out of hell. She hoped that's all it was. Yet something pulled at her, made her wonder why she hadn't been able to engage the way she normally did. She had been distracted and not feeling like herself. "Just a fluke, I'm betting. Luckily, number three on the leaderboard went down early as well. Not as early as me, but still helpful."

"And Elle?" Autumn asked.

"Held on until semis. She'll earn some decent points off that showing. Hold on to number one easily."

Hadley leaned in and whispered, "We still want you to take her down, right? Even though you're surfing's hottest new couple?"

"Definitely," Gia whispered back.

Isabel tapped a finger on her lips. "How's that going to work, exactly? You two are dating and also engaged in pretty heavy competition? Can both of those things exist?"

Gia squinted. "Haven't figured that part out yet."

"Sounds promising," Isabel said. "Nothing can go wrong there."

"Stop that!" Hadley told Isabel. "A minor detail. They'll figure it out. Love finds a way."

"Do not break into song," Isabel deadpanned.

"No promises," Hadley said, and reached for another croissant. She held it in the air. "I'm using these to cheer myself up. Work is not the picnic it once was."

"What's up?" Isabel asked.

"Trudy's still not happy with the direction our current roster of designers is taking. We've pulled in some new ones to shake up the store's image a bit. We're shooting for contemporary, with an edge. But not too edgy. It's a fine line, and apparently, I'm not delivering. Gotta drum up some new talent. Know anyone?"

Gia shrugged. "Fresh out of edgy-but-not-too-edgy designers."

"Forget that woman. You're awesome at your job," Isabel said. "Every time I go in there it's like I'm lost in a sea of amazing clothes I'm not good enough for."

"Hardly," Hadley said.

Autumn pointed at the plate in the center of the table. "And please eat all of those croissants or I'm going to blow up like a pregnant Macy's Thanksgiving Day balloon. Eating for three is feeling more like feeding an army." She placed a hand on her growing stomach.

Gia smiled. "Enjoy it. You should be pampering yourself. Eat all the baked goods."

Autumn stared at her and helped herself to one more. "You're a dangerous person."

"Let's hope I'm as effective on a surfboard." She stood. "Off to train before I fall off the leaderboard entirely." She pointed at Hadley. "Keep your chin up." She pointed at Isabel. "Write the hell out of that ex-CIA woman." She pointed at Autumn. "Keep making human beings."

Three salutes came her way.

She spent the rest of the day taking her body to task. A run on the beach, an intense ab workout, weight training, and a marathon surf session in which she put herself through the wringer, working through every skill she knew. She wasn't willing to let this opportunity slip through her fingers. Once the tournament concluded and the points were in, she'd held on to her number two ranking, but barely. She needed to buckle down and focus on not just defending her own position but moving up the board, which meant knocking Elle down. Refusing to let her personal life factor in would be key. When they were on tour, Elle had to remain just another competitor in her eyes. Away from the water was different. She could just be...Elle. Gia smiled at that version, picturing Elle, missing her. They hadn't laid eyes on each other since Gia departed the tournament the morning after she'd lost. They'd texted, chatted on the phone into the night even, but it was the live and in person Elle that Gia craved.

She attached her board to the top of her car, gave herself a quick dust off, and hopped inside. As she started her engine, she glanced at her phone.

I'm outside your apartment, and you're MIA.

She froze. The text was from Elle, but she wasn't supposed to be back until that night. Energized once she realized the text came in only minutes before, she put the car in drive and quickly drove the short two blocks to Seven Shores. If she was fast enough, maybe she could…

"You're here," Elle said, beaming at her from one of the outdoor couches. Gia didn't hesitate. She pulled Elle into an embrace and held on, burying her nose in Elle's hair, taking her in.

"Why are you early?" she murmured, still not letting go.

Elle laughed. "I canceled the last round of interviews. They only wanted to talk about one thing. Can you guess which?"

Gia released her, and searched her eyes. "Did you tell them to go to hell?" she asked, feeling extra protective.

"Not exactly my style. I told them when I was ready to talk about it, they would hear from me." She squinted. "I tend to think the kiss stands on its own, though."

"I guess that's true. How are *you* doing with it all? The attention?" She didn't allow herself to examine what it might mean for her if Elle wasn't doing okay. Underneath it all, she still hadn't entirely convinced herself that Elle knew what she was getting into or felt confident in this new life decision. Maybe she'd change her mind and, after trying it on, would realize this wasn't who she was after all. One of the reasons Gia had suggested moving slow. Self-preservation was important. Gia didn't put herself out there easily, and she was starting to do just that.

But Elle didn't look reluctant. In fact, she was luminous, glowing even. "I'm better now," she said, touching Gia's cheek softly. "I've just wanted to see you is all. Not saying it wasn't a roller coaster of a week."

"I can imagine."

"Did you just come out of the water?" Elle asked, her eyes dipping to Gia's bathing suit top.

Gia nodded. "Trying to keep up with you." She glanced at the stairs to her apartment. "Coming in? I have to shower."

The idea seemed to intrigue Elle. "Definitely. I need to see this place for myself at long last."

Gia sighed. "Okay. Not as fluffy and put together as yours. Fair warning."

"Bracing myself."

Gia's nerves hit as she led Elle to her second-floor apartment and let them inside. Her place would definitely not live up to Elle's. She surveyed the space now, seeing it how Elle might. She quickly dashed about the living room, straightening odds and ends, grabbing the sweatshirt (damn it) she'd left on the couch and tossing it into her bedroom.

Elle smiled. "Green surfboard on the wall."

Gia nodded. "One of my favorites from years ago. Couldn't bear to toss it when it busted." She was acutely aware that there was no other art, other than the surfing posters on her bedroom wall that now seemed juvenile and obnoxious. Elle didn't seem to mind.

"It's very you. Lots of bright colors."

Gia glanced around. "That don't exactly match." Her blue couch and red-cushioned dining chairs now seemed cringe-worthy. She really should have let Hadley go to town when it came to decorating.

"They match you," Elle said, meaning it as a compliment.

Gia nodded. "Can I get you a soda or something to eat?" She remembered that her fridge was mostly empty and hoped Elle would pass on that snack. Note to self: Buy groceries for guests. Always. Have. Groceries.

"I'm good. Go. Take your shower. I'll wander around your bedroom and snoop."

"Oh, that can't yield much good, but knock yourself out. I'm boring as hell." But she did a quick mental check anyway, realizing that there was nothing too incriminating lying around. She should be good.

She left Elle on her own and, moments later, stood under the hot water in utter surrender as the heat worked her aching muscles. She closed her eyes and dropped her head back, letting the pressure of the water massage her scalp, reaching blindly for the shampoo when Elle's voice from her bedroom interrupted.

"Are you singing in there?"

She straightened, horrified. She had been singing, hadn't she? It was her ritual, and so second nature, she hadn't even realized she was doing it—with company present no less. Not even company, *Elle*. "Oh, sorry!" she called back.

A chuckle. "Don't stop on my account."

But of course she would, and how long had she been going before Elle said anything? Didn't matter. Her singing was atrocious, which was why she only ever sang when alone in the shower, and now her singing was out there in the world, and someone she was interested in, and whose opinion mattered to her, had *heard*. She sighed, finished up, and stepped out of the shower, closing her eyes at a brand-new revelation. She'd left her clothes in her bedroom. That's right. When you lived alone and rarely had company, there was no reason not to walk naked from the bathroom to the bedroom and dress there. It was official, she was a bonehead. A very naked bonehead, with a newly minted lesbian (perhaps not ready for naked parades) on the other side of the door from her. Only one choice. Gia wrapped herself in a towel and casually walked to the bedroom, where she would quickly find appropriate attire and return to the bathroom to dress. That could work. With a solid plan in mind, she went for it.

As Gia entered the bedroom, Elle turned, mouth open, ready to speak. When she saw Gia clad in only a towel, however, the words died on her lips and she went still. "Oh," she said instead. She looked away to be polite, but only briefly. When her gaze returned to Gia, it moved unabashedly across every inch of exposed skin, sending a powerful shiver right through Gia. She was being objectified, and in this case, she didn't mind at all.

"Sorry. I just need clothes."

"Don't go out of your way on my account," Elle said, with a small smile, half joking, half not.

"You can't flirt with me right now."

"Yes, I can," Elle said boldly, tucking a strand of hair behind her ear. She had always been a go-getter, and apparently, that trait transferred to her personal life. Gia liked that about her. No game playing. No reading between the lines. With Elle, what you saw was what you got. Still, Gia wasn't ready to drop the towel just yet. Wasn't how she imagined that particular moment, and she did imagine it. A lot.

"Be right back," she said, dashing into the bathroom and throwing on her clothes.

Elle looked thoughtful when she returned. "That was Britney Spears, wasn't it? You were singing Britney Spears in your shower for me."

Gia held up a finger as she walked to the living room, Elle hot on her heels. "Technically, it wasn't for you. Britney and I go back years. And I wouldn't subject anyone to my singing."

"It's unique."

"C'mon, it's awful."

"I wasn't going to use that word. I prefer endearing with artistic license."

Gia winced. "You're kind."

"All my mother's work. You would like her."

"Would she like me?" The question had more to do with Elle's recent outing to her parents (and everyone else) than it did about Gia and her mother actually meeting.

"I think she would. She's going to need time to adjust to the idea of…a woman. Don't think she saw that one coming, but hey, neither did I. She's an open-minded person, though, and she loves her kids a lot."

"She sounds like good people." She pulled a bottle of water from the fridge and tossed one to Elle. "Are you doing okay?"

Elle nodded. "Um, surprisingly, yes. Did I hyperventilate in my hotel room when I realized what I'd done without even realizing it? I did. That happened. Would I take it back?" A small pause. "Uh-uh."

Gia exhaled in relief, doing her best to mask the reaction and play it casual. "I was worried…about you." She put her hand on her hip and then dropped it, not sure how to stand. Why did she suck so hard at sentimentality?

"Then come sit by me." The look in Elle's eye sent a flutter traveling through Gia's system. She really had missed her. She took a seat next to Elle and pulled Elle's legs across her lap. They couldn't seem to sit in close proximity without touching. It seemed to be an Elle and Gia rule.

"Hi," Elle said quietly.

Gia smiled. "Hi."

"There are no designers in LA," Hadley announced, breezing into the apartment in her upscale work clothes. "You would think I'm exaggerating. I'm not, I just—hey, there," she said, her eyes landing on Elle. A pause as a smile blossomed. "You're here."

"Hi," Elle said, standing. She certainly did know how to turn on the high-wattage smile, which seemed to make Hadley happy. Had liked friendly. She embodied it. "I'm Elle Britton, we haven't officially met."

"Not officially," Hadley said, beaming. "But I know all about you. I'm Hadley."

"I've heard of you, too," Elle said. "Want to sit?"

"Definitely," Hadley said, planting herself on the chair across from them. "I hear you did well at the tournament."

"Not the finals, but I'll take it. What were you saying about the designers in LA?"

"Oh, that they're ruining my life pretty much. I need new ones.

Lesser-knowns to bring into the boutique I work at, and they're just not out there. At least the caliber I need."

"Hadley's looking for high end but edgy."

"Still classy," Hadley filled in.

"I have a friend," Elle offered, looking thoughtful. "She's really quite good. I should have her look you up. She's gone viral on social media and looks to be the next big thing."

"Oh, my goodness, I would welcome that. I'm at Silhouette on Rodeo Drive. Tell her to ask for Hadley Cooper. I'd love to take a look."

Elle laughed at the sincerity of emotion. "Done. Her name is Spencer Adair, and I know she's got a lot on her plate. But I'll let her know you're looking."

"Spencer, okay. Great!" Hadley pointed at Elle. "I like her."

"I like her, too," Elle said, pointing back at Hadley. The two of them laughed and continued chatting away on a myriad of topics.

"I love your shoes."

"Tell me the best part about surfing."

"How many years have you and Gia been friends?"

It went on, and on.

There was never a lull, a gap, where one of them had to force conversation. Gia watched in awe. It was like two long-lost best friends sitting on her couch. They practically forgot she was in the room, and she wondered distantly if she should figure out something else to do.

"So, and stop me if I'm getting all up your business, but the kiss photo?" Hadley asked.

"Right. Not my most-thought-out moment, but sometimes you just have to follow your heart." Elle's cheeks colored and Gia felt warm all over hearing that it was Elle's *heart* that had compelled her to kiss Gia that day.

Hadley clearly liked that answer as well. "Yes! You completely have to." She furrowed her brow. "How are you handling it? Do you need anything? Baked goods?"

"You're so awesome to offer, but I'm actually hanging in there." She glanced over at Gia and smiled. "While it's scary to announce something so publicly without even thinking, this has been a really happy time in my life, and that beats all the side effects."

"So, no brownies, then?" Hadley asked.

"Unless you just want to be nice."

"Brownies it is!" Hadley's eyes lit up with a new project. She stood, energized now. "I'll let you two get back to making out or whatever it was you were doing on that couch when I barged in." She bowed. "As you were."

"Wait. Had, you okay?" Gia asked, wanting to make sure her friend didn't need her. "The work thing had you bothered when you walked in."

"Much better now," Hadley said, hand on her heart, and dashed out of the apartment.

Gia stared at Elle. "Did you just find a new best friend?"

She blinked back happily. "You know, I think I did. You come with a lot of perks. Britney Spears serenades and people like Hadley."

"I'm pleased and afraid."

"You should be both of those. What are our plans tonight?"

"Let's go to dinner," Gia said.

"Perfect. And then my place after?"

The implication was clear. Elle was inviting her to stay the night, and she wasn't sure she had the fortitude to resist any longer. "Are you sure about the after?"

"We could come back to yours. I'm open."

Gia shook her head, wanting to make sure this was truly what Elle wanted. "You know what I mean."

"Are you asking if I'm sure that I want you to take me home after dinner and have your way with me?" Elle nodded solemnly. "Very."

Gia inhaled at the potency of that word. She wanted Elle so badly, but her desire had just tripled with its utterance. "Your place it is."

❖

Elle wasn't generally a nervous person. In fact, she'd been told on multiple occasions that she had nerves of steel. She'd taken those words as a compliment and wore them like a badge of honor. Her courage had served her well in every aspect of her life, but as she got ready for dinner, she had a confession to make to the person looking back at her in the mirror. She was nervous for tonight. Deeply nervous.

She'd had sex for the first time at nineteen with a boy she'd gone to high school with, Grayson Trotter, who was dark haired, blue-eyed, and the captain of the tennis team. She'd thought he was the most good-looking boy she'd ever seen, and when his attention turned to her that summer after their senior year, she thought she was the luckiest girl ever. They had a good time together, went to movies, the beach. She'd even taught him to surf—with mediocre results. One night, when Grayson had his parents' house to himself, she'd come over. Marathon kissing on the cramped couch had turned into sex. Very, very disappointing sex. She'd always romanticized making love, had looked forward to it, waited for the right moment to take that leap. Grayson had seemed like the one to take it with. The end result had been fast, uncomfortable, and without pleasure. Thinking it had been a symptom of it being her first time, she'd not rushed to any conclusions. But her continued sexual relationship with Grayson, and the handful of men who'd come after him, had resulted in one lackluster sexual experience after another. It hadn't been a fluke.

While her experience thus far with Gia had been markedly different than with the men she had dated (and her lust meter was reading way off the charts), she still carried fear that sex would once again leave her on the outside looking in, wondering why the rest of the world found such power in an act she found relatively forgettable. On the other hand, where she and Gia were concerned, how could that be possible? The sex dream alone had been better than anything she'd experienced in real life. Still…as much as she looked forward to the night ahead, the fear shoved at her uncomfortably.

Selecting a casual white dress, Elle blew out her hair, opting to leave it down with a slight curl. She found her bag just as the doorbell rang. "You got this," she said to herself, and took a deep, fortifying breath.

Gia looked gorgeous, of course, and Elle's heart clenched pleasantly as she followed her out to the car. She wore black pants, heels, and a form-fitting blue top. But it was the way her gaze moved across Elle's dress, her body, that sent sparks racing across every nerve ending Elle possessed.

"I think white might be your color," Gia said once they were in the car. Elle kissed her, not caring if she ruined her lip gloss.

"If it always makes you look at me like this, then I may have to add to my wardrobe. Where's dinner?"

"Probably not somewhere you've heard of before. Is that okay?"

"I love new places. Take me there."

"I love how automatically adventurous you are."

Elle shrugged. "That's one of the best parts of life, discovering new things."

"I'm beginning to agree with that statement."

Gia was right. Elle had never heard of the small, out-of-the-way restaurant she had selected for them. The Orchard Inn, just beyond the outskirts of the city, was just as it sounded. The winding road up to the house was reminiscent of a fairy tale and the interior just as quaint. A small inn, complete with a downstairs dining room on the grounds of an apple orchard. Dark wooden floors and dark walls were accentuated with small candles on each table that gave the room an intimate, romantic feel. Dinner was served at 7:30 in one sitting to the various guests of the inn. Apparently, Gia pulled some strings to get them included.

"I don't know the owner or anything," Gia said, referencing Elle's outgoing disposition and the fact that she knew everyone. "Just a place I really like."

"I've never seen anything like it," Elle said, feeling special. Gia had put some thought into this. "It's perfect for tonight."

The menu was set and included a hearty green salad, likely from ingredients grown fresh on the property, filet mignon, vegetables, and a side of the most decadent potatoes, the likes of which Elle had never tasted. Dessert came in the form of a slice of lemon cake with a miniature chocolate milkshake on the side, a tiny red and white straw included. While the food was amazing, expertly prepared, it wasn't the star of the show. Gia was. The way she looked at Elle across the candlelight, listened to her with those big, brown luminous eyes like everything Elle said held the utmost importance for her. Their conversation came easily, too. Elle had never dated anyone who shared her affinity for surfing, and with Gia, she could lose herself on the subject for hours.

"Yeah, but the waves in Australia—I mean, no comparison. Bells Beach is insane. When I'm there, I never want to leave."

"We should go sometime," Gia said, seeming to latch onto an idea. "Outside of competition and just eat, drink, and surf."

Elle rested her chin on her palm dreamily. "Do you know how long it's been since I've taken a surfing trip that didn't require me to compete?"

"Which is why we should do it. Just think how romantic those beach sunsets are. I've never really gotten the chance to share them with someone I care about."

"I would love to watch a beach sunset with you, Gia. Your arms around me."

Gia smiled at her plate before raising her gaze to Elle's. "I can't come up with anything better than how that would feel."

"You don't have to twist my arm. I'm in. I'll even let you drop in on my waves." She winked and took a final bite of lemon cake and pointed at Gia with her fork. "That's a big testament to what I'm feeling for you."

Gia sat back appearing struck. "That's the nicest thing you've ever said to me. And I could watch you eat cake for hours, if we're being honest. The way you take your time, pull the fork slowly from your mouth…it's really something. I think you should do it again."

Elle obliged, only slowing down the process further.

They stared at each other as heat flickered between them. Elle set the fork down slowly. "Wanna get out of here?"

Gia nodded, her darkened eyes giving Elle serious heart palpitations. Gia gave the best looks, always clear in their meaning and unapologetic. The biggest turn-on, really. She felt that look all over.

Their intertwined hands rested in Gia's lap on the car ride home as soft music played from the radio. The city had never looked more alive or more beautiful than it did as they traveled its winding roads. The hillside and all of its twinkling lights looked down on them. As they neared Elle's neighborhood, the anticipation of what was to come was nearly all encompassing. Looking forward to finally capitalizing on all things she'd imagined doing to Gia rivaled the fear she had of not being able to engage the way she hoped. It was a mixed bag. What if sex was an utter failure for her yet again? What if she was broken?

As they crossed the threshold of her home, Gia gave Elle's arm a tug. She turned to face her, and Gia took both of her hands, intertwining their fingers. "You still sure?" The simple question, and the intention behind it, was all Elle needed. The nerves, her fear, disappeared in that moment, replaced by the warmth and strength radiating through to her from Gia's touch.

Elle took Gia slowly by the hand and led her through the darkened living room, down the short hallway, and into her bedroom. She turned on her small bedside lamp, because these were moments she needed to see. In fact, she wanted to keep every detail for herself.

Before Gia could even ask, Elle met her eyes and nodded, granting final permission. She unzipped the white dress and it fell from her shoulders and caught around her elbows, exposing her light pink bra. She'd worn the one that dipped steeply in front, because it made her feel sexy. She didn't need it, though, she realized. Gia made her feel sexier than she ever had in her entire life.

Gia took over at that point. Moving slowly, she cradled Elle's face in her hands, her gaze moving from her eyes, to her mouth, to her nearly exposed breasts. She didn't say a word, just kissed Elle with measured precision. But when she came up for air, her breathing was ragged, and that did things to Elle. She dropped her arms, allowing the dress to fall to the floor. She stepped out of her heels, which gave Gia the height advantage. With Gia's rapt attention, she unclasped her bra and watched as Gia took in her full breasts.

"Oh my God," Gia breathed, crushing her mouth to Elle's. She wrapped her arms around Elle's waist and hauled her close. She kissed down the column of Elle's neck, to her chest. Her hands moved up Elle's body, between them, to cup her breasts. She gasped as Gia increased pressure before dipping her head and lifting a nipple into her mouth. Elle threw her head back. She'd never experienced anything so physically powerful, and felt the acute results between her legs.

"Wow," she whispered, her own breaths came in fast little spurts. Elle's hands moved to Gia's shirt. She pulled it over Gia's head and quickly unfastened her pants. Gia obliged and slid out of them, and the skin on display to Elle now increased her desire exponentially. That body. God. Help. Her.

Gia lowered her onto the bed and lay down alongside her. Elle reached for Gia, needing more of the delicious sensations, craving something she didn't have a name for. But that was wrong, because she knew. She was on fire, and throbbing, and wanted Gia inside her, desperately. Now.

But Gia had other ideas and seemed to be taking her time. She looked down the bed at Elle's body, partially illuminated by the dim light from the lamp, and ran a finger from the waistband of her thong up to her breast, which she circled slowly. She kissed Elle and slid on top of her, placing a thigh between Elle's legs. Elle closed her eyes at the jolt that sent right to her center, and pushed her hips against Gia's thigh, once and then again. Gia, sensing her urgency, took the cue. "It's okay," she whispered, and slid her hand down the front of Elle's underwear. Elle squirmed and whimpered at the intimate touch. At last. She closed her eyes and rolled her hips against Gia's hand, amazed at the ever-building pressure and how fast it had all happened. She was *that* turned on. "Not yet," Gia told her, and returned to sucking her breast.

"Oh, God," Elle managed.

Before she knew it, her thong was off her body, which was good. So very good. Gia slid down the bed. The first sensation was Gia's warm breath, which was almost Elle's undoing. That was, until she felt her tongue. So many sounds came from her now. Sounds she'd never made before. With Gia's arms wrapped around Elle's legs, she held her in place and kissed her intimately, torturously so, before tracing patterns with her tongue.

That did it.

Elle raced toward orgasm, amazed by the power, the ferocity of the ever-growing tension. She'd never experienced anything like it, not even close. She twisted beneath Gia's touch, her mouth, desperate, searching for release, moaning quietly without even meaning to. She was not in control of her own body, an entirely new experience. Quite the opposite, in fact, and it thrilled her. When she finally came, she did so quietly, shaking, lost in pleasure, like an exploding star. The experience stunned her. Nothing she could have done would have prepared her for the mental or physical impact of that moment. "Oh my God," she whispered, as her hips thrust and Gia's tongue continued to dance across her delicately. When the pleasure ebbed, Gia held her legs, and kissed the insides of her thighs as Elle's body recovered, as she struggled to make sense of the very new experience.

She tried to find the words to explain how good it felt for Gia to touch her, to be inside her, but nothing she came up with seemed adequate.

"You're not saying anything," Gia said, after several extended moments passed. She'd joined Elle on the pillow, wrapping her arms around her protectively.

Elle turned in them and kissed Gia's cheeks, her nose, and sank into the warmth of her lips, kissing them extra thoroughly. "What am I to say about that unmatched experience?"

"That's a start."

She looked up, still searching for descriptors though her mind was at 50 percent. "It was dismantling."

"Dismantling," Gia repeated. "Is that good?"

Elle nodded, not quite finished. "And surprising. And torturous, until it wasn't."

"Okay." Gia smiled, picking up on the trend.

"Then it was simply…decadent." As they talked, Gia continued to touch Elle, who loved every second of it. Her stomach, her breasts, her collarbone, and more intimately along the insides of her thighs. "It still is, what you're doing to me. I'm still humming over here, because you're pulling new urges."

"That's a good report card," Gia said, and dipped her head to nibble on Elle's neck.

"Which should be rewarded, I would say."

Gia studied her briefly before going back to the tingle-inducing nibbling, probably unsure what to make of that sentence.

It was clear Gia hadn't come into tonight with any expectations, but Elle certainly had a few that had yet to be explored. "Which means it's time for you to stop that." She gently pulled Gia's face back to hers and kissed her hard and fast. Pulling her lips from the dizzying kiss, she sat up and pulled Gia with her. "You might have to be patient with me."

Gia nodded, her eyes dark once again.

Wordlessly, Elle unclasped the blue bra, freeing the breasts she'd been thinking about for weeks on end, anxious to get her hands on them at last. She looked up at Gia and smiled, her stomach dipping noticeably in appreciation of what she could only describe as simply beautiful breasts. Not large, but definitely not small. Perfectly round. She ran a finger from the top of each breast to the bottom before lifting one and taking the nipple into her mouth. The move pulled a groan from Gia, sending a bolt of arousal to Elle's center. She was lost again in a haze of lust, longing to do so many things at once, like a kid who had been long denied the candy store. She spent a lot of time on those breasts, bathing them, running her tongue across each nipple, sucking one, then the other firmly. Maybe even too much time, but the quiet sounds Gia made told her the attention was not wasted. Somehow, they ended up lying down, Elle's naked body on top of Gia's. Elle wasn't quite sure which of them had made that move, but she liked the feel of being on top, their breasts pushed together with delicious friction while her hips moved instinctively against Gia's. She gave her head a small shake, attempting to clear it from the rush of sensations it juggled. But maybe it was better this way. Unable to think, she was unable to second-guess her actions. She had zero experience in what she was about to do, and in her present condition, that didn't seem like a problem at all. She followed her instincts, her desire, and kissed a path down Gia's stomach, taking her time and savoring each response she pulled, memorizing it.

She kissed the insides of Gia's thighs, licked them, heady with power and longing to take Gia to the places she'd just taken Elle. She slowly parted Gia's thighs and delicately touched her on the outside of her underwear with one finger and first and then her entire palm. Gia hissed in a breath. Full of anticipation, Elle looped her thumbs through the black bikini briefs and pulled them down Gia's legs. She took a moment to just stare, now wet again herself. She leaned down and tasted Gia for the first time. Lightly with her tongue at first, and then more deliberately with her mouth, her lips. Just as Gia had done, she made small, gentle circles with her tongue. Gia moaned and bucked her hips, looking for more. Elle matched that rhythm with her tongue. She watched for signals, Gia's breathing, the increased movement of her hips, the intoxicating sounds she made. When she seemed close, Elle pushed her fingers inside, steadying herself from the overwhelming feeling of connection that hit all at once. Gia was no longer quiet, tossing her head on the pillow as Elle moved in and out, loving the sensation of Gia enveloping her. She didn't want this to end, but to her surprise, Gia grabbed a fistful of the blanket beneath her and cried out, her hips going wild and then still.

Elle exhaled in awe of the sight. Looking down at Gia's naked body, spent and glistening, was perhaps the most beautiful image she'd ever seen. She made a point to memorize it for all time. "Are you sure it has to be over?" Elle asked, kissing the insides of Gia's thighs, nibbling her way back to where she had been most effective just moments before.

"Not sure I can withstand much more of that," Gia said, with a laugh, and gently pulled Elle up the bed toward her.

"That was so different from what I expected it to be," Elle said, still processing.

Gia nodded, allowing her to do so. "Can you tell me how?"

"So much *more*," Elle said, staring out the ceiling. She flung her arm over her forehead and exhaled. "All this time, this was here, and I had no idea." She shook her head and looked over at Gia. "I've just been doing it wrong."

"I don't know if wrong is the word," Gia said, turning onto her side and smoothing Elle's hair.

"I do."

"So, are you okay?" Gia asked with a smile. Though it already looked like she knew the answer to that question.

"I'm more than okay." Elle sat up, not knowing what to do with herself. "I'm excited, and inquisitive, and also a little mystified. Did I say relieved? Because I'm that as well. So many battling emotions, but they're all good, and powerful. Did I mention powerful? God."

Gia laughed. "You're talking really fast."

"Am I? That would make sense."

Gia held out an arm. "Here. Why don't you lie back down and take a deep breath."

Because Gia looked more than a little inviting, Elle returned to the pillow next to her and slid her hand onto Gia's chest. "Yeah, this is better."

"Hi," Gia said, quietly.

Elle smiled. "Hi."

Maybe it was the proximity, or the few minutes it had been since they'd touched each other, but like a magnet they came back together. She wasn't sure who'd made the first move, but that was all it took to ignite their passion all over again. Kissing, touching, and so much more.

When they were happy and spent and barely able to move, they lay side by side facing each other, on the same pillow once again, in the very late—make that very early—hours. Neither one of them seemed to want to sleep. Elle, for one, needed to hang on to this night for as long as possible. It felt like her world had shifted dramatically, and she didn't want to miss a single minute.

"Why aren't people having sex all the time?" she finally asked.

Gia laughed quietly. "I mean...I think they are."

"They should. And like that. Exactly what we just did." She shook her head. "That was the longest sex I've ever had." She ran her fingers across Gia's collarbone, still marveling at how soft her skin was, and that she had free rein to explore it.

Gia grinned. "Really? I mean, I think we can beat that. You were... very much ready. It didn't take much."

"No, it certainly didn't," Elle said, remembering with a smile.

Gia's suggestion alone had Elle wondering about another go-round. "I can't believe it's taken me this long to...enjoy someone so much." She met Gia's eyes, relieved—no, ecstatic—at how the evening had turned out. Sex with Gia had far surpassed her expectations, obliterated them, and had certainly put her fears to rest. She was *not* broken. "You're beautiful," Elle said. "And tonight was mind blowing. And I think it's going to be hard to be a regular person out in the world when we could stay right here forever and just keep doing this. Forget everyone else."

Gia pulled Elle in and kissed the top of her head. "Then how will I conquer the surf world?"

Elle slid on top and rested on the backs of her forearms. "Well, you won't have to worry about that, because I've already done it."

Gia's mouth fell open. "Temporarily."

Elle shook her head and found those lips again, the ones she would never tire of. "You can be number one at kissing."

Gia considered this. "I accept. And while we're on such a roll, we should maybe try our hand at sleeping. Don't you have an early Trainers shoot?"

Elle sighed. "Yes. Damn it. Why do I always get the early slots?"

"Because you wake up looking beautiful."

She paused. She'd been complimented on her appearance before. But the words hit her in a whole new way, making her feel special. Maybe because Gia wasn't someone, like so many people she knew, who handed out compliments hand over fist. She was sincere and honest, and when she turned that attention on you, it felt like you were a hundred feet tall. "You're sweet to say that."

"It's true."

They shared a kiss and eventually drifted off, tangled up in each other in the most perfect way. Elle's heart felt as if it might burst, and she was pretty sure she fell asleep with a smile on her face. She was right earlier. The world would never look the same again, and that was beyond okay with her.

CHAPTER FOURTEEN

I could eat these guys all day," Autumn said, as she reached for another handful of fries. They'd met up at the Apple Pan in West Los Angeles because they apparently had the best burger and fries, at least according to Autumn's most recent research. These outings were something she and Gia tried to do at least once a month, steal some time for just the two of them to catch up. No matter how awesome their group friendship had turned out to be, one-on-one time was important.

Gia looked around the quaint diner outfitted with red and white décor, a faux brick wall outlining the pick-up window from the kitchen. "Yeah, we're gonna need some of that pie once we're done, too."

"You are the very best date for any pregnant woman. Has anyone ever told you that?"

Gia paused with a fry midway to her mouth. "Can't say they have."

"Well, it's true. Your athlete's appetite is the perfect match for my cravings. We could go far together over the next few months. You hear me?"

"I do, and you're on." They made the cheers gestures with their individual fries in a food pact neither would likely forget. "Next time, let's get these with cheese," Gia said, gesturing to the fries.

"Oh my God, it's like you're some kind of wizard."

Gia laughed. "Kate's not big on fun meals?"

"She indulges me in whatever I want. Makes midnight runs for sweet and sour shrimp if that's what I'm after, but I'm eating her under the table, you know?"

"Yeah, well, there's three of you."

Autumn pointed at her. "Thank you for saying that! You deserve a medal."

"Not necessary. And how long until we meet them now?"

"Twelve weeks and two days. I'm not counting or anything." In actuality, Autumn's stomach had grown considerably in just the past couple of weeks. She was tiptoeing her way into the third trimester, and it was clear this thing was actually happening, and soon.

"How are you feeling?"

"Got some energy back, which is nice for the afternoon rush. My feet are killing me, though, and I worry about you guys constantly. I'm a hormonal worrying person now. A mother hen on steroids!"

"What's got you worried? We're fine." Gia reflected on her night with Elle. More than fine, actually. She smothered the dreamy smile that threatened.

"No, you're not. Had's all stressed out about the store pressures, but she doesn't want to burden anyone with the details, so she holds it all in, which is not at all healthy. Izzy's buried under a mountain of work now that she's producing as well as writing, and I'm worried she's not coming up for enough air. And you—"

"What about me?"

"You're different lately."

"Different how? I am not."

"Your head is in the clouds, maybe in a good way. I can't tell, but my protective side is on alert just in case."

Gia nodded. That was fair. Her head *was* in the clouds. Part of her loved it. The other part was scared to death about who she was in the clouds *with*. Elle, in every way, was amazing, but what were the ramifications of sleeping with your biggest competitor? And what kind of implications would that have for her career, long term? Right now, she didn't seem to care. Elle had her feeling things, a lot of new and wonderful things, and she wanted to enjoy that before examining those feelings under a microscope. Because, in all honesty, who knew what she would find? "We slept together."

There.

It was out there now.

No taking it back.

Autumn, to her credit, kept her cool. She was always dependable for a mature reaction. "You and Elle?"

"Yep."

Autumn shoved a handful of fries in her mouth, and Gia grinned. She really adored the pregnant version of Autumn. The fries might have been a distraction to buy her a moment to compose her thoughts, but Gia didn't care.

"I feel like that's a big step for you," she said, around her mouthful. "It is."

"And I don't think you've ever volunteered information like that before. No, I can safely say you never have." Autumn paused. "This one matters, doesn't she?"

Gia sucked in air, hesitant to admit what she already knew. She nodded. "I can't believe I'm saying this, but I feel like I'm falling for her, and it's all happening really fast."

Autumn beamed. "I can tell. Just look at you, Gia-Pet. You look like I do when I'm daydreaming about junk food."

"What do I do now?" Gia asked. "I've never been here before. I need a map or a to-do list. I usually train for things I find difficult. How do you train for a relationship? For falling in love with someone."

Autumn reached across and covered the top of Gia's hand. "That's the best part. There's nothing to do, no training required. Just enjoy it."

"Except I still have to surf against her. My mission in life for years now has been to be ranked number one. I've never been so close."

"Yeah, that part's a little trickier, I admit."

"So, about that manual?"

"I'm afraid you're going to have to fly blind, my friend. Now I have a solid reason to worry about you."

Gia sighed and reached for a fry. She was worried, too, but the good overtook the concern in a welcome array of warm, sexy, and happy feelings that seemed to alternate, moment to moment. She'd never felt more like Hadley in her entire life.

The worry would just have to wait its damn turn.

❖

"So, how do you do it?" Gia asked, sitting up in bed, pulling the sheet with her. It was late morning on a Saturday, which meant she and Elle could be lazy, take some time off and enjoy the day…and each other. They certainly had the night before.

"Oh, that could go a lot of different ways. How do I do what?" Elle grinned, reaching up and tugging lightly on Gia's hair. "Might have to be more specific."

"The way you charm the public so effortlessly. I used to hate it. Now that I know the girl behind it, I'm impressed. Proud."

Elle smiled. "That's a really nice thing to say."

"Well, it's true. So, what's the secret? Because I'm clearly missing it. I come off like an idiot each time I open my mouth to those media types. Even when I don't mean to."

"You've never come off like an idiot. Even when I wasn't your biggest fan, I never thought so. You're just more reserved." Elle walked naked to the back of her bedroom door to retrieve her fluffy white robe as Gia watched happily.

"Okay. What's the cure?"

Elle came back to her, tying the sash as she walked. "Lots of smiling, lots of laughing, and honestly? The ability to listen and toss the ball back to them. Keep the conversation moving with a give-and-take."

Gia scrunched up her face. "Can you explain that last part?"

"Mm-hmm." She leaned down, stole a kiss, and sat on the bed across from Gia. "It's all about building rapport. Instead of answering a question and getting out of there, listen to what a reporter has to say, and try and continue the conversation. Do what you can to make it last. Let's try it."

Gia balked, completely out of her comfort zone. "No way. Absolutely not."

Ignoring her, Elle mimed an imaginary microphone. "Gia, as you struggle unsuccessfully to take down master surfer Elle Britton, what's going through your sexy mind?"

Gia darkened and leaned into the microphone. "That it's only a matter of time."

"Nope, that's borderline brooding and too competitive," Elle said, dropping the microphone. "Fail."

Gia laughed. "But you're a really cute reporter. Are you available later?"

"Oh my God. Yes!" Elle pointed at her, as the corners of that fantasy-inducing mouth turned up. "You're doing it right now! More of that."

"What? I was flirting with you."

"Then flirt with *them*. It's all a game. You were charming, and likable, and had the most wonderful smile on your face as you laughed. That's how you sell it. Worked on me."

"You're serious?"

"Beyond serious, and now I'm desperate to make out with you. That's how good it was."

"Wow, that's more than I was—" But she never got to finish her sentence because Elle's lips were on hers, and the sash on the robe was pulled, and the rest of their morning spiraled into one Gia wouldn't likely forget.

She loved Saturdays.

With the Cascais Women's Pro lurking in just a couple of weeks, both Elle and Gia spent most of their days training with their respective coaches and their nights dining out, watching movies, and eventually falling into bed together. Sometimes they even skipped those first couple of things.

Because they hadn't gone out of their way to be secretive about the time they spent together, photos and ridiculous headlines splashed across the trashiest of surf blogs about them. And suddenly Gia's requests for interviews had skyrocketed. Theo Trowebridge loved it.

"Okay, so maybe now we pivot," he said to the two of them, in his office. They exchanged a glance.

"In what way?" Elle asked, leaning forward with a squint.

"Now that you're linked romantically in the press, we play up the sex angle a little more."

"No," Gia said adamantly. Their personal life was theirs, and she wasn't about to exploit their relationship to sell chips. It was becoming too important to her.

"I agree with Gia," Elle said. "That part of our story is off the table. We still compete against each other. Let's keep it about the sport."

Theo looked bored and drummed his fingers. "Fine. If that's what you'd prefer. But for the record, it's me you should be thanking for your burgeoning love in the first place. You could show a little gratitude by keeping an open mind."

Gia studied him out of the side of her eye. He looked way too pleased with himself. "And why is that?"

He opened his mouth and closed it again, seeming to change direction. "For putting you together on this campaign."

Elle mulled this over. "I guess that's true to an extent."

"That, and the broken-down Jeep." He laughed. No, it wasn't a laugh. More like a childlike giggle. Was this guy serious?

"You screwed with my car?" Gia asked, completely floored.

"Nothing major. Just enough for you to need a ride, and I happened to know who was nice enough to offer one." He was still laughing at his own perceived genius.

"And let me guess? You called in the photographers who photographed us together?"

"Bingo," he said gleefully.

Which prompted the sex dream, which prompted the flirting, which prompted the holy hell sex life they were in the midst of, and cut to the deeper feelings.

With her mind completely blown, Gia didn't know whether to deck the guy or hug him. "Let's get one thing clear," she said, leaning forward across the desk. "You're done playing God, and you're done with games. If you pull a stunt like that again, I walk, contract or not."

Elle smiled at her briefly in solidarity. "I'm with Gia. It wasn't cool what you did, no matter what the outcome, Theo."

He held up his hands and had the decency to look contrite. "You have my sincerest apologies and assurances that I will behave myself from this moment forward. I honestly never thought it would go any further than a ride home and some photos that might stir the publicity pot. I thought you might see the humor in it, given the happy ending."

"We don't," Elle said.

"I understand. Shall we discuss the final series of ads?"

When they left the meeting, she and Elle walked to the elevator in silence. Once inside, they stared at each other from opposite ends of the car.

"So, it seems our whole relationship was built on an advertising stunt," Elle said solemnly.

Gia nodded. "We're a total sham."

A pause. "Want to get frozen yogurt and walk on the beach?"

Gia laughed and covered the distance between them until she was staring into gorgeous blue eyes. "You sure you want to be seen with your corporately engineered girlfriend?"

Elle pulled her face back in mystification. "Hey, you just called yourself my girlfriend."

Gia had heard it too. She hadn't meant to make that leap, but somehow, she had, and it was out there. "I'm sorry. It just came out."

Elle wrapped her arms around Gia's waist. "I love that you said it. Don't you dare apologize. I think you just made my afternoon, Two."

Gia shook her head at the stupid nickname, but it didn't distract her from the somersaults her heart was doing. They were a legitimate item now, and as odd a story as theirs might be, she was really, really happy about it.

❖

When Gia arrived at the resort in Portugal, she was greeted with full-on pandemonium, the likes of which she'd never experienced. She was a surfer, not a rock star.

"Gia! Can I get your autograph?"

"I love the Trainers commercials. Oh my God, you guys are hysterical."

"Gia, Billy from *Surfology*. Can we set up a one-on-one with you for tomorrow afternoon?"

"Gonna win the whole thing, Gia? What's Elle have to say about that?"

"Hey, your girlfriend's hot."

She hadn't so much as made it to the front desk for check-in yet, and already her life was a circus, and unlike any normal reception she was used to. She did her best to chat with each person, remembering Elle's unofficial media training. She smiled, she laughed, she lingered longer than felt necessary, and then she got the hell out of there, eager to catch her breath and regroup.

Quite purposefully, she and Elle had made the decision not to travel together, knowing how much attention it would attract. In retrospect, Gia couldn't imagine it being much worse than the flurry she'd just encountered. They were, however, staying in the same room, which had her slightly on edge. Distractions during a tournament were never a good thing, and part of her process was to strip each and every one of them away. That was an impossibility when it came to Elle, as she consumed so much of Gia's thoughts lately. This was new ground; she'd have to improvise as she went.

She found the room number and knocked twice. "Who's there?" she heard Elle ask.

"Your favorite surfer," Gia said, with a grin, knowing full well Elle would have already checked through the peephole before even asking.

The door opened and the most beautiful girl she'd ever seen was standing there smiling at her in jeans and a pink T-shirt. The wonderful tingle that smile inspired always amazed her.

"I haven't seen you in two days. Do you realize that? Sight for sore eyes," Elle said.

"It felt longer."

"Get in here so I can say hello the way I want to." Elle stepped aside to let Gia enter. And once she was safely in the room, and the door closed, she caught Elle by the waist and hauled her in for a long and heat-inspiring kiss. The thing about kissing Elle was that Gia never wanted to stop. The warmth of her lips, the way they clung to Gia's, the way she tasted, the way her hair tickled the side of Gia's face, the way she murmured adorably into the kiss: It was a perfect package of everything Gia never knew she wanted. She kissed Elle in the middle of the room, up against the wall, and they worked their way to the bed, undressing as they walked.

"You're early in heat three tomorrow," Elle said between kisses. "We need to remember to set eight alarms."

"Good thing I brought ten."

More kissing, and groping. Gia gasped at the way Elle tortured her relentlessly before lifting her to shattering orgasm. When Gia went to turn the tables, Elle held up a finger. "No time. We're meeting my parents for dinner, remember?"

She did remember.

Two days before she was set to leave for the tournament, Gia had glanced down at her phone.

Think you'd want to meet my family? the text from Elle read. *They're coming to Portugal.*

Gia held up the phone and looked around the table at her friends, who were halfway into Breakfast Club. "Would you say it's a turning point to meet someone's family?"

Isabel glanced at Hadley, who glanced at Autumn, who glanced back at Isabel.

Isabel set down her coffee. "Got it. I'm nominated." She turned to Gia. "That's the big leagues, my friend. I didn't meet Taylor's parents until she was a hundred percent certain I was her penguin for life."

Hadley looked at Gia. "Aww, I think you might be Elle's penguin. That's so cute."

"So, what do you say? Do you want to be penguins with Elle?" Isabel asked with a smolder.

Autumn smiled at her supportively across the table.

"That's the thing." Gia reached for a sleeve for her coffee. "We haven't discussed penguins just yet."

"Yeah, but surely the penguin conversation is coming," Autumn said. "You guys are spending more and more time together. You get the faraway look in your eye all the time like you're thinking about her when she's not even here."

"That's because I am. I don't know how it happened. But that's where we are. I don't want to screw up the family thing. That could be disastrous."

Isabel smiled into her coffee. "Good, then don't. Families can make or break you."

Hadley waved off the comment. "Stop scaring her. Everyone likes you, Gia. You have nothing to worry about."

"That's not true. There's definite worry to be had." They glanced up to see Larry Herman, their ultra-uptight landlord, peering over them, holding a coffee. "Ms. Malone is not perfect. Her rent's not always on time."

"I was two days late," Gia said. "One time."

He pushed up his eighties plastic glasses. "If a doctor's late for surgery, everyone dies."

"They do not," Isabel interjected. "That makes no sense. Do you even hear yourself when you talk, you weirdo?"

Hadley passed Isabel a look. "He's just being Larry."

"Thank you," Larry Herman said, standing a little taller. His cheeks dusted with pink right on schedule, his love for Hadley on full display. "Good luck, Ms. Malone. You'll need it." He walked away on that line.

She heard the foreboding sentence play again as she sat in that hotel room in Portugal. Gia blinked at Elle, who'd started dressing for dinner with her parents.

"I'm sometimes late on my rent," Gia blurted. "Like one or two days. I just forget."

Elle paused, one arm frozen on the way to its sleeve. "Was there a segue that I missed?"

"I have my own issues, is what I mean. I come with flaws, and what if they don't like me for you because of them? What if they don't like me at all? You didn't." She closed her eyes, terrified she wouldn't make a good impression. She wanted to so badly. For herself. For Elle.

Elle softened and came and sat on the bed next to her. She gave her those earnest eyes that always stole Gia's breath. "Are you planning to blow off one of their greetings, or shoot them a competitive stare, or drop in on one of their waves?"

Gia shook her head. "Not on my to-do list, that I know of."

Elle smiled. "Then I'm confident you'll do just fine." She kissed Gia softly. "But we should get you dressed, because we're about to find out."

CHAPTER FIFTEEN

E lle felt on edge.
       Not because she was afraid Gia would make a bad impression, not at all. But rather, because her parents would be meeting someone important to her for the first time. She hadn't introduced them to a significant other since her senior prom, when the corsage hadn't gone on right and the photos had been a comedy of errors and her dad had to drive them when the hired car hadn't shown up. It only heightened the intensity that, this time, she would be introducing them to a woman. Her mother had been surprised, but supportive, when she'd broken the news. Her father had said...less. Though she knew inherently that he loved her very much and would be there for her when she needed him, she needed him *tonight*.

This was going to go well, wasn't it? It would be fine. Just fine. She should suck it up and get out of her own head.

"Oh, there's my girl," she heard her father say, as they rounded the corner into the restaurant. She held firmly to Gia's hand and passed her a supportive smile. And then there they were, standing in the entryway of Monterios, the high-end seafood restaurant attached to the resort. Her father wore a crisp suit that matched his gray hair, feathered back. Her mother had assembled her blond locks into a pile on her head and looked elegant in a turquoise cocktail dress with a solitary diamond hanging around her neck. They looked happy, tan, and like the stereotypical California parents.

"Hey, you guys," Elle said, pulling her mother into a hug and then accepting a hug and kiss on the cheek from her father. "Been here long?"

"We had a glass of wine at the bar and headed over about five minutes ago," her mother said.

Elle turned to Gia. "I want to introduce you both to Gia Malone. Gia, this is my father, Blake Britton, and my mother, Dee. They live in Laguna Beach."

She looked on as the three of them exchanged handshakes and pleasantries.

"You're a talented surfer," her father said. "Right on Elle's heels."

Gia looked off balance. It would be in her nature to say something competitive. It was what they did with each other. Instead she pivoted. "She makes it hard."

Her father wrapped an arm around Elle and smiled. "That's my girl. Shall we go inside?"

Dinner got off to a decent enough start. Her parents were friendly. Gia was charming. The food was wonderful and the restaurant quiet enough that they could all talk comfortably. That's when it happened.

"So, Gia," her mother said, cutting into a scallop, "are you seeing anyone?"

Gia went still. Elle swallowed the bite of chicken in her mouth before choking. "Mom," she said, setting down her knife and fork, "Gia and I are seeing each other. You know that."

Her mothered dropped her voice. "I know there was a kiss and a lot of hubbub about it, but I didn't know you were moving toward an actual relationship. That seems like a big leap."

Elle went numb. Her mother thought this was a phase. She'd been supportive while quietly waiting for it to pass. Elle met Gia's sad and uncomfortable eyes and sent her a reassuring smile. "Well, we are."

Her father sat taller. "It's surely difficult, dating someone you're in such close competition with." He directed the question at Gia.

"I think we take that part one day at a time. Having a sense of humor about it helps. I think we both do."

Elle nodded. "Definitely some razzing."

"And you think that's sustainable?" he asked them both.

"I guess that's what we're hoping," Elle said. Gia attempted a smile, looking nervous as hell.

"And this is what you *want*?" her mother asked, looking pained.

"This is what I want," Elle said, matter-of-factly, embarrassed in front of Gia and disheartened for herself. This wasn't like her parents. Not at all. Her coming out had apparently hit them harder than she had realized.

Her father forced a smile as the waiter removed his plate. "Where did you go to school?" he asked Gia, with a new level of scrutiny.

"High school?" Gia asked, thanking the waiter with a smile.

"Where did you get your *degree*?" he amended.

She glanced at Elle and back to her father. "I didn't go to college. I went straight away onto the qualifying tournament, hoping to rack up enough points to join the Championship Tour."

"Which I see you've managed to do," he said. "Elle took a similar route, but got her degree from UCLA at the same time."

"Education is important," her mother said, gently.

Her father nodded. "It's everything."

"Some people, however, are students of the world," Elle told them. There was now a negative undercurrent to the entire conversation. The room felt tense and Elle's senses moved into a heightened state.

"I wish I had gone to college," Gia said quietly, in explanation. "It just wasn't possible at the time. I didn't have any help financially. My parents could never have afforded the entry fees. As you know, professional surfing isn't cheap." It was her way of subtly pointing out that Elle had Britton money backing her, which was true. With the help of her parents, she'd been able to afford classes on the side, which had led to her degree in sports medicine. It wouldn't have happened otherwise. Elle was very much aware of that.

"And what will you do when you can't surf anymore? How will you make your living then?" he asked.

"That's a bridge I'll cross when the time comes." Gia took a sip of her water, the vibrant color now gone from her face.

"Could really come at any time, if you think about it. Injuries change lives at the drop of a hat."

"Dad."

"What?" he asked, with a smile. "We're just getting to know each other a little."

"It's okay," Gia said to Elle. "I would imagine I'd turn to coaching."

"And you have the skillset for that?"

"I do."

Elle couldn't take much more. Dinner was over, and she certainly didn't want to stay for dessert. "Mom, Dad, I've got an awful headache. Let me get the check."

"Don't be silly," her father said. "I'll take care of it. Go rest up for tomorrow. We'll be in the stands rooting for you."

Elle squeezed her mother's shoulder. "I'll look for you after."

She gave Gia a moment to say goodbye to her parents, took her hand, and got the hell out of there.

"I'm so sorry," Elle said to Gia, once they were alone on the elevator.

When Gia raised her gaze, the vulnerability Elle saw looking back at her left her struck, staggered.

"That didn't go well at all," Gia said.

She wanted to argue. To reassure Gia and make her feel better. Unfortunately, she couldn't. "I was expecting so much more from them. They're good people, Gia. They are. You just wouldn't know it from tonight."

"I know." Gia blinked and pretended to study the lights on the ceiling. But Elle caught the welling of tears she was hoping to hide. Her heart ached for Gia, who had a much more tender side than she ever would have imagined just a year ago. She'd grown to understand that Gia was a softie underneath it all, with very real and fragile feelings. She cared about other people and put the needs of those she cared about before her own. But right now, she was hurting, and that hurt Elle.

"I guess it didn't go as well as I planned." Gia smiled in spite of her tear-filled eyes.

Elle took her hand. When they were together, they seemed to touch more than they didn't. She needed that connection now. "It's not your fault, okay? You were wonderful. It's theirs. They behaved badly. Apparently, they have a lot to work through. Let me talk to them."

"Don't do anything to make it worse," Gia said. "Okay?"

Elle nodded. "Okay."

Things felt tense between them the rest of the night. A distance cropped up. Gia recessed behind her self-made armor and didn't say a whole lot, and Elle wasn't sure what to do to close the gap that now existed between them.

"Does it bother you that I don't have a degree?" Gia asked finally, just as she was about to turn off the light for bed.

Elle tucked a strand of Gia's hair behind her ear. "Not in the slightest. What bothers me is that you surf like a champion." A pause. "I also think that's pretty hot."

Gia nodded, offered a halfhearted grin, and kissed her softly. "Good night."

❖

No, no, no. Gia was screwed. Fucking screwed.

She blinked at the scoreboard. She'd turned in a dismal combined score of 10.2 in round one of the tournament. Luckily, two of the three surfers competing would move forward to round two. She'd made it by two tenths of a point. The conditions were utter perfection, the weather was on point, and she was in the best shape of her life. Yet Gia couldn't seem to get her head in the game, no matter how hard she tried.

"What was going on out there?" Elle asked, once Gia made her way back to the beach. She offered a reassuring smile, but Gia could see the concern all over her face. She'd sucked, and not just by her own standards.

"I don't know. I just wasn't…me. I wasn't taking risks and then when I forced myself to be more aggressive, I bombed epically. Wiped out, lost all form."

"Okay, look at me." Elle took Gia by the shoulders in a manner that said she meant business. "It was a weird heat, okay? You're gonna go back out there in the next round, clear your head, breathe, and take it one wave at a time."

Gia nodded. "I can do that." In her peripheral vision, she saw a number of cameras pointed their way and heard the telling click, click, click of a dozen shutters. Apparently, they'd just served up another good photo op. She shrugged it off in annoyance. "You're up in twenty. You ready?"

"More than ready."

That's when Gia caught sight of Elle's parents in the surfers' reserved section, which meant they'd just seen her tank out there. Another chance to make a decent impression gone. Her muscles tensed and frustration flared. She shook it off and made a point to focus on Elle. It helped. Her encouraging face alone, her kind smile, made everything extraneous calm down. "All right, go get 'em. I'll be watching."

Elle took the heat and easily advanced to round two, but not by the impressive margin she usually did. They were off, both of them, and it transferred to their lives outside of competition.

"So today sucked," Gia said, over what had been a quiet dinner so far.

Elle nodded. "Tomorrow will be better. Tomorrow we kick ass." She rested her foot on top of Gia's underneath the table and they shared a smile.

"Damn right we will."

But Gia was out by round three, barely even making it there. Her surfing had come apart. She returned to the hotel room in tatters, not understanding any of it.

She tossed her water bottle onto the bed with force. She was angry with herself, disappointed in the final results, and helpless to find a way to turn it all around. It would be near impossible to hold on to her number two ranking at this point, simply from a mathematics perspective. She'd fall to three or four, depending on the outcome of the tournament she was now out of. "Fuck!" she yelled to the empty room.

❖

Elle went down in round four. Not even a shot at the quarterfinals. She was dazed, in shock, and furious with herself by the time she met her parents at the hotel café late that afternoon. Their faces held the disappointment she would have expected, and that sliced at her. She'd give anything for a do-over, a chance to surf the way she wanted to. The way she knew she could. She'd invested a lot in this tournament, imagined a triumphant outcome a thousand different times, planned on that finals heat, on earning those much-needed points, and still, she'd let the whole thing slip through her fingers in the most embarrassing manner.

"It just wasn't like you," her father said. "I'll take a Pellegrino, with three limes on the side," he told the waiter, with a smile that he promptly dropped when they were once again alone.

She nodded. "Can't agree more. I had a bad day." Lindy Ives, who she gone head-to-head with, had surfed a clean set in the fourth, but on any other day, she'd have been no match for Elle. And that didn't even take into consideration her less-than-stellar performances in the heats prior. Something was definitely wrong.

"Have you kept up with your training?" he asked, skepticism creasing his brow.

She resisted the urge to snap at him, instead maintaining control of her voice. A deep breath. Slow and steady. "I most definitely have."

"I don't know if you want our opinion, but I'm just going to say it." Her mother set her tea cup on the table with the most delicate of clinks. She met Elle's gaze. "I think you let yourself get caught up with whatever you have going with Gia Malone."

Elle took a breath and let it out slowly. "I don't think that's the issue."

"Hear me out, because I happen to know you very well," her mother said. "When something has your attention, you fixate like nothing else matters. Just think back to when you wanted that puppy we saw for sale in the supermarket parking lot." She turned to her husband. "When was that? Was she nine?"

"Ten," he corrected, with a nostalgic smile. "You couldn't eat. You couldn't sleep. All you thought about was how much you wanted that puppy. Brought it up every day. Your grades fell."

"Please tell me you're not comparing Gia to a childhood whim, to a puppy I never got and haven't thought about in years."

"The behavior's the same. And maybe this is another whim," her father said with annoying confidence. "She's not who I imagined for you, Elle. Not even close, and that has nothing to do with sexuality. Are you willing to throw away your career for an exciting few months?"

"We're just worried about you," her mother said. "We love you so much, Elle, and want to make sure that your eyes are open."

"They are, and this isn't some tryst."

"All right, then. Let's say it is more. What then?" her father asked. "Are you going to be able to handle the hit your surfing is going to take? Because I can all but guarantee there'll be more days like today if you're splitting your focus between yourself and your top competitor. That's a lose-lose every which way you look at it."

Elle felt like the world was shifting, because not only did his words anger Elle, they forced a trickle of terror down her spine. What if, by some slim chance, he was right? What if the connection she and Gia had forged was the very thing that was taking her down, and Gia right along with her? While their relationship was one of the most remarkable things that had ever happened to her, she'd spent her whole life working toward one goal, and she couldn't give up on it now. She wouldn't. Elle gripped the table, rejecting the unsettling idea and the implications that came with it.

"Just wait for the Rip Curl Pro," she said, with a serenity she did not feel. "You'll see. This tournament was nothing but a fluke."

Her parents exchanged a defeated look. Her mother sighed. Her father shook his head. "It's your life, sweetheart. You get to make all the decisions."

❖

Elle was quieter than normal on the flight back to California. Gia gave her the space to think, go over the events of the past couple of days, as awful as they were. After losing in the fourth, she'd hold on to her number one ranking, but barely, as Lindy Ives finished second in the tournament, narrowing the gap between her and Elle, which was awful. If Gia couldn't top the leaderboard, the next best thing was that Elle did, the woman who had her heart.

"What do you think happened in Portugal?" Elle asked, still in defeat mode, as they drove back to Seven Shores from the airport.

Gia was afraid to say what she suspected was the truth. "We were distracted." She parked the Jeep and turned to Elle. "We're letting ourselves get caught up."

Elle nodded. "In each other."

"In each other, in the drama with your parents, in the crazy attention we pull from reporters now."

"It's gotten out of control." Since the Trainers ads started running, attention from the sports media and bloggers had tripled. When their relationship had come to light, it exploded even further. All eyes were on them, and not just in regard to their surfing. They'd created a proverbial circus. "So, what do we do?" Elle asked.

"I don't know."

They sat there in the car, defeated, before finally making their way to Gia's apartment. Along the way, the noise from Isabel's place snagged their focus. "Oh, I think we have to stop," Gia said.

Elle looked intrigued. "I'll follow you."

Not bothering to knock, Gia let them into the one-story unit and found Kate sitting on the floor, controller in hand as Ms. Pac-Man flew around the screen. Isabel and Larry Herman stood behind her cheering. "She's a beast! Kate's broken her personal record!" Isabel yelled, and flung herself into Gia's arms. "Hi! Glad you're back. Hey, Elle. Come in! Quick. This is crazy. So crazy. I'm losing my shit."

Gia darted farther into the room and stared at the screen, noting the importance of such a feat. Kate, their up-and-coming *Ms. Pac-Man* prodigy, fairly new to the game, was wrecking shop. "Don't let the banana into the warped tunnel!" Gia yelled.

"Fucking get it!" Isabel yelled. "Hurry! Grab that bastard banana!"

"Ms. Carpenter, oh no! Be aware of the blue ghost on the left-hand side of the screen," Larry Herman said, with more intensity than volume. He pointed at the edge of the television. "Right here!"

"So, this is one of the retro video games you told me about?" Elle asked, a hint of a smile on her face.

"The most important one by far. Ms. Pac-Man is a big part of our lives. She's everything."

"I get that distinct impression. You guys are hard-core. Maybe even—"

"What a fucker!" Isabel yelled, slamming a throw pillow to the ground as if the midst of a wrestling match. She threw her body on top of it.

They turned to the screen to see Kate's Ms. Pac-Man shrink and shrink into a sad little death.

"It's okay," Kate said, standing from her spot on the floor. "I had a good run."

She may have gone down, but it had been an admirable fight that would up her high score on the refrigerator. "You killed it," Gia said. "Update the board."

With a nod, Isabel headed to the fridge where Kate's level and score would be upped. "This is big," Gia said to Elle.

Elle nodded reverently. "Oh, most certainly. I can tell."

"It seems weird at first," Kate said. "But I promise, it's fun. Do you want to try?"

Elle shrugged. "What the hell? I like games."

"Who are you?" Larry Herman asked, stepping between Elle and the television as Isabel handed her the controller. "Who is this, please?" he asked the room, as if this new individual were invading the stasis of his perfectly assembled Larry Herman world.

"My girlfriend, Elle," Gia said. "She's never played."

He hesitated. "All right. But you need to understand the importance of not letting the colored ghosts touch Ms. Pac-Man. She loses lives. And they will chase you, quite vehemently. You need to be prepared for that inevitability. Do you feel prepared?"

Elle broke into a high-wattage smile. The kind she charmed the world with effortlessly. "I do. Those are all very helpful tips."

Larry blushed on cue, and stepped out of the way.

"Hadley might have herself some competition," Isabel whispered to Gia.

Gia laughed. "He should get in line."

"Hey, sorry the tournament didn't turn out as you'd hoped."

"Next time. Trust me. Next time." They fist-bumped and focused on Elle's atrocious first attempt at *Ms. Pac-Man*. Oh, it was *bad*.

"See, you want to go the opposite direction of the ghosts," Kate explained calmly.

Larry shook his head in disdain, crossing his arms in a huff.

"Guess you can't be number one at everything," Isabel murmured.

"That's a fun game," Elle said, as they left the apartment a short time later. "Not sure I have much future on the refrigerator, though." But she was smiling and lighthearted, one of the qualities Gia loved most about her. "Who knew you were such a nerd?" she asked and bumped Gia's shoulder.

"Total nerd, with lots of dedication to the job." Gia bumped her back. "You've been forewarned."

"Nerds aren't always so sexy. You are, though. What do you have to say to that?"

"I'll take it." But she felt her cheeks heat. So lame. So easy.

"Look at that," Elle said, touching her face. "Look how easily affected you are by just a compliment."

Gia laughed and looked away. Her heart was full. "Know what I could go for after traveling? A really hot shower."

Elle raised an eyebrow, and Gia laughed. "What?" Elle asked. "I'm doing the Gia. You always raise your eyebrow just like this." She offered a second overexaggerated raise.

"No, I don't. I don't know who you've been talking to."

"More like, who I've been studying." She hurried up the stairs. "Shower is this way, if memory serves."

Gia raised her eyebrow.

"See? There it is. More of that. Just like that. Now turn your head to the left. Give me sexy eyes," Elle said, mimicking the photographer from their numerous Trainers shoots. Gia chased her up the stairs as she screamed.

Nine minutes later, the steam from the hot water had nothing on them. Elle had her up against the wall of the shower and at the mercy of her amazing mouth. With Elle's fingers pushing into her and her tongue tracing unbelievable patterns between her legs, Gia moaned low from her throat, grasping for something to hold on to, finding very little, until the release she craved came over her in an earth-shattering wash. Elle held her steady, then kissed her way up Gia's body, licking droplets of water off her as she went, until they stood face-to-face.

"We've been derelict. We've been letting showers to go waste," Elle said, breathless and looking pleased with herself. Her blue eyes danced. "For two people who excel in water, how did we miss this?"

"We won't ever again," Gia said. "I always thought shower sex was overrated. It's not. I should damn well apologize to the universe for my naïveté." She sucked in more air and reached for Elle, eager to get her hands on her and to repay the overly generous favor, and then some. Elle swore when Gia's hand landed between her legs.

They might have lost out in Portugal, but it was a glorious homecoming.

❖

"It's been forever since we've dished. So, tell me, if you had to categorize things with Gia, what you would say?" Holly asked, as they dragged their boards back to the shoreline. It was a beautiful Saturday that came with relatively calm waters, but they'd managed to get in a good couple of hours on what swells they could snag. It was the kind of morning Elle lived for. No competition, no judges, no coaches. Just the unhurried love of the sport alongside her best friend.

Elle dropped her board and looked over at Holly. "Surfing is over, and now we girl talk. I see how it is."

"Hell, yeah. My two favorite things, and I prefer them in that order."

For once, Elle didn't have that dreaded feeling that she was about to crash and burn. Bring on girl talk! This time, she was ready and well-equipped.

"It's honestly more than I ever thought possible. I still can't wrap my brain around how well we work together."

"That sounds promising, which I already knew would be the case, as evidenced by the glow radiating off you like rays off the sun."

Elle smiled. "Is it that noticeable?"

Holly shielded her face. "Sweetheart, I need sunglasses." Elle nodded, enjoying that her happiness was that obvious. "What's the best part?"

Elle considered this. "Knowing I have this amazing other person, who is nothing like me, by the way, to share everything with now. When something happens in my day, she's the first one I want to tell. No offense."

"I'm only partially offended. I'll accept second place in exchange for this whole new you. What else?"

"She makes me feel special. Has coffee waiting in the morning when I come out of the bedroom. If she makes herself a smoothie, she makes one for me, too, just in case. She sent me flowers yesterday."

"Flowers?" Holly practically yelled. "I never get flowers!"

"That's what I mean. She goes out of her way."

"And the sex is still good?"

Elle covered her eyes. "Oh my God. I don't have words to do it justice. I can't keep my hands off her, and I think it's mutual. I thought that, by now, maybe the newness would have worn off, but, Hol, it just gets better as we go."

"I hate you."

"I know. I hate me, too."

"I will punch you in the face."

"You damn well should."

Holly sighed. "But I'm also very happy for you, because it's about time. You deserve this."

Elle took a moment. "But it's not perfect. The scenario."

"Let me guess. There might be a little conflict of interest when it comes to your jobs?"

"Well, yes. I think we were both very aware of our rivalry, and if we ever forget, the media is right there to remind us. Not to mention, a chip billboard every five miles. But it might be more than that. I'm not sure yet."

"You're gonna have to explain."

Elle stared off at the horizon and watched as the seagulls dove to the waterline, knowing that if she voiced her fears, it might actually make them true. Nonetheless, she needed to get them out of her head. Maybe talking to Holly would offer clarity. "Gia's bombed the last two tournaments since we started up, and I crashed and burned at the last one."

"And you're wondering if the relationship was part of it?"

Elle nodded. "It's occurred to me once or twice."

"Whoa."

They paused as a rowdy group of teenage boys tore down the beach carrying boards. Elle shook her head. "It's probably something that's going to work itself out. Maybe it's even just a coincidence." A pause. She couldn't seem to leave it there. "But what if it's not?"

"Then you'll figure it out, right? You have to. I don't want you to lose that glow."

Elle met Holly's gaze as fear crept in, making her feel smaller by the second. "This is all I've ever wanted, to be at the top of my sport. I've worked my whole life for this. I can't completely lose my head and watch it fall apart now."

"Have you said as much to Gia? What does she think?"

"We haven't discussed it fully, but trust me, she's concerned. She has to be."

"Talk to her about it."

"Maybe. We have the Rip Curl Pro coming up pretty quick. I gotta train my ass off, if I have any hope."

"Australia, huh? Well, all the coolest things happen *down under*." Holly winked.

"Is that a euphemism?"

Holly's mouth fell open. "It's like you don't know me at all."

CHAPTER SIXTEEN

The sound of Gia's heart beat loudly in her own ears. Too loudly. Round three of the Rip Curl Pro in Australia was playing out like a bad dream of the haunting variety, where everything seemed to happen in slow motion, but you had no means to correct anything or make a difference at all—no matter how hard you fought. She felt like her board was moving through molasses out there, and the more she realized it, the further into her head she fell—the worst possible place for her to be. She felt the tension from the crowd, and knowing Elle was out there cheering her on should have carried encouragement, but it only added to the palpable pressure that closed in on her, more and more, as each second ticked by.

She saw her shot and went for it, increasing her power as she charged the wave. A big guy, too. She was up on her board, steady and strong. She turned to the left, shredding, spray on her face as she moved straight up through the lip. But her timing was off and she got caught behind the wave instead of with it and wasn't able to make the exit happen, disappearing with a mouthful of water she promptly spat out. Her leash yanked her back under and she took in another mouthful. Fuck. She pulled herself to the surface just as rescue approached. She swore loudly and waved them off, grabbing her board and swimming the hell out of there.

A one-maneuver wave wasn't going to bring the points. The clock was ticking, and she'd yet to land a decent ride. Priority ran out and she shifted her attention to her competitor, Alia Foz, who seemed on fire today. She, too, went left, though her effort was a little more drawn out, the wind edging her forward, fueling her momentum instead of detracting from it. And then, bam. She found the perfect wedge section, held her form, and found her way out easily for the perfect ending maneuver.

This wasn't good.

Gia waited, watching the clock for another shot to up her score. It never came. She set out for a final wave, but it totally fizzled before she so much as made any significant connection.

Foz ended up a solid 13.2 combined score to her even 11.

She was out.

Again.

With a solid lump in her throat, she carried her board, which felt heavier than it ever had, past reporters, fans, and friends, not saying a word to anyone. This couldn't be her new reality. It just couldn't.

She walked the distance of her hotel room and back again, trying to work through the disappointment, the humiliation. Going over each moment of the heat second by second, she came to one very upsetting conclusion: She was screwed. This was not a fluke, nor was the last tournament or the one before that.

"Hey," Elle said, entering the hotel room. "I know you must be pissed right now, but it's just a continuation of some sort of phase. You'll figure it out."

"Will I?" Gia snapped. She'd never spoken to Elle that way before, and hated that she did it now. The anger-laced adrenaline had hold of her and wasn't letting go. It wasn't Elle's fault. Except it was. Even though it wasn't.

"You will," Elle said calmly, taking a seat on the bed. "We both will. What do you think happened today?"

"Just like we suspected before. I'm forgetting why I'm here. *You're* making me forget." Whether she wanted it to or not, it sounded like an accusation.

"How is that my fault?"

"I don't know, but just give me some space, okay? I need to just feel awful about myself for a little while." Gia paced the floor, finally falling into a chair and holding her head in her hands. She couldn't believe this was happening all over again. Three tournaments in a row.

"It's not your fault," she told Elle finally, finding a modicum of equilibrium. "Not intentionally, anyway. But it's like I'm not myself anymore."

"Yeah, well, I'm not either, okay? So, what are we supposed to do now?"

"You're still *in* the tournament," Gia pointed out. "So I guess you'll surf, and I get to watch you. Maybe that's how it will always be. I can be your cheerleader."

"You sound thrilled about that."

"It wasn't exactly how I imagined my life playing out. No."

"And you resent me for that. You can just say it."

Gia shook her head. "I don't want to."

"But you're thinking it." Elle reached out her hand to touch Gia's face, but she moved quickly away.

Elle took a moment, stunned.

Gia felt awful. It had been a reflex, motivated by her hellish mood, but now it was like toothpaste you couldn't put back in the tube. She wasn't in control, and she was lashing out unfairly at Elle. "I'm sorry."

"Okay. Would you, maybe, like me to get my own room? Give you some space?"

"Whatever you want," Gia mumbled. She couldn't seem to push past it in the moment, even for Elle, which said a lot about her level of devastation.

With a singular nod, Elle began moving about the hotel room, folding clothes and layering them into her suitcase.

Gia blinked. "Wait. I don't want you to go. You shouldn't have to."

"Which is it?"

Gia sighed, at a loss. "Both. Neither. I don't know. Little out of my depth here."

Elle straightened and turned to her, the hurt apparent on her face. "I know. Me, too. But maybe it's better for both of us if we gave each other a little breathing room tonight."

"Whatever you say."

Moments later, Elle pulled her case to the door. "We can talk tomorrow. I'm really sorry about the round." And with a click of the door behind her, she was gone.

Gia felt the loss immediately. She wanted to go after Elle, tell her she'd been an ass, pull her into her arms and not let go. Yet something held her back. She was falling for Elle, and quickly. Her heart was no longer her own, and at the same time, she watched her career crumble, piece by piece, in front of her. How much deeper was she willing to let herself fall before having to throw in the towel altogether, losing her spot on the tour?

The questions haunted Gia. The uncertain future did. She had no clue which way was up.

❖

"Wakey, wakey, surf fans. This is Shoshana from Surfline coming at ya with all the updates from the Rip Curl Pro you'll ever want in my hot little hands, and let me tell you, it was a doozy from down under today. The women, as always, are keeping it interesting. Lindy Ives advances to the final round in glorious style and will meet wildcard Heather Cho. In a surprising turn of events, number one Elle Britton went down in the semis. This means, win or lose, Ives takes the yellow leader jersey from Britton, who will now reside in the number two spot. Ouch. Tough break for a fan favorite. You'll get 'em next time, Elle. In the meantime, go, Lindy! You earned that jersey!"

Elle closed her laptop, deciding to maybe stay off the surf websites for a while.

She was back stateside after the demoralizing loss in the tournament. Gia had gone home a day ahead of her. They'd kissed and talked briefly and left things on a positive note, but things felt markedly different now, and Elle didn't know how to fix it. Everything in her life was a giant question mark and she was having trouble getting her brain to focus on something as simple as making breakfast.

"You home?" a voice called from her entryway.

She popped her head around the corner and smiled widely at Christopher, happy to see a friendly face. "What? You don't knock? You think you live here now?" she asked playfully.

"I've been waiting for my key." He strolled into her house looking handsome as ever, wearing salmon-colored shorts and a trim white polo. She was fairly certain he'd gotten laid recently. "Glad you're back," he said, and kissed her cheek.

"Not exactly as victorious as I'd planned, but back all the same."

"Yeah, was sorry to hear that." He pointed at her floor. "What in the world is that thing?"

"Foam roller. For my muscles before and after training. You work out. How do you not know this? You're getting one for Christmas."

He picked up the long foam tube and examined it. "Looks sexual to me."

She shook her head. "Such a guy."

"So, how are things?"

A normal answer would have been "They're okay" or "I'm getting by." Instead she went with "I feel like my world is imploding. My relationship and my job don't seem to get along, and I'm caught in the middle and I don't have a clue what to do."

"Okay, okay," he said, moving to her and wrapping his arm around her shoulders. "Sounds like you have a lot going on in there."

"You have no idea."

"Well, let's break it down," Christopher said. "Sometimes that really helps me gain perspective. It's like crunching numbers."

"We could try," Elle said, sounding pathetic even to her own ears.

"What's the most important thing in the world to you?"

"Surfing my best. Rising to the top. It's been my lifelong dream. It was right there for, well, a few fleeting months, and now…gone. Poof."

"That sounds like it's weighing on you. And the new girlfriend? The other surfer."

"Gia."

"What about Gia?"

"She's amazing. When we're together I feel fifty times lighter, and I look forward to seeing her again and again. But we're both paying for it dearly because of the toll it's taking on our scores. It's adding a whole new layer of tension, and I hate it and have no idea what to do."

"It's a legitimate problem. There are football players who won't have sex during the playoffs because it takes them off their game. Some avoid it for the entire season."

She laughed. "I'd like to think I'm a little more complex than just that."

"But maybe not. Cut yourself some slack. It's a common problem for athletes."

She sobered, understanding it was time she faced that reality. "If that's the case, then what?" She resisted the urge to throttle something, because this was so not fair. For the first time, she was with someone she had honest-to-goodness feelings for, who she thought about constantly and planned her proverbial future around, and the matchup came with these kinds of consequences?

"I don't envy you," Christopher said.

"It's a Sophie's choice that I'm not prepared for."

His eyes carried sympathy. "What can I do to help?"

"Feel like listening? Take me out for sushi and listen to me lament my long list of problems."

He pulled his keys from his pocket. "I'll drive."

As they walked to his car, Elle's phone buzzed in her pocket. A check-in text from Gia. *You doing okay? Thinking about you. Miss you.*

While her heart fluttered pleasantly at the sight of Gia's name, her warring emotions took hold.

"You ready?" Christopher asked, car door open.

"Yeah, let's go." She hesitated, then shoved the phone, and the unanswered text message, back into her pocket.

❖

The Cat's Pajamas was closed for the evening, but Gia and her friends had gathered there anyway.

Needing someone to talk to, Gia had gone to Autumn, knowing she'd be on her own and going about her typical closing duties. Autumn in turn had called Hadley, who'd promptly texted Isabel, which brought them to this moment where they'd congregated in the shop with the darkened sign out front, all positioned around their normal breakfast table. Only at night.

"You haven't been yourself since you got back from Australia," Autumn said, gently.

Feeling under the microscope, Gia closed up, finding it hard to express all that was going on in her head. She nodded, with an uncomfortable lump in her throat.

"I know you were hoping for a better finish," Isabel said. "We all have slumps. I'm sure that's what this is. It's just a bitch is all. Whisky hit?" She pulled a flask from her bag.

Gia reached for it and a took a quick swig, passing it to Hadley, who demurred, and then back to Isabel. "Maybe. But it's more than that."

Hadley scooted her chair closer to Gia's and looped their arms. "Is everything okay with Elle?"

Gia took a deep breath, hating the fact that tears filled her eyes. She was so not a crier, especially when it came to her own issues. She usually sucked it up and dealt with it. Apparently, this time was different. Her stomach felt off and her muscles tense. Not to mention, her coping skills were at an all-time low. "We haven't talked in a couple of days. We've hit some issues, and I don't know that there's a solution."

"Why is that?" Autumn asked, quirking her head to the side.

"Elle's lost number one, I've fallen to five with no clue how to get any better except to go back to what I was doing before."

"Living the boring single life," Hadley said with a pout.

"Trust me, not what I want. But am I supposed to give up everything I've ever dreamed of? Not to mention, she's pulled away exponentially."

"Maybe you could just put it on hold, until the season plays out," Isabel said. "I'm just thinking out loud here."

Hadley shook her head firmly. "And then Elle, who it turns out is wonderful, meets someone else and gets confused about what she wants, which is Gia. Or worse, resents Gia for pulling away from her to begin with. No."

"I agree with you," Gia said. "But what's the alternative? Watch everything I've worked for evaporate?"

"Yes!" Hadley exclaimed.

Autumn held up a hand. "Gia has to do what's right for her."

She shrugged. "If only I knew how."

"You have to talk to her," Autumn said, gently. "See what she thinks."

Gia nodded and blew out a breath. "What kind of wuss am I that the concept terrifies me?"

"You're a wuss with a very big heart," Isabel said, "which is the main I reason I let you win at *Ms. Pac-Man*."

"Thanks, Iz," Gia said, ignoring that last part, because it was asinine. "I guess I should give her a call. Or should I maybe wait until tomorrow?"

"Tonight," her three friends said, in unison.

Gia stood, feeling unsteady on her feet. "Maybe one more sip." Isabel passed the flask. It was now or never. "Tonight it is."

❖

When Elle opened the door, it was close to eleven p.m. Seeing Gia standing in front of her after days apart left her breathless. Gia's hair was down and tousled from the wind. She wore jeans and a baseball T-shirt, white with navy sleeves. Elle wanted nothing more than to walk into Gia's arms and inhale the scent she'd come to love and miss. Yet their circumstances kept her rooted right where she stood.

"Hey," she said, as nonchalantly as possible, knowing their conversation would likely be anything but. Fear prickled at the back of her neck. She stepped aside. "Come in."

"Thanks." Gia smiled as she passed. But it was the way she smiled that sliced at Elle. Politely, as if they hadn't just shared a handful of amazing months together. Was this who they were now? Elle wasn't sure she could wrap her mind around this new dynamic, if she even wanted to try.

"I'm sorry it's so late," Gia said. "I just had a lot on my mind and thought maybe you did, too."

"Yeah. I do." Elle nodded and headed to the couch, her stomach tight. "Why don't we sit?"

"The fluffy couch," Gia said fondly, almost as if she were saying goodbye to it.

Elle wanted to scream. She hated all of this so much. "I just think—"

"Lately, it's seemed—"

Elle smiled at their overlap. "You go ahead."

"No, you can."

"All right." Elle took a moment to order her thoughts, to steady her heart. "I think it's safe to say that we've both been feeling the stress of competition and our lack of performance."

"Lack of performance is kind." Gia attempted a smile. It didn't fully manifest. "But yeah, that part's true."

Elle took a deep breath and just said it. "I don't want to lose you, Gia. I don't want to lose us, but if *we're* the problem, what's the solution?"

"I've been asking myself that for days."

"So I can let myself fall helplessly in love with you, which I'm confident I'll do, and—"

"Pay for it every step of the way."

"Or we can take a step back from us, before we're any further in, and try and salvage what's left of the season and beyond. I don't know about the future, but maybe we do what's right for us now."

Gia stared at the carpet, her jaw set. "Sounds like you know what you want to do."

"It's *not* what I want. I'm improvising here, and I need your help. What do you think?"

Gia didn't say anything at first, studying the hem of her jeans. She raised her gaze to Elle's, and the sadness spoke volumes. She couldn't stand to see Gia looking that way, the very same way she felt herself. "Isabel mentioned that maybe after the season, we could see where we're at. Maybe hit a pause button and focus on the tour."

Elle nodded, afraid to speak. "Maybe," she said quietly.

"But who knows where we'll be then. Who you'll have met. And honestly, why would next season be any different?"

"Right," Elle said, allowing the tears to come. Their potential future was looking bleaker and bleaker with each moment that ticked by. "So we just go back to being competitors who see each other in lobbies of hotels? That sounds awful."

The corners of Gia's mouth turned down in a helpless fashion. "I think we agree on that."

They stared at each other, the sadness palpable, overwhelming. "I guess we're doing this," Elle said, not quite believing it.

Gia stood and shoved her hands into the pocket of her jeans. "Walk me out?"

Elle took her hand, and together they walked to the entryway of the house. Once in front of the door, Gia took Elle's face in her hands, stared long and hard into her eyes, and kissed her, thoroughly. Elle stepped into the kiss, memorizing that mouth, Gia's scent, the feel of her skin, unsure how she was going to get by without these very important things in her life.

"I should go," Gia whispered, her forehead pressed to Elle's. "Goodbye, Elle."

Elle swallowed, as the tears fell. "Goodbye."

She didn't watch Gia walk down the sidewalk to her Jeep the way she so often had in the past. She couldn't do it. Instead, she closed the door to the familiar image, and to what had been a wonderful time in her life, wondering, all the while, if this might be her biggest regret.

Chapter Seventeen

O h, my goodness. We're here!" Hadley said, wide eyed. She twirled in a circle at baggage claim, and Gia looked around to see who noticed. "It feels like France, you know? The ground is French."

"It is," Gia said conservatively.

"Hello, France!" she said to the air all around her, then turned back to Gia. "And we're going to see French things, and talk to French people, and find a café and dream big dreams like they do here. I can't wait till we can see French stars in the sky."

Gia nodded, doing her best not to kill Hadley's buzz, but really not feeling it herself. "Sounds exciting, and I want you to be able to get all of that in. We'll see what kind of downtime I can come up with." Hadley had been more than generous and agreed to accompany Gia to the Roxy Pro when she'd asked. Knowing Hadley's affinity for Paris, offering to take her anywhere in the same country was a pretty sure bet. Having a friend with her would be helpful, she decided, and bolster her courage to face this tournament…and Elle.

It had been a good three weeks since they'd said their tearful goodbye in her doorway. Since then, Gia had put every waking moment she had into being a better surfer, to satisfying results. She was currently in the best shape of her life and taking on waves like Ms. Pac-Man downing pellets. She had high hopes for her chances this week, though she was less optimistic about the toll it would take on her heart.

She missed Elle. Even her crazy affinity for organization and the way she was capable of charming every person she met. She smiled thinking back on the way she'd flick her hair behind her with her hand, often smacking Gia in the face. The buzz about them in the media had died down, as they'd given them zero public interaction to scrutinize.

It was almost as if the whole thing never happened, except for the lasting impression it left on every inch of Gia's being. She longed for Elle and wondered if there would ever be a time when she was over her. Didn't seem possible.

"No, no. Don't get me wrong." Hadley said, yanking Gia back to the conversation. "We're here for surfing and so much more surfing. To surf like we've never surfed. To win it all and climb that leaderboard." Hadley grabbed her light blue suitcase with the pink heart sticker on the handle from the carousel. "And we will." A pause and another twirl. "But we're in France!"

"You guys here for the Roxy Pro?" the guy next to them asked, clearly having overheard their conversation.

"Yep." Gia nodded, keeping an eye out for her suitcase.

"My friend here is one of the best surfers in the world," Hadley said proudly. "Gia Malone. Write that down."

"Oh, yeah. I know you. I wish you all the best." He gestured to his buddy. "We're big fans of the sport. Gonna try and catch some of Elle Britton's heats."

"She's pretty great," Gia said, and attempted a smile.

She felt Hadley watching her just before Hadley sprang into action. "Hey, maybe if we moved closer, we could grab your bag sooner. C'mon."

Gia dutifully followed her friend, the conversation having plunged her into another dark depth. "You're good, you're good. Just shake that off," Hadley said, giving the side of Gia's shoulder a smack. "Did that hurt?" she asked quietly, with a squint. "I always feel like athletes like to be hit when they're pep talked, but that didn't feel right."

"I'm fine," Gia said. "You're a great coach."

"But do I need to hit?" she asked reluctantly.

"No," Gia said, and slung her arm around Hadley's shoulder. "But I see my suitcase, and then we can get the hell out of here and let you see some of the French countryside."

❖

"I'm serious about exploring the idea of a clothing line," Kip said, as they hugged goodbye.

Elle smiled. "And I told you I would consider it. Which I will. Thanks for breakfast."

"My pleasure. Any chance to get in some one-on-one with a valuable client and write off a trip to France is a win in my book."

She laughed. "Say hi to that gorgeous husband of yours."

"Will do," he said, leaving her in the lobby of the resort. "I expect a win."

"Not a problem. Trust me."

Kip headed off for the next few days of vacation, and Elle made a mental checklist of all she had to do. Meet with Bruce and wax her board, make sure that it was in tip-top shape, sponsor stickers in place. She had a media thing in an hour and her first heat the following day. She'd need a good night's sleep and—

"Hadley," she said, startled to see a familiar face from home strolling through the hotel lobby.

"Elle!" Hadley said, beaming. She pulled her into a tight hug. "How are you?" The words were casual, but the sympathetic eyes gave her away. Of course Hadley would know all about her and Gia. In fact, everything these days was a reminder, especially—

Her thought ended there, because trailing Hadley, and just feet away, stood Gia herself. Elle swallowed, caught off guard by how beautiful Gia looked, and how desperately she'd missed her.

"Hi," Gia said, with a half smile.

"Hey," Elle answered, resisting the urge to hug her, touch her, something. It was one thing to try and erase someone from your mind when they were out of sight, but with Gia standing right there in front of her, it was a losing battle. God, she looked good.

Hadley looked from Gia to Elle and thankfully took the reins. "You guys are gonna kill it this tournament. No doubt in my mind."

Elle squeezed her hand, always grateful for Hadley's positivity. She was good people. "Thanks, Hadley. I know we're both hoping to."

"It'll be weird not seeing you wear the yellow jersey," Gia said.

Elle winked. "Won't be for long."

"See ya out there," Gia said, with a smile and sliver of their old competitive banter.

Elle smiled. "Yeah. I look forward to it."

The rest of the week couldn't have gone any more according to plan if Elle had mapped out each detail herself. She sailed through the first four rounds without so much as a glance behind her. She was in top form, and everyone noticed.

"Elle, how have you recaptured that old magic to take France by storm?" Shoshana from Surfline asked, as Elle trotted in from round four with a smile on her face. "We've all missed you!"

"It's just about giving all you have to each and every turn out there. Every ride is different. I just have to keep listening to the waves. And can I just say that I love my fans? They're the best around, and I appreciate them sticking with me even through the down times."

"Doesn't look like there are too many more of those on the horizon. Not the way you're surfing."

"You're sweet to say so. Looking forward to the semis!"

"We'll be watching," Shoshana said, and offered her a high five.

When the cameras were gone, the fans all signed for, Elle returned to the locker room and gathered her belongings. She'd walked away triumphant once again, doing what she did best. Somehow the wins felt hollow, however. She knew why, of course. She just couldn't allow herself to dwell. When she learned just an hour later that she'd be going head-to-head with Gia in the tournament's semifinals, she knew she had more than a little mental prep ahead of her. Just the thought had her hands sweating, her shoulders tensing, and her heart squeezing uncomfortably.

Whoever said life was easy?

"You're going to go out there and tackle each and every wave that looks like it has possibility. No holding back for the perfect specimen. You hear me?" Hadley asked, with her serious face on.

"I hear you," Gia said. "You're scarier than Katrina with that glare."

"Yeah, well, she's not here, so you're stuck with me."

"Got it, Coach. Taking the aggressive approach, right out of the gate."

"And you're not going to worry about surfing against Elle. It's impossible for both of you to win, so take this one."

Gia softened, less emphatic about this point. "That's the plan."

When she and Elle paddled out, she was feeling less sure. But she'd laid the proper foundation and had her focus steady up until this point. There was no way she was gonna falter now.

"You okay?" Elle called from several yards away. Gia nodded and offered her the thumbs-up sign. She had priority and would be up first. She waited, letting one wave after another pass without engaging. All eyes were on her, but she just couldn't seem to make herself attack. In her peripheral she saw Elle paddle over to her.

"Hey, what's going on?"

"Just need to shake loose a little."

"Okay," Elle said, calmly. "I want you to turn your brain off, okay? This next one's yours. See it out there?"

Gia nodded.

"Good. Now take a deep breath and get ready to charge."

Gia met Elle's eyes and took on strength. She remembered herself, took that breath, and went for it.

From that point forward, the heat was a back and forth of innovation. One killer ride after another from both her and Elle, making the final margin a very tight one. In the end, Elle took the semis with four tenths of a point over Gia. One of the best damn matchups she'd seen in a while.

Didn't matter that she'd lost. It was the kind of competition, the kind of surfing Gia lived for. Would the win have been nice? Of course, but it wasn't meant to be. Elle had earned it, and there was a big part of Gia bursting with pride for her. She'd kick ass in the final, and that was the way this tournament was meant to go. A showing in the semis would still prove good for Gia's ranking, and she'd take it.

Underneath all of that, she wished she'd be there to celebrate this victory with Elle and to cheer her on in the finals. She'd do that silently, but it wasn't the same. In fact, had she hung around, maybe there wouldn't even have been a final for Elle. That was still a bitter pill to swallow.

"You put up a good fight," Hadley said, as they walked back to the resort together.

"Thanks, Had. I'm proud of the way I surfed. And of Elle."

"You know something? You're a good egg, Gia, and you deserve the world. I wish you could find a way to take it for yourself."

Gia felt that familiar ache as she ruminated on all she'd lost. "Yeah. Me, too."

CHAPTER EIGHTEEN

Two weeks later, it was a beautiful morning in Venice Beach, relatively warm and bursting with the kind of sunshine that makes a person want to stay outdoors all day. Gia had gotten in an early morning surf session when the waves were hoppin' and stopped by Pajamas late morning for a second pick-me-up. She waited in line patiently behind Larry Herman, who ordered his very specific drink and stepped down the counter.

"Caramel lattice drizzle for you, too?" Autumn asked with a wink.

"I'm gonna mix it up. How about a cappuccino, extra foam."

"My kind of girl. Any special art on that?"

"Can you do a peace sign?"

"You're insulting my talent."

Gia laughed. "I'll let you choose, then."

Moments later, Autumn delivered a cappuccino with a startlingly accurate depiction of the Pink Panther created in foam. "You continue to outdo yourself," Gia told her. But Autumn wasn't smiling proudly like usual. In fact, she was frozen in what could only be described as a pain-filled wince with one hand on her pregnant belly. Gia snapped to attention. Her stomach dropped out from beneath her. "You okay?" A pause. "Autumn, talk to me. What's going on?" She was up and standing next to Autumn in less than a second, her hands trembling.

"Not sure." She shook her head over and over. "Doesn't feel right."

"Pain?"

Autumn nodded, gripped a nearby chair for support, but didn't say anything, almost as if she couldn't.

"Okay, no panicking. Got it?" Gia said calmly, though every ounce of her wanted to climb on top of the table and scream for help. Why was her voice so calm? Shouldn't it be trembling, too? "Should I call an ambulance? I think maybe I should." She searched the counter for Steve but didn't catch his gaze.

"No," Autumn managed, shaking her head. "Can you drive me? That would probably be quicker at this point."

"Of course. Can you walk?"

"I think so. I don't know what's going on. I've never felt like this." She winced again and gripped two chairs, her face contorting in pain. Customers turned their concerned gazes in their direction.

"Take my arm," Gia ordered. She didn't know how much time they had and felt her sense of urgency triple. *Deep breaths*. She could do this. She had to do this for Autumn, for the kids. "Steve?" she called.

He whipped around and, catching sight of Autumn, practically leapt over the counter. "What's happening?" he asked.

Autumn shook her head, unable to speak.

"She's in pain. We're not sure. I'm going to drive her to the emergency room."

"Good idea. You're going to be okay," Steve said to Autumn, but the terror that crisscrossed his features said he was just as worried as Gia was. Steve and Autumn were like family, and he would do anything and everything for her.

Autumn nodded and squeezed his hand. "Watch the shop?"

"You got it. Don't give it another thought."

Steve helped Gia get Autumn to her Jeep. As she drove, Gia placed a call to Kate, who was at work. She was forced to leave a voice mail but would call again once they arrived. Still in what seemed to be crippling pain, and taking very deep breaths, Autumn called her doctor and in a shaky voice explained her symptoms.

"She says not to worry," Autumn told Gia as they drove. "She's going to meet us at the hospital. But I feel like something is *really* wrong. It's not just the pain, G. It's instinct. The babies are in trouble. I can feel it."

Those words were enough. Autumn had always been intuitive, and when it came to her children, that intuition would only be magnified.

Gia pressed the gas and got them there in half the time, dodging cars and taking every shortcut she knew. All the while her heart thudded away in her chest. Her breathing came in shallow spurts. Regardless, she would stay calm. She had to.

Once they arrived, a nurse took over and ushered them to an exam room. With the professionals there, she could breathe a small sigh of relief. It was fleeting, however, as she remembered there was still a larger problem. Nothing could happen to these babies or to Autumn. Not sure what to do with herself, she decided to walk to rid herself of the extra energy, which she did in the hallway while Autumn was examined. Now feeling nauseous, she texted her friends. They had a right to know. She would want to.

Then she waited.

The seconds ticked by like hours, and with each one that passed, Gia was just certain the prognosis was grim. Just as Autumn's had, her gut told her something was very wrong.

She had to prepare for that. They all did.

❖

"Why am I never a match for the giant ones?" Holly asked, swimming back to Elle, dragging her board behind her. They'd been out in the water for a couple of hours now, having taken the Jet Ski to catch some bigger action. "I watch you practically dance across those monster waves, making it look so easy. When I try it, I get smashed to pieces and left sucking water."

Elle flashed her a smile, her hands resting on top of her board. "That's why I'm a pro. I spend hours and hours practicing in order to make it look easy. All part of my scheme."

"Nope. You've always been a prodigy and I've always been a hobbyist. Just how things are, Wave Weasel."

Elle laughed, because the comment mirrored the lightheartedness of their entire morning together. "If you're asking my advice, and I'm not sure you are, it's because you chicken out at the last minute and it shows all over your stance. You edge away from the action."

"Are you saying I cower in fear?" Holly splashed her.

Elle blinked to clear her vision, and splashed her back even harder. "I would never say that."

"Fiction. I can read between the perfectly crafted Elle Britton PR routine. All right, so the next big one? I'm on it, and I will hold my ground, and my stance, and stick to that wave like we're in long-lost love."

"Don't think too much, and don't back down, whatever you do. You're a great surfer, Hol, but you're in your head a lot."

"Good point. No thinking. Got it." She paused and watched the horizon and her incoming options. "Okay, here comes a big guy. What do you think?"

"Nope. Let that one go. It's going to fizzle early. Watch the edges. You can tell."

"I'll just rely on your inarguable instinct."

They stared off at the incoming waves, until a solid, sturdy one headed their way. "That's the one. You ready?"

"Ready."

"Fearless?" Elle asked.

"Check." With a funny little salute, Holly was off and paddling like a maniac as Elle called after her, egging her on.

"You got this, Hol! Take your time. No rush to stand. There ya go! Yeah! Killing it!"

It was gorgeous, the turn Holly took right off the bat. Nothing tentative about her. She found the barrel and sailed right through it with the most perfect of S-curves. But she didn't quite make it out in time and the wave, a monster one too, came right over the top of her. Elle winced, knowing how those things could take the wind right out of you. Silence hit. She swam closer, waiting for Holly to surface. It was getting to be lunchtime, and maybe a wipeout like that was the perfect time to call it a day. Though the first part of that ride had been beautiful, and she was ready to let Holly know.

Elle scanned the water for her friend. Nothing yet. She swam farther out, popping up in the water for a better vantage point, and so she'd be sure to spot Holly right away. But still no sign. Weird. She was starting to get nervous. Her blood pressure edged up and her heart rate escalated the way it did when something felt off. Where in the world was Holly? She unleashed herself from her board and dipped under the water, but saw no sign of her. "Holly?" she yelled, once she surfaced. Nothing. Under again, swimming farther and farther down, until she needed air. "Hol?" She blinked the salt water out of her eyes, ignoring the sting. This couldn't be happening. She scanned the horizon, but the nearest people were out of earshot. Down again, this time farther out. She saw movement to her left and followed it. As she approached a small reef, there was Holly tethered to it by her leash, which had apparently gotten caught. Holly blinked at her in terror as she approached. Elle had to think fast. Holly was still conscious, thank God, but she wouldn't have long. Elle reached for the safety latch to release Holly from the leash altogether, but the current made it nearly impossible to open. Damn it. She didn't have time for this. The clock seemed to tick away at exponential speed. The other end of the leash was jammed around a rock. She tried again, screaming inside her head, her adrenaline pulsing. She wasn't going to let this happen, but without air herself, she was no good to either of them. Her lungs were throbbing painfully, stretched to their limit.

Calling on her muscles to move her as fast as possible, she raced for the surface, fully aware of her enemy, the ticking clock. With a deep inhale, she headed back, more determined than ever. Holly's eyes had fluttered closed when she returned to her, which meant time was running out.

The scenario was a nightmare come true, but she wasn't about to let it end that way. She could not, would not, lose Holly. Not on her watch. Impossible.

She tugged the leash, wishing to God she'd carried a knife that morning, as she'd been known to do in the past when they'd gone out so far alone. She pulled, and yanked, and wrestled the leash, expending all of her strength. Though she couldn't break the material of the leash itself, she was able to move the latch to the other side of Holly's ankle, giving her better leverage to negotiate the release.

She gave it a final tug, the last of her energy, and to her surprise, it opened. Thank God. But they still had to make it to the surface, and getting them both there when her levels were depleted would be a feat. Elle couldn't think about it. She ignored the pain in her chest, the numbness in her limbs, and fought with everything she had to return with Holly to the surface. She looked upward as she swam, focusing on the goal, the sunshine that guided her way. This couldn't be the end. If Holly wasn't okay, she'd never forgive herself.

She hoped with everything she had that it wasn't too late.

❖

"The pain can luckily be attributed to Braxton Hicks contractions," Kate calmly explained to Gia, Hadley, and Isabel, who'd gathered in the hospital waiting room, bonded together like one friendship unit. Autumn's doctor had arrived and assessed the situation while they'd waited patiently to hear. They each had their own unique way of dealing with stress, though it was so much more comforting to do it together. Isabel talked nonstop at a high rate of speed, Hadley offered only positive words of encouragement coupled with the occasional uplifting metaphor, and Gia walked incessantly, needing to release extra energy. To each her own.

"What are Braxton Hicks contractions?" Isabel asked with a worried squint.

"They're basically false labor pains that can hurt just as much."

"Oh, no," Hadley said. "Poor Autumn, having to go through all of that before any actual labor begins. That doesn't seem fair."

"But that's good, right?" Gia asked. "That means nothing's wrong with the twins or Autumn?"

"That part is good," Kate said. "But unfortunately, Autumn's blood pressure has bottomed out, which has the doctor very concerned."

"Fuck," Isabel whispered, shoving her hands into her back pockets. "What can that do?"

Kate exhaled slowly, which told Gia that she was doing her best to hold it together. But when Gia looked further, she could see that Kate's hands were shaking, a sure sign that, internally, she was a wreck. Her eyes fluttered closed briefly and she swallowed before continuing. "Apparently the danger for Autumn is high. If her blood pressure gets any lower, we're looking at the potential for organ damage or a heart attack. For the twins, it could decrease their blood flow."

"What's the plan?" Gia asked, wanting the doctors to solve this problem before those awful consequences were even possibilities.

"They're going to treat her BP and keep her overnight for monitoring. We don't want to deliver the babies at this point, at only thirty-two weeks, but the doctors say it's something we'll have to consider if Autumn's life is at risk."

"Oh, no," Hadley said, hugging herself.

"It's going to be fine," Isabel said, putting her arms around Hadley. "The doctors know what they're doing."

Gia nodded, needing to believe that. "Yep. They do. By tomorrow, that blood pressure will be much more in range." There was an old saying, *fake it till you make it*, and Gia planned to apply that adage here. Everything would be just fine. She would cling to that until told differently.

Kate nodded, worry now creasing her face. "Autumn's asleep right now. But I can call you guys if anything changes."

"Thanks, Kate," Gia said, and gave her pal a hug, as did Hadley and Isabel. But when Kate disappeared down the hall again, nobody made the move to leave. They looked at one another.

"I don't think I can just go home," Hadley said, finally. "Not until I know more."

Isabel returned to her original chair in the waiting area and took a seat. "Me neither."

"Then we're all in agreement," Gia said. "Let's order in some food. Could be a long night."

When she reflected on it, staying wasn't even a question in their minds, really. Gia understood that her friend was in trouble, and it wasn't an option for her to go about her day as if that weren't the case. With her shoulder, she nudged Hadley, who nudged her back. Isabel smiled over at them. She would sit here with Hadley and Isabel, and they would be there…just to be there.

It's what friends did.

❖

Two hours later, after a round of Chinese delivery, the three of them recessed to the quiet of their own thoughts and keeping-busy tasks. Hadley read a mystery novel. Isabel tick-tacked away on her laptop, most likely writing something brilliant, and Gia kept herself occupied on her phone. She returned some email, looked over her most recent stats, and headed over to Surfline.com to catch up on the latest round of projections and interviews with her competitors and colleagues. She didn't get very far. The headline, splashed big and bold across the top of her screen, brought the world to a stop. She slid to the edge of her chair and blinked hard to be sure she'd read it correctly.

Elle Britton Rushed to Hospital in Ambulance from Hermosa Beach

She stood up and reread the headline. It didn't fully compute until it did, and she couldn't find her breath. She opened her mouth to tell her friends, but the words failed her. She closed it again.

"G, what's wrong?" Hadley asked, looking alarmed.

Isabel stood up next to Gia. "Hey, you're white as a sheet. Paler than me. Say something."

She thrust the phone at them. "I think something bad happened," she finally choked out.

Hadley took the phone as Isabel peered over her shoulder at the headline. Gia felt their sympathetic stares turn to her, but all she could concentrate on was the fact that the floor felt uneven and the air had disappeared. Or maybe her throat had constricted. She looked around for help, but what help would there be? "It doesn't say much other than there was a surfing accident, and an ambulance on scene that left with lights and sirens," Hadley told them.

"Does it say where they took her?" Gia asked, attempting to establish logical thought progression.

"She could be here," Hadley offered.

"What do I do? How do I find out?" Gia asked. Her brain wasn't hers. She needed guidance. She needed information. She needed Elle. God, hadn't she always?

Isabel leapt into action. "Let's do this. Had, stay here in case there's word about Autumn. Text me if there's anything. I'll walk with Gia to the admissions desk and see what we can find out."

"Okay, but let me know," Hadley said. "I'm just going to be sitting here worried."

"Will do."

Gia followed Isabel down the hall like a lost child following a dependable adult. Her hands were numb, and her thoughts jumped from one awful conclusion to another, never settling for long. She flashed on happier images, too. Of Elle, her face when she smiled, her fist curled beneath her chin as she slept. If anything happened to her, Gia wouldn't recover. There would be no point. If she was hurt, Gia wasn't sure how she'd cope. The idea alone had her feeling nauseous. She wanted to trade places with her, to do something to erase whatever horrible thing had happened and take it on herself. God, what in the world had happened out there anyway?

"Hi," Isabel said, to the woman at the circular desk in the lobby of the hospital. "Hoping you can help us. We were told our friend had been brought in following a surfing accident."

The woman nodded, as if confirming the information, but offered nothing further.

"Can you tell us where we'd find her?"

"Relationship?"

"I'm a close friend."

The woman sighed, as if Isabel had just lost the grand prize on an all-important game show. "I'm afraid I'm not authorized to release that information."

"But her sister is here, too," Isabel said quickly, and grabbed Gia, dragging her front and center. "Right here. Certainly that rule doesn't apply to family."

"You're the sister?" the woman asked, clearly skeptical.

"Yes. I'm the sister. Can you tell me how she is?"

"All I know is that particular patient is in intensive care on the fourth floor. They can tell you more about her condition there."

Gia's heart fell further. Intensive care? She looked to Isabel, who squeezed her hand.

"It's gonna be okay. It will. You need to be strong right now. Can you do that?"

Gia nodded, but didn't believe it for a moment.

By the time they arrived on the fourth floor, Gia was a basket case, watching her entire journey with Elle play back in her mind like a cherished home movie. This couldn't be the end. They'd barely even had a beginning.

"Hi," Isabel said to the woman behind the nurse's station. "We're looking for my friend's sister, Elle Britton. She was brought in a short time ago."

The nurse squinted back at Isabel. "One moment." After a quick perusal of her screen, she came back to them. "No patient by that name."

"Are you sure?" Gia asked.

"Positive."

"Maybe they have her listed under another name for privacy," Gia offered. "Is that possible?"

"Not that I'm aware of."

"She was in a surfing accident," Isabel said.

"Oh! Well, why didn't you say so?" The nurse pointed with her chin down the hall. "Four-eleven."

Isabel tapped on the counter. "Thank you." She headed off in the direction the nurse indicated, but turned back when she realized Gia was not with her. "You coming?" Isabel asked gently.

But Gia couldn't move. Nope. In this moment, as far as Gia knew, Elle was going to be okay. If she walked down that hall and learned the reality of the situation, that might no longer be the case. She just needed to hang on to *this* moment for a beat longer. It was all she had.

Isabel returned to her. "Whatever we're facing, I'm right here with you. Look at me. Not going anywhere."

Gia nodded and accepted Isabel's offered hand. With each step toward room 411, Gia's fear catapulted. Tears pooled in her eyes, and her stomach dropped out from beneath her.

"Gia?"

She knew that voice as intimately as her own. She turned around. Was she hallucinating? The image was too beautiful to be real. Too wonderful, which meant her mind was playing tricks on her. She was afraid to believe what was right there. Elle walked toward them, wearing a pair of scrubs, a curious look on her face. Her hair was damp and her eyes were red. "What are you guys doing here?"

It took Gia a moment to speak. She was too overcome with emotion. Before she knew it, she was moving to Elle and pulling her into a crushing hug, which Elle slowly returned. Gia heard the sounds then and realized they came from her. She was sobbing, unable hold back the flood of emotion a moment longer. She gripped the back of Elle's scrubs and held on, crying into the crook of her neck. "Are you okay?" she sobbed, pulling Elle in tighter, inhaling her scent.

"Hey, hey, hey," Elle whispered to her. She stepped back and took Gia's face in her hands. "Look at me. I'm okay. See? I promise."

"I thought you were badly hurt. I thought maybe it was worse than that." Gia began to cry again, this time from relief as the understanding that Elle was all right slowly crept in.

"Shhh," Elle said, steadying her by the shoulders. "I'm right here, and not going anywhere. Please don't cry." With her thumbs, Elle gently swept away the tears on Gia's cheeks. "I can't stand to see you cry."

Gia nodded, slowly finding her footing. She took a deep breath and found her still-shaky voice. "I still don't understand. What happened?"

The reassuring smile on Elle's face dimmed, a clue that everything wasn't okay. "It's Holly. We were surfing and took the Jet Ski quite a way out. She wiped out pretty hard and her leash got caught on a reef. She was under for too long."

"Oh, God. Is she okay?" Gia asked, glancing behind her at room 411.

"She has to be," Elle said with determination, tears appearing in her eyes this time. "But they're not sure of the extent of the damage. She lost consciousness and her brain was deprived of oxygen. They have her sedated and on a ventilator until they can run more tests. Figure out if there's any cognitive impairment. An MRI will tell us more. I just…" She shook her head, looking lost. "I don't know what to do."

"You were there?" Isabel asked gently.

Elle nodded. "It was like an awful dream. I pulled her out as fast as I could, but it took a while to get the damn leash free. I did CPR until she sputtered and threw up a bunch of water while some guys on the beach called nine-one-one."

"I can't even imagine," Gia said. It was a nightmare scenario. Something they all looked out for and feared.

"The ambulance came, and they've had her on oxygen ever since. She was in and out on the ride to the hospital, but never said anything. I'm not sure she could." She shifted her focus between Gia and Isabel, her eyes a little wild with fear. "The doctors are worried about something called brain hypoxia. The damage could be extensive or none at all." She shrugged helplessly as the tears fell. "We just don't know yet."

Isabel took Elle's hand. "Your friend sounds strong."

"She is. She always has been." Elle seemed to seize on this notion like a much-needed lifeline.

"Remember that. She's gonna fight this."

Elle nodded. "Thanks, Isabel. I called her parents in North Carolina. They're hopping a flight but won't be here until tomorrow. Dash is in with her now. So I guess I'm just waiting."

"We're just waiting," Gia corrected. She needed Elle to know that she wasn't alone in this. She didn't plan on going anywhere.

Isabel looked from Gia to Elle. "I'm gonna check on Autumn. Give you guys some space. I'll check in a little later."

Gia nodded. "Thanks, Iz. I mean it. Please keep me updated. I'll be down to check in in a little while."

Isabel nodded. "I'll check in on you soon, too."

When they were alone, Elle turned to Gia. "What is she referencing? Is Autumn here?"

"Admitted downstairs for false contractions and low blood pressure. They're keeping her overnight. That was horrific scare number one."

"Really?" Elle shook her head. "I can't believe all of this happened in one day." She reached for Gia's hand. "I'm sorry you were worried about me on top of everything, but I would be lying if I said that I wasn't happy that you're here. It helps so much just to see your face right now."

"I'm glad." Gia inhaled deeply, still feeling shaky and off-kilter from the shock. It was awful that Holly was hurt, but knowing Elle was okay was the only thing holding her together. She turned to Elle with forceful purpose. "Listen, you gotta stay safe, okay? Always. No matter what the cost. No getting hurt, because that?" She shook her head and placed a hand over her still delicate heart. "I can't take."

Elle smiled and touched Gia's cheek softly. "I will do my very best."

"No, not good enough. I'm serious. I don't know what I would do if something happened to you, logistics of the word aside. You're too important."

Elle softened. "I feel the same way. I get it."

"Do you?" Gia said, unrelenting.

Elle took her hand. "I do."

Maybe it was because they were alone in the hallway and her emotions hung so plainly on her sleeve, but Gia couldn't stop herself from taking Elle's face in her hands and kissing her. In her current reality, restraining herself was not an option. Not on a day like today, and what point would that serve anyway? For one moment in time, her career could kick rocks. Elle was what mattered. She had Gia's focus, and through that kiss, she made a point to channel every iota of feeling she had for Elle, which was staggering. Elle didn't stop her, didn't pull away or merely accept the kiss. In fact, she kissed her back with the same urgency and cradled the back of her head.

"God, I miss you," Elle whispered into her hair, which prompted Gia to hold her tighter, never wanting to let go. But underneath, she knew their circumstances hadn't changed. This was about raw and honest emotion, what they felt for each other, and her feelings for Elle hadn't wavered. In fact, she loved her. She knew that as true as what day it was.

"I miss you, too," she whispered. "I keep thinking it's going to get easier." Gia pulled back and lifted Elle's chin. "Listen to me. Holly's going to be okay. I can feel it."

Elle offered a wobbly smile. "Thank you for saying that. I think it's going to be a long night."

"We'll get through it together," Gia said, and wrapped an arm around Elle as the routine sounds of the hospital continued around them.

"You're really going to stay?"

"Would you if it were me?"

"Without hesitation," Elle said.

"Exactly," Gia said, kissing the top of Elle's head. "I've got you. You're not alone."

The rest of the evening was quiet. Elle was allowed ten minutes every hour to visit Holly, which she shared with Dash, who mainly stared at the wall and flipped through magazines. Gia stayed close, offering Elle her hand to hold, and made a point to keep their supply of coffee and snacks intact. Somehow having a job made her feel useful. She walked down to check on Autumn every hour or so as well. Isabel and Hadley were adorably snuggled into each other like kittens at her three a.m. check-in.

"I can't believe you guys stayed," Kate said, standing in the entryway of the waiting room. She'd spent most of the night at Autumn's side but looked in on them occasionally. "You didn't have to do that."

"Yes, we did," Gia said, quietly so as not to wake the others.

Kate smiled. "I guess you did. You guys are such great friends. Truly."

"Any updates?"

She nodded. "The medication seems to be having a positive effect. Autumn's blood pressure is up a bit. Everyone says this a great sign. We'll likely go home mid-morning, once the doctor weighs in."

Gia grinned and placed a hand over her heart. "Best news ever."

"And Elle's friend? How is she?"

"Hard to say. She's still sedated and the doctor won't be by until morning. Elle's a wreck."

"I can relate. Tell her we're thinking about her."

"Will do. Thanks, Kate."

When nine a.m. hit and there was no word from Holly's doctor, Elle turned to Gia. "If I had only been a little faster."

"Could you have been?" Gia asked the question not because she was curious, but to make a point.

Elle thought on it and finally shook her head. "I don't think so."

"Me neither. And if it had been anyone else out there with her when this awful accident happened, she likely wouldn't be here anymore. She was so lucky you were the one there."

"Yeah," she said, with only slight commitment.

"I'm serious. With your swimming skills, your knowledge of the equipment, and your speed? She won the rescuer lottery."

"I hadn't actually thought of it that way." Elle seemed to ruminate on the comment before going quiet again. She still wore the scrubs the hospital had supplied her, but she now also wore Gia's maroon hoodie because the waiting room was cold. Elle had snuggled into it almost immediately after Gia offered it, as if the simple garment were a valuable security blanket, her hands disappearing beneath the sleeves.

"You should keep that," Gia told her hours later.

"Thank you," Elle said, snuggling into it further. "If it's okay with you, I would like that."

The automatic doors that separated intensive care from the waiting room opened just before ten, and a male doctor with an iPad emerged. "For Holly Sinclair?"

Elle and Dash, who had just briefly fallen asleep, sat upright. "Over here," Elle said.

The doctor took a seat in the chair across from them and offered a warm smile. That had to be a decent sign, right? "I'm Dr. Kulka. I believe we met briefly yesterday. Let me tell you where we're at." They nodded and sat forward. Elle squeezed Gia's hand extra tight as the doctor turned the iPad around to show them the images from the MRI. "This is all looking very promising. I'm not seeing any of the standard warning signs on the gray matter structures of the brain. Everything is actually looking quite clear on the scan. Because of that, I'm not anticipating any long-lasting effects from the accident." Elle exhaled in relief. Dash smiled widely and began nodding. "Though it's possible Ms. Sinclair could experience some minor difficulties."

"What kind?" Dash asked. He and Elle exchanged a glance.

"For a while, there may be some short-term memory obstacles, but those will most likely resolve themselves over the next month or two. She'll also need to continue respiratory therapy to get her lungs back in shape. In fact, we'll have a therapist with her as early as today to get started."

Elle and Dash exchanged a hug. "We can deal with those things," Dash said.

Dr. Kulka nodded. "The nurse will have more information for you, but I'm optimistic, given the test results. She was very lucky. We'll keep her another night or so to be sure we're in good shape, and then send her home with you." He turned to Elle. "You were the one who pulled her from the water?"

"Yes."

"Your CPR training prevented severe damage and likely saved her life entirely. Without it, we would be having a very different conversation right now. You did a good thing."

Elle nodded, emotion clearly constricting her throat. Finally, she managed a "Thank you. I'm just glad to hear she's going to be all right."

Gia hoped Elle finally understood how heroic her actions were. She was grateful the doctor took the time to say so.

"When will she wake up?" Dash asked.

"Anytime now," Dr. Kulka said, and shook all their hands.

He was right. An hour and a half later, a very groggy Holly opened her eyes. Dash and Elle stood at her bedside. Gia watched from a cautious distance away at the door. They gave her a minute to orient herself.

"Hey, Weasel," Holly said in a raspy voice.

The sound of Holly's voice brought with it a wave of comfort. "Hey, yourself," Elle said, holding her hand. She brushed the happy tears from her cheeks. "Dash is here, too."

"Hi, sweetheart," he said. "You don't know how good it is to see you."

Holly nodded but didn't say anything further after that, her droopy eyes closing once again. But she was breathing on her own, and awake, and speaking, which felt like a big step forward. With a positive prognosis, Gia was feeling hopeful, amazed that they'd made it through this night unscathed. She gestured behind her to silently communicate to Elle that she was off to check on Autumn. Elle smiled and mouthed the words "Thank you," and blew her a final kiss. Things were going to be okay on the Holly front.

She found Isabel, Hadley, and Kate all gathered around a smiling Autumn sitting on the edge of her hospital bed. The image was like a much-needed breath of fresh air.

"Check this out! You're looking much better than the last time I saw you," Gia said, grinning from the doorway.

"Gia-Pet! I'm sorry if I scared you yesterday," Autumn said. "I'm so grateful for all you did."

Gia shrugged, embarrassed to have the spotlight shift to her. "No big deal."

"It is, too," Kate said. "We're incredibly grateful."

"And she's getting sprung in a matter of minutes!" Hadley said, radiating the kind of sunshine they all needed. Her exuberance pulled a laugh from the room.

Isabel sat on the bed next to Autumn and bounced. "That's right. Fucking free as a bird. Well, for at least a few more weeks."

Autumn grinned. "I feel like we dodged a bullet. Oh! And how's Holly?"

"Awake and going to be okay."

Hadley leapt up. "That's fantastic. This is a huge day and we can't let it go unnoticed. I feel like we have to celebrate." An idea seemed to occur to her and she beamed. "Later, I'm bringing you all ice cream! Meet me in the center of the complex at two this afternoon. Forget it," she said, gaining momentum. Her smile tripled. "Not just ice cream, I'm bringing *toppings*, too!"

"Whoa," Isabel said. "Toppings? That's quite an offer."

"Nothing will keep us away," Autumn said happily. "Thanks, Had."

Isabel turned to Gia and Hadley. "You guys ready to head out? Let these folks get discharged in peace?"

Gia nodded. "Just need a moment to say goodbye to Elle. You two can go ahead." She kissed Autumn's cheek. "I'm so glad you and the babies are okay."

"Thanks, Gia. See you at home soon."

She waved to her friends and headed to the fourth floor. Gia found Elle in the hallway when she returned, appearing more relaxed now, which made perfect sense. She reached out and tugged on Gia's sleeve, drawing her closer. "You're about to leave me, aren't you?"

Gia nodded. "Autumn's being discharged, and Holly's on the mend. Everyone seems to be doing okay."

"I'm so glad," Elle said. She placed a hand over her heart. "Thank you, Gia, for being here for me, staying with me last night. I can't imagine what it would have been like without you here. It means…a lot to me that you were."

Gia nodded, not sure what else to say. It was almost like the spell had been lifted. Without the drama of the past twelve hours to hold them together, they were left in the very same spot as before. She didn't want to leave Elle, but she knew that it was the mature thing to do. "I guess we go back to our status as acquaintances now."

"Tour mates," Elle said, flatly.

A long pause hit, anything to delay Gia saying goodbye. They'd felt like *them* in these desperate hours, and she didn't want to let go. She studied Elle's features, her blue eyes, that mouth that communicated so much with a smile or grimace. The way it felt against Gia's. She blinked against the ache. "I guess it's been good for you, though. You're back at number one."

Elle smiled, but her eyes carried regret. "You're climbing your way up the board yourself."

"Yeah." They nodded and stared and steadied themselves against the blanket of sadness that fell over them. She met Elle's eyes and touched her face gently. "Take care, Elle. I'll see you in Honolulu. Final stop of the season."

Elle leaned into the touch and closed her eyes briefly, as if to hold it in for just a little while longer. "I'll see you there."

"Tell Holly I'll be thinking about her."

"Of course."

Gia could feel Elle's gaze on her as she headed down the hallway, which made sense because their connection hadn't dimmed. While more than anything she was grateful for Elle's safety, her well-being, underneath it all, she carried regret about the way things stood between them. The familiar lump in her throat presented itself as she made her way to the front of the hospital. It didn't seem fair that, at long last, she'd found someone who'd grabbed hold of her heart so fiercely, and it was the one person she couldn't have.

Suck it up, she told herself, doing her best to remember the bigger picture.

Champions didn't wallow in their feelings.

CHAPTER NINETEEN

N o one said this ice cream gathering was a theme party," Gia said, surveying Hadley, who was dressed, as best she could characterize it, as a cow who walked upright.

"It's not technically a theme gathering," Hadley said. "I have a Beach Blanket Bingo party on tap for next week, but I couldn't resist adding to the festivities a little today."

Gia nodded stoically. "Right. As a cow."

"Cows make milk, G. And milk is used to make—"

"Ice cream," Gia finished.

"Now you're with me!" Hadley fluttered away, tail swaying, to make sure no one needed any extra hot fudge.

Their friends were gathered outdoors around the couches in the center of the complex, making sundaes from the vast buffet Hadley had assembled on the coffee table. She was happy to see that Taylor and Kate had joined them, as had Barney and their surliest neighbor, the heavy-eyelinered Stephanie, who only emerged from her apartment for free food and disparaging remarks in a monotone delivery. Oh, and of course, Larry Herman was there, never one to miss an event thrown by his beloved Hadley. Apparently, Gia was the last to arrive. She made herself a mint chocolate chip bowl smothered in Oreo crumbles, perfect for the warmer weather that had blown in with the summer, and joined Isabel on the couch.

"Whoa. You've made the most colossal sundae I've ever seen," Gia said, taking in Isabel's towering bowl of ice cream, covered entirely with large pieces of candy of all varieties.

Isabel pointed with her spoon. "I don't mess around when it comes to food. It's too important. How'd things go at the hospital?"

"With Elle? As good as can be expected."

"It was cool of you to stay with her."

"Thanks, Iz. Wasn't as easy a decision to leave her there, though."

A pause. Isabel opened her mouth and then closed it.

"Were you about to say something?" Gia asked, squinting.

"I don't know if you want me to."

"Well, now it's out there. You have to."

"What's out there?" Hadley asked, trotting over in her ridiculous getup. "Autumn, what are they talking about without me?"

Autumn, who sat on the couch across from Gia with Kate, didn't miss a beat. "Pretty sure Isabel is about to get real, real honest with Gia over there. Gia looks curious. Taylor looks concerned. She's probably thinking Iz should throttle back."

As if on cue, Taylor leaned in to Isabel's ear. "You sure you want to do this?"

"No," Isabel answered loudly. "But if I'm the one who got her into this mess, I should at least be ballsy enough to try and get her out of it."

"You go, little pale girl," Stephanie said, with zero inflection, as she slowly walked past.

Gia exhaled. "I'm ready, Iz. Go."

"I get that jobs are important. Hell, I almost ruined my entire relationship over one. But at the end of the day, you don't grow old with your job. You don't kiss it good morning. It doesn't hold your hand when your friend is sick in the hospital. So, I guess what I'm saying is…fuck surfing."

"Language," Larry Herman mumbled between bites of caramel fudge ripple.

"I can't temper it, Herman," Isabel bit out, "because this is my friend's future we're talking about."

"Fuck surfing, huh?" Gia said. "How is it that easy? It's my entire life."

"Didn't look like it yesterday," Hadley offered quietly, and went meekly back to her ice cream. That one hit a nerve. Because no, all that had mattered to her in the world twenty-four hours ago was Elle, and that she was okay. When she left her at that hospital, all she wanted to do was run back to be by her side. But no, it wasn't that easy. She had a whole life to consider and all the time, energy, blood, sweat, and tears, and that wasn't even taking into account what Elle had on the line, too.

"It's a nice thought, and trust me, I'd love to buy into the happy fairy tale, too, because that would make everything so much easier.

But, listen, there are real-world logistics at play. I can't just throw away everything I've dreamed of because my emotions got in the way."

Hadley intervened, playing mediator as she so often did. "It's okay, G. We all just want to see you happy. That's the only reason we check in on you."

She nodded, letting her blood pressure simmer. "I know."

"And nobody faults you for following your dream," Autumn said.

Isabel opened her mouth and, with one look from Taylor, seemed to think better of it. "Agreed," she said finally.

"Great! We should probably have more ice cream," Hadley said, clapping once and scrambling to get them back on track. "Larry, what can I get you for round two?"

"I'll stick with vanilla," he said, straightening, as if having been called on in class.

"How 'bout some caramel lattice drizzled on that?" Autumn asked with a knowing wink. That seemed to perk him up.

As the group chatter took over and the afternoon blossomed into laughs and their typical fun-loving antics, Gia found herself unable to fully engage. When everyone agreed to head to the beach to watch the sunset, she opted out altogether.

"I think I'm gonna hang back," she said, trying to appear casual.

"You sure?" Hadley asked. She studied Gia with sympathy, which just made the whole thing feel worse.

"Yep. I need some downtime."

"Okay," Had said reluctantly, and caught up with the others.

Gia didn't sleep well that night.

Or the night after.

Too many emotions that she didn't know what to do with swirled and circled endlessly. She attempted to take it out on her board and spent the third morning surfing. Not just any surfing, either, angry surfing that released a great deal of that pent-up energy she hadn't been able to shake for days. By the end of the marathon session, she was raw, exhausted, and spent. With literally nothing left to give, she stared up at the clouds that moved quickly across the sky, signaling an impending storm. Something important was brewing in her, too.

She dragged her board back to her Jeep and fastened it to the rack.

The drops fell about that time, but she welcomed them. Feeling more than a little sliced in half, she trudged back out to the sand and took a seat as the drizzle evolved into a downpour. She watched as stragglers raced to their cars, but Gia didn't move. For the first time, she allowed herself to be open to what the universe had in store for her. As the rain fell in a blinding onslaught, and the wind whipped past, and the waves crashed, for the first time, she admitted to herself what was most important. Scary? Hell yeah. But it was the most honest moment of her entire life.

"Fuck surfing," she mumbled, and a smile crept onto her face. Then and there, she understood. She wasn't the same person as she was six months ago, so why would she expect her priorities to be the same? Honestly, how could they be? She loved surfing with all her heart, yes, but taking control of her life and living it with Elle didn't mean she had to give it up entirely. She stood up and stared into the tumultuous ocean, recognizing the parallel in herself as of late. She laughed. No more.

In the scheme of things, did it really matter if she dropped a tournament here or there if she was in love and happy? So she'd be number six or seven instead of number one or two. She was ranked seven just a year and a half ago and had been pretty thrilled about it at the time.

She ran a hand through her drenched hair. She could have Elle and still surf. It would just take some readjusting in her head. Gia squinted happily through the pouring rain and kicked a puddle with renewed energy. And what was more? Maybe, over time, she and Elle would figure out how to be together and still surf their best. Crazier things had happened in life, and wasn't it worth the risk? Wasn't Elle?

"Hell, yeah," Gia said to the empty beach, reaffirmed and ready.

She had her path.

❖

Elle watched the storm on the beach not far from her back door. The sky had gone dark and swallowed up most of the morning's light altogether. The beach was desolate, and she'd given up her morning workout entirely as a result of the unexpected storm.

"She's doing much better," Elle told her mother as she watched the rain.

"Fantastic to hear. And her strength?"

"We took a short walk last night. I think it's slowly returning. Don't want to rush it, though."

"I'm glad you're there with her. She's lucky."

"Thanks," Elle said, taking a sip of the vanilla coffee she'd brewed. She closed her eyes and the liquid warmed her throat. A loud clap of thunder struck, shaking the house.

"And how are you?" her mother asked.

"I'm okay."

A pause on the other end of the line. "That doesn't sound convincing at all."

"Well, I have a feeling you don't want to hear the reality of my situation. I thought I'd spare you."

Her mother's voice was softer, warmer when she replied. "I don't want anything softened when it comes to you. What's got you down? Is it the breakup with Gia?"

The walls came tumbling down. "She came to the hospital. She was so wonderful, Mom, and life without her is just not the same. It feels pointless."

"I've been thinking," her mother said. "And just let me get this out before you say anything."

"Okay." Elle traced the drops of water on the window as she listened.

"I'm not proud of the way we handled your relationship with Gia."

Elle perked up, intrigued now. Was this really happening? She stood and crossed to the center of her living room, pleasantly surprised by what she was hearing. But to honor her mother's wishes, she didn't interrupt.

"You have a plan on how you'll react to any given situation that involves your children, until you're in the middle of it and lose your way. I feel like that's what happened when I found out you were dating a woman. I let my alarm take over, and, Elle, that's not how I feel at all. I'm not alarmed."

"You're not?"

"No." Her mother sighed into the phone. "I just needed a moment to find my bearings. All I've ever wanted is for you to be happy. If you find that happiness with a woman, then I'll be nothing but thrilled for you."

Elle gripped the phone tightly, closed her eyes, and allowed the tears that threatened to fall fully. She swallowed back the emotion. "Does Dad feel the same?" Elle asked, her heart in her stomach.

"He does. We've talked in depth on the issue, and we're both ashamed of how we behaved in Portugal. I'm sure you'll be hearing from him at some point once he's ready."

Elle opened her eyes and studied the ceiling as the wash of warmth came over her. "You don't know how much of a relief it is to hear all of this. I really needed it."

"Just know that I don't claim to have all the answers, and I might say something stupid or awful again, especially if you give me a martini. I hope you can be patient with me."

"I can," Elle said. "It's new for all of us. I get that."

"Oh, and now I'm all misty," her mother said, laughing, "which is my cue to let you go. You don't need an old woman blubbering on the phone to you."

Elle laughed. "Mom. Stop."

"It's true! Please send our love to Holly. We dropped a care package in the mail for her yesterday. It has some spaghetti fixings. Maybe you can help her out with that."

"Of course, and thanks, Mom. For all of it."

"Just part of the job."

When they clicked off the call, Elle wasn't sure what to do with herself. The storm, the one that, just a few moments ago, seemed threatening and dark, was now beautiful and mysterious. She snuggled further into the maroon hoodie she'd grown to love and watched the rain in wonder. She didn't know what came next, but Elle knew one thing for certain: The world never ceased to amaze her. She tapped her lips in anticipation.

Chapter Twenty

It was seventy-four degrees in the west corner of Maui, typical for July. Gia liked the even temperatures of these summer tournaments. There was something motivating about them that made her fight that much harder to win. If the conditions were ideal, her surfing should be, too. And while winning was nice, it was not her top priority for the trip. She had her sights set on another goal: taking control of her life, instead of letting her life control her. She just needed to talk to Elle, convince her of the same.

Gia knew in her heart they belonged together, and if she had to sacrifice to make that a reality, she was ready to do that. She only hoped Elle would be willing to do the same.

The tournament had gotten off to a positive start. Gia had easily advanced through rounds one and two. Elle had crushed them. She was unstoppable lately, which made Gia keep her distance. She wanted more than anything to talk with Elle right away, to confess all, but she knew the ramifications it could have on Elle's tournament performance.

She'd simply have to wait. Even if it killed her.

Instead of talking to Elle, she watched her, attended every heat, and cheered her on each step of the way. She'd glanced up at the competitors' reserved section during her own heats, but Elle hadn't made an appearance. Given what they'd decided—no distractions—it made sense. It didn't stop her from hoping.

Midweek, they ran into each other in the lobby of a café attached to the resort. Gia had agreed to have dinner with one of the surfers on the tour, Sasha Christianson, to catch up and hang out. Elle was there with her media manager.

"Hey, you," Elle said, as they waited to be seated.

Gia smiled. "Hi. Congrats on such a great showing."

"Yeah, well, you're not doing so bad yourself." The words trailed off, the conversation finished, but their eye contact held. So many unspoken words passed between them in that moment. Gia felt just as connected to Elle as ever. She longed to reach for her, to trash their respective dinner plans and eat together, talk for hours, and maybe sneak away to her room later, just the two of them. What she wouldn't give to do just that.

Elle's table was ready. "You two enjoy your meal," she said to Gia and Sasha. She looked back once over her shoulder at Gia as she walked, and every part of Gia went warm. She blinked. She longed for Elle, but she could be patient. She could do this.

The next day, Gia and Elle both cruised into the semis in a glorious showing but faced off against different opponents. Elle brought in a solid 14.5 to advance to the finals. If she won there, she'd end the year as world champion, which had Gia tingling with excitement for her at just the idea. In many ways, she wanted Elle to take the tournament for that very reason, her own results be damned. This was huge!

A day later, Gia went down in the semis against Lindy Ives, who would now challenge Elle for the top spot in a finals heat not to be missed. Gia took the loss in stride, keeping her eye on the bigger picture. She'd had a great time surfing that week and had so much more to look forward to. What would have once crushed her was just another day at the office. The new outlook was a wonderful weight off her shoulders, and she wondered now why it had taken her so long to get here. She could definitely get used to this and realized, suddenly, she'd found the joy of the sport all over again.

This year's world title would literally come down to who took the final heat, Elle Britton or Lindy Ives. The media was having a field day with the matchup, recounting the careers of each and what brought them to this final showdown. The entire resort was tied up with ribbons of anticipation. Gia's heart was in her throat just thinking about it. She was nervous as hell. This was everything for Elle, and for Gia by default.

The next time she saw Elle was in the lobby that night. Her gaze was pulled to Elle like a magnet, and the beauty she saw stole her breath. Elle wore a black cocktail dress and was clearly headed out for a nice evening. Her hair was pulled partially back, with blond layered on blond, cascading down her back. With her clutch bag in hand, she paused when she saw Gia, who felt drab compared to Elle, in just jeans and a zip-up hoodie.

"You're off somewhere important," Gia said as they neared each other. They exchanged a smile and Gia shook her head in wonder. Elle radiated in that dress. It came in at the waist and dipped just low enough in front, not to mention the glamorous addition of the high heels and diamond earrings. The way she looked, Gia was confident Elle's photo would headline every sports gossip site by morning. Rightfully so.

Elle sighed. "Rip Curl is hosting a party for its team of surfers and a string of VIPs."

"Those tend to be fun."

"Yeah," Elle said, unconvincingly. "I hope so."

"Congratulations on the finals. I'm thrilled for you, Elle. It's yours tomorrow. There is no doubt in my mind."

"Thank you." A pause. Elle met her gaze. "Will you be staying for the heat?"

Gia smiled. "I wouldn't miss it for anything." They stared at each other until Gia finally remembered herself. This wasn't the time for that. "You have a good night, Elle."

"Yeah. You, too."

Gia headed to the elevator, all set for her own very wild night of flipping through the local stations and ordering in. Maybe a pizza. She was done for the season. She could indulge with a few extra carbs. As the elevator doors closed, she pressed the button for her floor and waited, watching the numbers above the door. Only they didn't move, nor did the elevator.

Instead the doors slid opened and Elle stepped inside. "This is stupid," she said.

"The party?" Gia asked, confused. What was happening? The doors closed behind Elle, and the elevator kicked into action, taking them to the eighteenth floor, just as Gia had requested. Gia squinted at her, perplexed.

"Not the party," Elle said, clearly worked up. She gestured between them. "This. Us. What we're doing. It's the most ridiculous thing I've ever been a part of, and I refuse to be ridiculous anymore."

"What does that mean?" But underneath, she knew. God, she knew.

"I love you," Elle said quietly.

Gia blinked, not quite believing what was happening. That Elle had just said the words before she'd even had a chance to lay out her case for them. The doors to the elevator slid open, revealing Gia's hallway, but neither one of them moved. The gravity of the moment outweighed all else. The doors closed again, and the elevator continued climbing to who knew where.

Elle shifted nervously. "Do you have anything to say to that? Tell me I'm crazy or that that ship has already sailed? I can take it. I just need to hear where your head is so I can breathe again."

"I love you so much," Gia said, her heart racing, her emotions bubbling to the surface. "That's what I have to say to that. I couldn't stop loving you if I tried, and I did try."

Elle closed her eyes as if to savor the words. "That's all I needed to hear."

The elevator opened and a group of teenagers stepped forward. Elle held up a hand. "I'm so very sorry, but this elevator's going in for service. We'll send another." She pressed the button and closed the doors again.

"Maybe we should table this discussion. You've gotta keep your head clear," Gia said. "What about the finals?"

"They don't mean as much to me as you do." Elle closed the distance between them, pressed her entire body up against Gia's, and wrapped her arms around her neck. Everything in Gia's being cried out, her body no longer hers in the midst of their contact. She sucked in a breath as Elle continued. "Win or lose, the most important thing is that you're waiting there when it's all over. I'm sorry I didn't realize that sooner."

"That's all I want, too." Gia's arms slid around Elle's waist, holding her in place. "So maybe instead of calling me Two, you'll call me Six."

"Six has a nice ring. Maybe I'll be Four."

Gia closed one eye. "I don't know about that. Four is ranked higher than six, so..."

Elle stared for a long moment into Gia's eyes, then kissed her thoroughly, expertly, her hands sliding into Gia's hair and angling her mouth for better access. Their tongues danced, and Gia's body thrummed pleasantly. The door to the elevators opened yet again, this time to the lobby, Gia realized distantly. Moments later, a flashbulb went off. They laughed in the midst of the kiss but didn't stop. Wouldn't. Even with guests now piling into the elevator.

"Can someone hit eighteen?" Gia murmured against Elle's mouth. She couldn't be bothered to. She was too busy kissing the woman she loved.

❖

It had to be close to midnight, Elle thought, as she traced the line of Gia's collarbone, placing soft kisses along the way. She never got tired of touching her, looking at her. They lay facing each other, cheeks on pillows, spent from their long-overdue reunion. She closed her eyes and smiled, because what a satisfying reunion it had been. In every delectable way. Her body still sensitive to every wonderful thing Gia had done to it.

"We should get some sleep," Gia said, tickling Elle's bare shoulder with one finger. "You have a big afternoon tomorrow."

"We *should* get some sleep. That part's true. But I'm afraid if I close my eyes, you'll be gone. All of this will have just been a wonderful dream."

"I'm not going anywhere. I promise." Gia kissed her. "Excited for tomorrow?"

"Damn straight." She sighed. "I really want this one. I'll go out there and do my best, and whatever is meant to happen will happen. And then we'll go back to California together. That last part's decided, by the way. I'm switching my flight to yours."

"Or I can switch mine."

"Or that." Elle slipped a hand between Gia's legs. "Maybe just one more time? I'll work fast."

Gia gasped at the touch she instinctually moved into. "Your never-ending appetite still amazes me. Oh, wow." Her eyes fluttered closed and she sucked in a breath. "Yes. Right there."

"Get used to it. I think you're stuck with me."

"Can I quote you on that?" Gia asked as she grabbed a fistful of the bedsheet.

Elle slid down the bed. "I'll send out a whole damn press release."

❖

Gia surveyed the finals crowd as she took her seat. All those eager faces waiting for the same thing, to find out who would be this year's world champion. Some wore sunglasses and bikini tops, others carried giant signs that cheered on their competitor of choice. They all had one thing in common, a deep and abiding love of the sport. In the midst of competition, Gia sometimes forgot that pure-hearted enthusiasm. She felt it in full force today and made a vow to never forget again.

After a few standard announcements, the clock started, and the heat was under way. Gia rolled her shoulders, more nervous than if she were the one surfing.

Elle drew first blood with long walls stretching out ahead of her, the perfect canvas for her turn out. Her back foot drove way off the traction pad, allowing her to pick up speed and power. She leapt off her board, missing the exit, but overall, it had been a decent enough ride It would pull a solid number from the judges. Gia allowed herself to take a fortifying breath. This was good. This was a step in the right direction.

Lindy was up next and no shrinking violet out there. She charged hard, but it was a short in-and-out ride. Okay, okay. This was even better. If only her heart would stop thudding its way out of her chest. She placed a hand over it as she looked on.

"Think Britton's gonna pull it out?" Alia Foz called to Gia from a few seats down. "She's been looking good out there this week. I'm thinking it's hers to lose."

"If she can stay the course, she'll be fine. She's a fighter."

"Would be a shame to see her lose the title after holding it for so much of the year."

"I don't think that's gonna happen."

Elle set out on her second effort, starting with a promising opening turn. "C'mon, c'mon," Gia murmured. She had command of the wave, with perfect form and flow. She attacked the pocket hard, bringing Gia to her feet, then out of nowhere went down.

"Fuck," Gia said, under her breath. "What the hell happened there?"

Elle emerged with a smile on her face and shake of her head at the lost opportunity. But the clock was ticking.

Lindy delivered on her next three outings, turning in three solid rides, hanging on to the corner each time in an impressive showing. She wasn't the most creative surfer, but she was solid. Elle didn't fare as well. A couple of shorter efforts, ending early, followed by a simple series of turns on a smaller swell. The waves were not on her side today, but it wasn't over. Timewise, she would have one last shot before the heat ended. Gia swallowed back the fear and said a silent prayer. If she could nail this one, she'd have a chance. If not, the title would most assuredly go to Ives.

"Come on Elle. Wait for your wave!" she called. "You got this."

Elle paddled out, leapt to her board, and went for it. The wave was monstrous, and if she could capitalize, it would score huge. She swung big into the wall and down again, pulling a big cheer from the crowd. Then the nose of her board dug in on one of the ripples, and she fell fast over the top of the board into the surf below. Gia blew out a defeated breath as a hush fell over the crowd. Awful. Had she just put her head down, she could have balanced herself and ridden out of it. No, no, no. This couldn't be happening.

With the final seconds of the heat ticking away, there was nothing to do.

Lindy Ives came away with a combined two-wave score of 15.2. Elle scored a 14.5, bringing the season to a disappointing close.

"I think the world champ's run just ended here at the Maui Pro," she heard the announcer say over the loudspeaker. "A round of applause for your new champion, Lindy Ives." The crowd went wild, enjoying every second of the nail-biter they'd just experienced. People would be talking about this upset for a while, watching replays and analyzing every moment online.

Gia had only one thing on her mind. Elle.

She waited for her alongside the roped-off competitors' walkway. She expected sadness, defeat, and someone who would need to be picked up off the ground. She got none of those things.

"There you are," Elle said to Gia as she approached, a small smile on her face.

"It was close out there, Elle. You should be proud of yourself."

Elle nodded with a confidence that caught Gia off guard. "I am. For a variety of reasons." She touched Gia's cheek briefly. "I've got a little bit of press to attend to, but maybe we can grab dinner? I could use a mai tai or two."

"You sure you'd be up for that?"

"More than up for it." She squeezed Gia's hand. "I'm good. Better than good, actually. Just one tournament of many, right?"

Gia understood exactly what Elle meant, because in the scheme of life? She was on top of the world herself. Together, they could handle anything. Each setback, each defeat, each injury. Anything that came their way. They shared a smile in recognition of the new frontier.

"Elle, how about a quick wrap-up interview for the doc?" Jordan called from across the ropes.

She held on to Gia's hand. "Can we do it together?" she asked, and tilted her head toward Gia.

"Even better," Jordan said with a grin. Once Jordan had them situated in a two-shot with the beach behind them, she fired off her first question. "Elle, I'm sure the loss of the title today was a hard one. Can you talk about how you're feeling?"

Elle nodded and gathered her thoughts. "I'm disappointed to not end the season as world champion. It's not what I expected, and certainly not what I planned on. But I know I gave it everything I had, and I'll come back next season ready to do it all over again."

"It's been a long journey," Jordan said. "Lot of ups and downs for you, Elle. Looking back, was it all worth it?"

This time Elle didn't hesitate. "One hundred percent. I met the most wonderful woman, and fell head over heels in love. Did I mention that? I mean, did you guys know?" She laughed, looked over at Gia and then straight into the lens. She paused. Sincerity took over. "It's been the most satisfying year of my life, and I wouldn't change a second."

Standing next to Elle, who, after a devastating loss, was more focused on what *they* had together, had Gia feeling like the luckiest woman on the planet. She couldn't wipe the grin off her face if you offered her a million dollars.

"What about you, Gia? You're ending the season as number four instead of battling it out for one. Any final thoughts?"

"I've never been happier to be number four."

Jordan laughed. "I suppose it's safe to say that you two are an item?"

"What is it they say?" Elle asked. "Love conquers all?"

Gia nodded. "That's exactly what they say." She looked at Jordan. "And it has."

EPILOGUE

I love your house," Hadley told Elle, as she carried in her empty plate from the beach out back. The back patio still smelled like the wonderful hamburgers they'd grilled two hours ago. A tad chilly for August, which signaled that an early fall might be on the way. Elle was grateful for the chance to host Gia's friends. Well, hers now, too. The afternoon had been relaxed and fun, with a little beach volleyball and delicious mudslide cocktails for all.

"Don't give her too many compliments," Holly said. "She got all her decorating tips from me."

Elle laughed and turned to Hadley. "That's only partially true."

"Doesn't matter," Hadley said. "I want to move in."

"You can't," Autumn said, entering through the back door. "I'd miss you too much. Who would walk across the courtyard and keep me company?"

"Me," Isabel said, from the hallway. "Sorry, Elle. I just gave myself a grand tour of your ridiculously cute house. Seriously, you're too cute. I don't know how you survive. I might have to murder you in your sleep."

"Please don't," Gia said, slinging an arm around Elle's shoulders.

"Fine, but only because you asked."

"I think Kate and I are gonna take off," Autumn said, patting her ridiculously large stomach. Elle was really amazed at how such a small woman could carry two full babies. Somehow Autumn was handling it like a champ. "Late-afternoon nap is calling."

Elle opened her arms and pulled Autumn into an embrace. "Thank you so much for coming, and hang in there."

"Less than a month," Autumn said. "I got this."

"We're right behind you," Taylor said, corralling Isabel, who still wandered the expanse of the living room in a curious daze, taking in each piece of art.

"And me," Hadley said. "The lonely fifth wheel! Don't forget me."

Isabel grabbed Hadley, put her in a headlock, and gave her hair a tousle. "I have a feeling you won't be lonely for long. Good things are coming for you, Hadley-Pants."

"That's a new nickname," Gia said, quirking her head.

Isabel grinned. "I'm keeping it. Gonna get all Had's stuff embroidered with it for Christmas."

Holly pointed at Isabel. "I like you."

"I like you back," Isabel challenged.

Elle smiled as everyone gathered their belongings and headed for the door. These women were endlessly entertaining, and she enjoyed getting to know them more and more. Gia, who was wonderful enough on her own, came with a lot of perks.

"You were so great to have them all here," Gia said, once they were alone. "But halfway through, all I wanted them to do was leave, already."

"Leave? Really? Why?" Elle asked, clearing a tray. "Everything okay?"

"More than okay." Gia came behind Elle at the sink, wrapped her arms around her from behind, and kissed her neck slowly. "I was just dreaming about doing this…and more. You were so cute in your hostess mode." She slid her hands up the front of Elle's shirt to her bare stomach.

"Yeah?" Elle asked. She turned in Gia's arms and stared into those chocolate brown eyes. "Is there anything I can get for you, ma'am?"

"Now you're just trying to torture me with your hostess voice."

"No, ma'am. I'm just happy to help with anything you need."

"Well…in that case." Elle's phone rang, interrupting them. She held up one reluctant finger, because this conversation was on its way to somewhere really good. Her temperature had already risen multiple degrees and her body tingled wonderfully. Cleanup from the barbecue could definitely wait until other matters were attended to.

She found her phone by the couch, clicked over to the call, and took a seat. "Hey, Isabel. You guys forget something?" Gia was hot on her heels, not ready to pause what they had going.

"Not at all," Isabel said. "I guess I'm just feeling a little glowy for you two, and I also realized that I forgot to thank you for having us over. Today was fun. You're a cool chick." Gia knelt in front of her. Elle passed her a questioning look.

"You're so sweet to call," Elle said. "You didn't have to do that. We had fun with you guys, too."

"Oh! And Taylor wanted me to thank you on her behalf as well." Gia ran her hands up the back of Elle's calves and pulled her forward to the edge of the couch. Elle sucked in a breath, holding Gia's heated gaze.

"Please tell Taylor she's very welcome. The cake she made was amazing." Her eyes fluttered as her pants were unbuttoned, her zipper lowered. In a quick motion, Gia slid her jeans right off her body. Elle's eyes went wide.

"Don't tell her I told you this, but the cake was from a box. She excels at finding the best boxes, though, and now she's poking me in the arm for telling her secrets. I'm fucked."

Elle shivered at the use of the word coupled with Gia's hand sliding slowly between her legs. When that hand applied pressure to the square of fabric, she bit her lip hard. "Boxes can be just as good," Elle said evenly. "Who doesn't, uh, love a boxed dessert?"

"Right? She's a whiz of innovation," Isabel said, just as the fabric square was moved to the side. With just a touch of her tongue, Elle dropped her head back. Gia groaned quietly.

"Thanks so much for calling, Iz. I'm sure I'll be...seeing you soon."

"No doubt. Take care, Elle. Oh! I forgot to tell you. We'd love you both to drop by set sometime. I know you're a fan of the show, and it might be fun to see the shooting of a scene or two."

Elle dug her fingers into the couch as Gia worked her magic and the pressure built steadily.

"We wouldn't miss it."

Moments from orgasm, Gia took the phone. "Hey, Iz. I gotta steal Elle for a second. Household matter. We'll talk later." She clicked off the call and tossed the phone behind her onto the carpet. "Where was I?" she asked, moving in for more.

Ten seconds later, Elle knew exactly where she was: enjoying the blissful payout from just one of the many sexy moments that came with life alongside Gia, whose name she repeated as she savored the wash of pleasure.

Elle never knew such happiness was possible for her. Looking back on her life just one year ago was startling, almost unrecognizable.

Her mundane existence had shifted dramatically to a full and rich life alongside one of the kindest and most beautiful people she'd ever known.

She looked forward to waking up each day, seeing what the world had in store. For the first time…she felt alive.

"What about a little surfing at dusk?" Gia asked. "Would you be up for that?"

"Yes, Four," Elle said with a sated smile. "I would love to surf with you tonight. And after that, I have a few plans of my own for you."

Gia blinked back at her. They shared a lingering kiss as, through the window behind them, the sun descended slowly to the water.

"This has been a really good day," Gia murmured.

Elle smiled against her mouth. "I have a feeling we can top it."

About the Author

Melissa Brayden (www.melissabrayden.com) is a multiaward-winning romance author, embracing the full-time writer's life in San Antonio, Texas, and enjoying every minute of it.

Melissa is married and working really hard at remembering to do the dishes. For personal enjoyment, she spends time with her Jack Russell terriers and checks out the NYC theater scene as often as possible. She considers herself a reluctant patron of spin class, but would much rather be sipping merlot and staring off into space. Coffee, wine, and donuts make her world go round.

Books Available From Bold Strokes Books

Alias by Cari Hunter. A car crash leaves a woman with no memory and no identity. Together with Detective Bronwen Pryce, she fights to uncover a truth that might just kill them both. (978-1-63555-221-8)

Death in Time by Robyn Nyx. Working in the past is hell on your future. (978-1-63555-053-5)

Hers to Protect by Nicole Disney. Ex–high school sweethearts Kaia and Adrienne will have to see past their differences and survive the vengeance of a brutal gang if they want to be together. (978-1-63555-229-4)

Perfect Little Worlds by Clifford Mae Henderson. Lucy can't hold the secret any longer. Twenty-six years ago, her sister did the unthinkable. (978-1-63555-164-8)

Room Service by Fiona Riley. Interior designer Olivia likes stability, but when work brings footloose Savannah into her world and into a new city every month, Olivia must decide if what makes her comfortable is what makes her happy. (978-1-63555-120-4)

Sparks Like Ours by Melissa Brayden. Professional surfers Gia Malone and Elle Britton can't deny their chemistry on and off the beach. But only one can win… (978-1-63555-016-0)

Take My Hand by Missouri Vaun. River Hemsworth arrives in Georgia intent on escaping quickly, but when she crashes her Mercedes into the Clip 'n Curl, sexy Clay Cahill ends up rescuing more than her car. (978-1-63555-104-4)

The Last Time I Saw Her by Kathleen Knowles. Lane Hudson only has twelve days to win back Alison's heart. That is, if she can gather the courage to try. (978-1-63555-067-2)

Wayworn Lovers by Gun Brooke. Will agoraphobic composer Giselle Bonnaire and Tierney Edwards, a wandering soul who can't remain in one place for long, trust in the passionate love destiny hands them? (978-1-62639-995-2)

Breakthrough by Kris Bryant. Falling for a sexy ranger is one thing, but is the possibility of love worth giving up the career Kennedy Wells has always dreamed of? (978-1-63555-179-2)

Certain Requirements by Elinor Zimmerman. Phoenix has always kept her love of kinky submission strictly behind the bedroom door and inside the bounds of romantic relationships, until she meets Kris Andersen. (978-1-63555-195-2)

Dark Euphoria by Ronica Black. When a high-profile case drops in Detective Maria Diaz's lap, she forges ahead only to discover this case, and her main suspect, aren't like any other. (978-1-63555-141-9)

Fore Play by Julie Cannon. Executive Leigh Marshall falls hard for Peyton Broader, her golf pro…and an ex-con. Will she risk sabotaging her career for love? (978-1-63555-102-0)

Love Came Calling by C. A. Popovich. Can a romantic looking for a long-term, committed relationship and a jaded cynic too busy for love conquer life's struggles and find their way to what matters most? (978-1-63555-205-8)

Outside the Law by Carsen Taite. Former sweethearts Tanner Cohen and Sydney Braswell must work together on a federal task force to see justice served, but will they choose to embrace their second chance at love? (978-1-63555-039-9)

The Princess Deception by Nell Stark. When journalist Missy Duke realizes Prince Sebastian is really his twin sister Viola in disguise, she plays along, but when sparks flare between them, will the double deception doom their fairy-tale romance? (978-1-62639-979-2)

The Smell of Rain by Cameron MacElvee. Reyha Arslan, a wise and elegant woman with a tragic past, shows Chrys that there's still beauty to embrace and reason to hope despite the world's cruelty. (978-1-63555-166-2)

The Talebearer by Sheri Lewis Wohl. Liz's visions show her the faces of the lost and the killers who took their lives. As one by one, the murdered are found, a stranger works to stop Liz before the serial killer is brought to justice. (978-1-63555-126-6)

White Wings Weeping by Lesley Davis. The world is full of discord and hatred, but how much of it is just human nature when an evil with sinister intent is invading people's hearts? (978-1-63555-191-4)

A Call Away by KC Richardson. Can a businesswoman from a big city find the answers she's looking for, and possibly love, on a small-town farm? (978-1-63555-025-2)

Berlin Hungers by Justine Saracen. Can the love between an RAF woman and the wife of a Luftwaffe pilot, former enemies, survive in besieged Berlin during the aftermath of World War II? (978-1-63555-116-7)

Blend by Georgia Beers. Lindsay and Piper are like night and day. Working together won't be easy, but not falling in love might prove the hardest job of all. (978-1-63555-189-1)

Hunger for You by Jenny Frame. Principe of an ancient vampire clan Byron Debrek must save her one true love from falling into the hands of her enemies and into the middle of a vampire war. (978-1-63555-168-6)

Mercy by Michelle Larkin. FBI Special Agent Mercy Parker and psychic ex-profiler Piper Vasey learn to love again as they race to stop a man with supernatural gifts who's bent on annihilating humankind. (978-1-63555-202-7)

Pride and Porters by Charlotte Greene. Will pride and prejudice prevent these modern-day lovers from living happily ever after? (978-1-63555-158-7)

Rocks and Stars by Sam Ledel. Kyle's struggle to own who she is and what she really wants may end up landing her on the bench and without the woman of her dreams. (978-1-63555-156-3)

The Deep End by Ellie Hart. When family ties become entangled in murder and deception, it's time to find a way out… (978-1-63555-288-1)

The Boss of Her: Office Romance Novellas by Julie Cannon, Aurora Rey, and M. Ullrich. Going to work never felt so good. Three office romance novellas from talented writers Julie Cannon, Aurora Rey, and M. Ullrich. (978-1-63555-145-7)

A Country Girl's Heart by Dena Blake. When Kat Jackson gets a second chance at love, following her heart will prove the hardest decision of all. (978-1-63555-134-1)

Dangerous Waters by Radclyffe. Life, death, and war on the home front. Two women join forces against a powerful opponent, nature itself. (978-1-63555-233-1)

Fury's Death by Brey Willows. When all we hold sacred fails, who will be there to save us? (978-1-63555-063-4)

It's Not a Date by Heather Blackmore. Kade's desire to keep things with Jen on a professional level is in Jen's best interest. Yet what's in Kade's best interest…is Jen. (978-1-63555-149-5)

Killer Winter by Kay Bigelow. Just when she thought things could get no worse, homicide Lieutenant Leah Samuels learns the woman she loves has betrayed her in devastating ways. (978-1-63555-177-8)

Score by MJ Williamz. Will an addiction to pain pills destroy Ronda's chance with the woman she loves, or will she come out on top and score a happily ever after? (978-1-62639-807-8)

Spring's Wake by Aurora Rey. When wanderer Willa Lange falls for Provincetown B&B owner Nora Calhoun, will past hurts and a fifteen-year age gap keep them from finding love? (978-1-63555-035-1)

The Northwoods by Jane Hoppen. When Evelyn Bauer, disguised as her dead husband, George, travels to a Northwoods logging camp to work, she and the camp cook Sarah Bell forge a friendship fraught with both tenderness and turmoil. (978-1-63555-143-3)

Truth or Dare by C. Spencer. For a group of six lesbian friends, life changes course after one long snow-filled weekend. (978-1-63555-148-8)

Children of the Healer by Barbara Ann Wright. Life becomes desperate for ex-soldier Cordelia Ross when the indigenous aliens of her planet are drawn into a civil war and old enemies linger in the shadows. Book Three of the Godfall Series. (978-1-63555-031-3)

Hearts Like Hers by Melissa Brayden. Coffee shop owner Autumn Primm is ready to cut loose and live a little, but is the baggage that comes with out-of-towner Kate Carpenter too heavy for anything long term? (978-1-63555-014-6)

Love at Cooper's Creek by Missouri Vaun. Shaw Daily flees corporate life to find solace in the rural Blue Ridge Mountains, but escapism eludes her when her attentions are captured by small town beauty Kate Elkins. (978-1-62639-960-0)

Twice in a Lifetime by PJ Trebelhorn. Detective Callie Burke can't deny the growing attraction to her late friend's widow, Taylor Fletcher, who also happens to own the bar where Callie's sister works. (978-1-63555-033-7)

Undiscovered Affinity by Jane Hardee. Will a no-strings-attached affair be enough to break Olivia's control and convince Cardic that love does exist? (978-1-63555-061-0)

Between Sand and Stardust by Tina Michele. Are the lifelong bonds of love strong enough to conquer time, distance, and heartache when Haven Thorne and Willa Bennette are given another chance at forever? (978-1-62639-940-2)

Charming the Vicar by Jenny Frame. When magician and atheist Finn Kane seeks refuge in an English village after a spiritual crisis, can local vicar Bridget Claremont restore her faith in life and love? (978-1-63555-029-0)

Data Capture by Jesse J. Thoma. Lola Walker is undercover on the hunt for cybercriminals while trying not to notice the woman who might be perfectly wrong for her for all the right reasons. (978-1-62639-985-3)